A TASTE OF CHRISTMAS POISON

There was another delay as Nathaniel Poe proposed a toast. Reluctantly putting down her silverware, Louise pickd up her wineglass and all ten at the table raised their glasses together. "Let us drink to all of our good healths," said Poe, "and to a friendly dinner together."

No "hear, hears" or amendments to the toast, just the tipping up of the glasses and the drinking of the wine. Then there was that moment of delighted murmurs and rustling silverware as people prepared to take their first bite of a magnificent dinner.

Bunny had settled in her seat and turned her undivided attention on Bill. "Too much excitement, isn't there luvy?" she asked him. And with that she picked up her wineglass and gulped the contents down. Suddenly she jerked to her feet, scraped her chair back, and dropped the goblet onto the table, crashing it into her water glass and sending shards of glass flying.

Both of her hands went to her throat and she hoarsely cried out, "One of you bloody sods *poisoned* me!"

D1449301

Books by Ann Ripley

HARVEST OF MURDER

THE CHRISTMAS GARDEN AFFAIR

DEATH AT THE SPRING PLANT SALE

Published by Kensington Publishing Corporation

A GARDENING MYSTERY

THE CHRISTMAS GARDEN AFFAIR

ANN RIPLEY

KENSINGTON BOOKS
Kensington Publishing Corp.
http://www.kensingtonbooks.com

KENSINGTON BOOKS are published by

Kensington Publishing Corp.
850 Third Avenue
New York, NY 10022

Copyright © 2002 by Ann Ripley

All rights reserved. No part of this book may be repro-
duced in any form or by any means without the prior
written consent of the Publisher, excepting brief quotes
used in reviews.

If you purchased this book without a cover, you should
be aware that this book is stolen property. It was reported
as "unsold and destroyed" to the Publisher and neither
the Author nor the Publisher has received any payment
for this "stripped book."

All Kensington Titles, Imprints, and Distributed Lines
are available at special quantity discounts for bulk purchases for sales promotions, premiums, fund-raising,
and educational or institutional use. Special book ex-
cerpts or customized printings can also be created to fit
specific needs. For details, write or phone the office of
the Kensington special sales manager: Kensington
Publishing Corp., 850 Third Avenue, New York, NY
10022, attn: Special Sales Department, Phone: 1-800-221-
2647.

Kensington and the K logo Reg. U.S. Pat. & TM Off.

First Kensington hardcover printing: October 2002
First Kensington mass market printing: October 2003

10 9 8 7 6 5 4 3 2 1

Printed in the United States of America

To Tony

ACKNOWLEDGMENTS

Many people helped me with this book, including a number of garden experts: Cindy Owsley Lair of Boulder County Department of Open Space; Jim Knopf, garden writer and professor; Panayoti Kelaidis of the Denver Botanic Gardens; nurseryman Tom Throgmorton; garden magazine editor Thomas Cooper; Peggy Stanley of Greenworks Florists in Washington, D.C.; orchid expert Paul Lembeck; restoration ecologist Ken Lair; Carolyn Crawford of the Colorado Native Plant Society; Mary Cressel of the USDA Department of Natural Resources Conservation Service; and Dr. H. Marc Cathey, president-emeritus of the American Horticultural Society.

Others adding their expertise were Captain Blaine Corle of the Alexandria, Virginia, Police Department; Trux Simmons, producer at KRMA-TV, Denver; Steve Berry of the FBI; former detective Tom Lynch; garden magazine editor Jane Shellenberger; Barbara Emerson of *Horticulture Magazine*; Jessie Mahoney; Irene Sinclair; Margit and Mike Percival; and Pat Rogers. Sybil Downing, Karen Gilleland, and Margaret Coel were, as usual, immensely helpful readers, as were Sarah Ripley, Emily Ripley, and Beverly Carrigan.

Additional thanks to my editor at Kensington Publishing, John Scognamiglio, and to Jane Jordan Browne, my agent.

1

December 1

Louise Eldridge came to the end of the chapter in her mystery novel, reluctant even to tear her eyes from the page. She knew the moment she reentered the real world, she'd feel serious pangs of guilt. After all, she'd been lying on the living room couch reading for two hours now. She was still wearing her charmeuse nightie and fleece robe, an almost empty coffee cup on the table beside her, crumbles of toast on her bosom, and her cat, Hargrave, asleep in the curve of her arm.

Since the Protestant work ethic ran strong within her, Louise knew it was dissolute to be reading in one's nightclothes at ten in the morning. On the other hand, she reflected, it was a very good book. She suppressed these bothersome feelings, took a sip of cold coffee, and read on. Not until some time later, when a high beam of sunlight cut through the windows and virtually blinded her, did she finally stir from her snug nest. It was getting on toward eleven. With a sigh, she set the book aside and carefully stood up, brushed the crumbs into her hand, and headed for the bedroom, Hargrave in pursuit, hoping she'd detour to the kitchen and put fresh food in his dish.

As she approached her Winthrop desk, she promised herself she wouldn't look at that damned invitation again. She'd fixated on it too many times already.

Once alongside the desk, however, she found the temptation was too large. Fancy and gilt-edged, the invitation sat primly closed on top of her neat stack of papers. The real trouble, however, like Pandora's box, was what was inside. She opened it to reveal an inset sheet containing the names of forty-eight people, forty-eight very important people. Scanning the prestigious roster, her gaze was drawn to the name on the top of the list: Bunny Bainfield. Louise thought of herself as an easygoing person, someone with no enemies to speak of, except for a couple who were doing time in prison. She'd never hated anyone before, but now she despised the person who bore that name, Bunny Bainfield. It was a woman she'd never met.

Closing the invitation, she wandered back through the living room, giving her nearly finished book a covetous look, and passing the piano without caressing a key. She went over to the tall windows and stared broodingly into the woods. Returning to reality was a bummer. Usually, this modern house set in its forest of tall trees was her spiritual retreat, but not these days, when envy was growing inside her like the moss on her front flagstone walk.

Sunlight was playing hide-and-seek in the trees. And where there was sun, Louise told herself, there might be hope. If she went out and worked in the garden, maybe she could shake these dark thoughts.

Besides, there were the bulbs. Purchased late at the nearby nursery and sitting in paper bags in the storeroom, they had to be planted right now, before a cold front blew into Washington, D.C., and froze the ground solid. She expelled a deep breath, relieved to know she had no more time to wallow in her misery.

She put on her gardening clothes—worn Japanese farmer pants, metal-toed work boots, and a big gray wool sweater—and went outside with the cat. Fetching bulbs, tools, and wheelbarrows from the toolshed, she went to the front garden and got to work digging a big hole. By the time she'd finished, thoughts of Bunny Bainfield, the rival who'd moved in on her territory, had receded, if not totally disappeared.

It was an interesting hole. Even the cat thought so: better than the ones *he* dug. Louise thought of how, as hostess of her Saturday morning *Gardening with Nature* TV show, she would have described it to her audience: *"Big and irregularly shaped, like an amoeba, with steep sides and a flat bottom like a caldera created by an active volcano . . ."*

Unfortunately, her thoughts began to stray like an untethered balloon. How would Bunny Bainfield have described it? Bunny, the garden maven *extraordinaire*, had burst upon the American scene six years ago from England and since then had become arbiter of America's lowbrow home-and-garden style, monopolizing every part of the gardening world that she touched, selling nursery plants, floral arrangements, and garden design and art. Two months ago, Bunny's rival garden show was launched on the House and Garden network in the same time slot as Louise's show on PBS.

Since then, Louise hadn't had a decent night's sleep.

Bunny would have said something different to her TV audience about the hole Louise had dug: *"Make it as curvy as your sweetheart's hips, luv, and deep, very, very deep!"* She shook off these thoughts and got back to business. Alongside her was a mound of mulch she'd removed from the site, and her two small red wheelbarrows. One held the dug-out earth; the second, fresh soil laced with superphosphate, as well as the epimedium plants she'd uprooted before digging. She tucked a loosened strand of her long, brown hair back into its scrunchy, and commenced planting.

This was Louise's favorite garden, a half-hidden place nestled against the front walk. To get the best view of it, one had to push aside a low-hanging yellowwood tree limb. With its irregular drifts of mahonia, epimedium, liriope, and toadlily, it was the ultimate in understatement. It had a random beauty, the kind that she liked best. In some things Louise was compulsively neat; the business papers on her desk, for instance, were set in anal little piles with no paper out of line. In gardens, her model was the randomness of the lava lamp. She set out plants in irregular patterns, allowing them to move and change by seeding themselves or expanding their swollen roots and growing outside the bounds of where they started. Though she certainly didn't do anything kooky like *talking* to plants, Louise thought she understood them, how they moved around and multiplied, and how they liked to be treated.

By spring, these bulbs would become asymmetric drifts of flowers in grape, white, and pale yellow. Nothing too bright or intrusive, for this woods by nature was filled with soft tints only, the white dogwood being the brightest of its pale native plants.

She scooped some topsoil from the nearer wheel-barrow and spread a couple of inches in the bottom of her crater. On top of this she placed the biggest of the bulbs, the rough narcissus with attached bulblets. Next she added a layer of the enriched soil, a dusting of superphosphate that she hoped was not overkill, and then five *Fritillaria persica* bulbs, which would bloom tall, grape-colored, and exotic-looking. Now came the bulbs of ten pale yellow and white striped lily tulips, and, in the shallowest level of this garden grave, the small *Fritillaria meleagris* bulbs, which would arise from the ground as petite lilies checkered as finely as if an artist had painted them.

The dirtier Louise's hands got, the purer her soul felt. Bunny was forgotten.

As she back-filled the hole, she left half a dozen gaps for the epimedium plants. By April, there would be a swarm of heart-shaped epimedium leaves out of which the bulbous flowers would rise like phoenixes, then die back again and hide in those leaves.

After replacing the rough bark mulch on the planting site, she sat back on her heels and let out an audible sigh of pleasure. Who could guess that beneath this patch of dirt there was such potential? It was one of the immense joys of gardening, to hide secrets under the soil—bulbs and seeds— and watch them evolve into flowers. For a moment, it made her feel powerful and godlike.

A shaft of sunlight from on high sliced through the tall trees, touching Louise's face and setting her quickly back in her place as a mere mortal. She smiled, realizing that these woods had a claim on her stronger than she knew. Maybe she was changing, becoming more of a pantheist than a Presbyterian. She felt closer to God when working in her gardens than she ever did in church. It was as if she were the servant of the woods, the sweet gums and oaks that reached one hundred feet into the sky, the dogwood, wild cherry, and sassafras that swarmed through the understory. Since her house almost disappeared in the forest depths, the place was as if untouched by time. Louise's mission, she'd often told her husband Bill and daughter Janie, was not to ruin what was already here.

She collected her equipment and put it away, and returned indoors, walking slowly, reluctant to go back inside. But at least she'd cleared her mind a little of the I-hate-Bunny clutter.

Once indoors, she heard the phone and caught it on the fourth ring. It was her producer, Marty Corbin.

"What's up, Marty?"

"Bad news, Lou."

She suddenly felt cold. "The results of the November sweeps are in."

"You guessed it," said her blunt producer. "Bimbo in the Garden—I mean, Bunny in the Garden—"

Louise laughed appreciatively; Marty had a way of taking pressure off these tense moments.

"Bunny's made whopping gains. Her average for the month was a six rating with an eleven share. That's up from October."

"I'm not surprised." She recalled seeing the tapes of the bawdy Bunny during sweeps, with half her breasts exposed, her bottom half-exposed as she leaned over in her short shorts. Leaving no sexual simile unexploited as she rattled on about gardening. "And what about us?"

"Now, Lou, you know we don't live and die on ratings and sweeps: we're not delivering eyeballs to advertisers like commercial stations do." His voice was a little too casual. "Just the same, it's not good that *Gardening with Nature* is down a point."

"Oh."

Her show had gained audience share steadily over the past year. And now this, and all because of Bunny and her libidinous assault on viewers.

"I know what you're thinkin', Lou," said Marty. "Me, too. We just gotta keep doing a class show, because that's what we started with. It's going to take a lot bigger drop before they replace us with a cooking show or something. We're getting a four point three rating, with an eight share. Still, this isn't good news; it's rough being up against a sex kitten like that. I don't want you to think it's your fault. Hell, the way I hear it, you're not the only one in the garden industry who's being drubbed by this Bunny character."

Louise's stomach was in a knot. Whatever inner peace she'd gained out in the garden had fled. Her mind was back in the old rut, nurturing the three monsters of anxiety, envy, and hatred.

"*Say,*" said her producer, "*you've* been invited to the new First Lady's fancy Christmas garden party. I bet you'll meet Bunny there."

"I'm sure I will. That's just what I'm afraid of."

2

In the newsroom of the *Washington Post*, like most newsrooms across the country, informality was the word. Still, *Metropolitan* editor Warren Rugaber stared in annoyance at the reporter's butt reposing on the corner of his mahogany desk. But then, from the minute he'd been hired through some special pull with the publisher, Charlie Hurd, owner of the butt, had been a source of annoyance to the editor.

"Look, Warren," said the pinchy-faced young man, in a tone that unwisely implied they were equals, "like you say, every new president's wife has a right to cut new turf for herself. But I see a way to play this story—*I'm* guessing that James Anderson, our shiny new president, is *pussy-whipped!* Otherwise, like I've been telling you, why would a self-respecting, newly elected leader of the free world let his wife have the first shot at all the publicity with a weed-inspired Christmas ball?"

Warren raised a warning hand and kept it up, hoping Charlie Hurd would recognize it as he would a red light. *Stop, Charlie, you asshole!* He could feel the muscles of his back tighten against his leather chair. He deliberately flexed them so they wouldn't crab up during this exasperating meeting. After two years of service, the reporter remained an irritation to his editor: although he still seemed wet behind the ears, he'd come up with some remarkable scoops that had ended up spread all over the front page. On the other hand, Charlie was a screw-up. Recently, his high-handed methods had required a long, contrite skinback to save the paper from a lawsuit.

Warren wished he had some farther corner of the suburbs to send him. As it was, since northern Virginia was his territory, the twerp naturally inherited the story of the president's wife's Christmas party and native plant conference in Alexandria.

"Listen, Charlie, I'm not kidding," said the editor. "I want you to treat Maud Anderson benignly."

Charlie's lip curled in a little sneer.

"I mean it. Write it straight—we'll center it in local news, and Graphics can put a twiny flower border around it. It's not up there with interpretive stories about the bitter aftermath of the election, or Anderson's cabinet picks— those will be the stories that dominate our front pages in the next few weeks. Besides, she's following in the footsteps of the unimpeachable Lady Bird Johnson; it's going to be hard to fault her. So try to make nice with the story, huh? For Chrissake, who can quarrel with using more native plants in America?"

With that, Charlie's butt slid off the desk. He stood accusingly in front of his editor, like a righteous six-year-old. "I get it, Warren. You don't want me to politicize the story. Well, maybe it doesn't matter that the first move of this administration is a goddamned *garden* party."

Now the editor flipped his hand in a dismissive motion. "Missing the point again, Charlie. Her *garden* party and her little 'advisory' conference are jackshit. What we really will need to cover—but that will be someone else's province, not yours, since it will all be happening in the District—is how the new First Lady influences her husband on other issues. That's the much more important story."

"You mean she's hot on global warming?"

Warren permitted himself a smile. Sometimes this guy Hurd was funny. "She is, and environmental issues in general. She's very much against environmental degradation, just like all of us who like to breathe. Especially worries about that ozone layer. But this lady's a true believer, puts her money where her mouth is: did you know that years ago she was chained with nineteen others to a sequoia tree for a *week*?"

Warren caught a sheepish look overcoming Charlie's face. He'd out-researched the cocky little bastard. "I hadn't known that," said Charlie, "but I would have found it out when I checked her out."

"Yeah, you would have. You can go into some of her background in your story, but let's not make it into an exposé, when it isn't. In other words, let's not *make* news, just report it."

Charlie started to leave. Then he wheeled around and stood at Warren Rugaber's office door, rocking back and forth from his toes to his heels. "Y'know," he said, "they're not letting any of the press *attend* this fancy ball. Just what does that mean, Warren? I say, something's going on." Then he turned his pointy nose up to the ceiling and snapped his fingers as if he'd had a revelation from on high.

"I *know* how to get the goods on that party. Louise Eldridge is on the guest list."

The editor's signaling hand went up again hurriedly. "No, no, Charlie, not that woman again. You've already defamed our local TV garden host once in our paper—our friendly *Post* ombudsman had a helluva time straightening things out."

But the reporter was not ready to give up. He came back to the mahogany desk, leaned forward and spread his hands down on the wood surface to support his weight. The editor suddenly wanted to reach over and slap the young fellow's face. Instead he sat back and relaxed his shoulders and waited for Charlie to make his final pitch and get the hell out.

"Look, Warren, Louise will be there, at both the party and the conference. So will that British gardening dingbat, Bunny Bainfield. She has become to gardening what Donald Trump is to New York real estate. I mean, her company trades on the NASDAQ for thirty dollars a share, for God's sake. Why, just the two of them alone ought to create some real fireworks—" Seeing the editor's continued chilly reaction, he quieted his voice a little. "All I mean to say is that if anything interesting happens at all, I'll at least have an inside source. Why, the top Department of Agriculture people will be there. How do we know—maybe Maud's deciding to wage a war on behalf of some endangered warthog or something—"

Warren glared at the reporter. Wouldn't he ever give up? *"Drop it,* Charlie," he growled. *"*The Eldridge woman's off limits, and that's *that. "* Then, he turned to the pile of stories lying before him on the desk and shut Charlie Hurd out of his mind.

3

Richard Ralston coaxed the flower stems into the slippery green oasis and felt the magic flowing from his fingers. He'd achieved his success by creating with these hands. Yet he rarely did flower arranging anymore, simply because running his floral empire—four shops in Washington, D.C., and branches in New York, L.A., and San Francisco—left him no time for it. Bouquets were left to two designers and a dozen floral arrangers, just as sales were left to his two account executives, bridal consulting to his bridal consultant, and bills to his bookkeeper. Richard, who'd topped off a floral design degree with a master's in business administration, spent his time thinking of creative business strategies.

Today was different, though. He was having fun, exhilarated by having been handed the biggest job of his career. He was experimenting with a floral concoction that was out of place for sophisticated

Washington, D.C., and out of season for December. But it was the kind of thing his new commission called for.

His cell phone rang. "Damn," he muttered, hating the interruption. He looked down at the screen and saw the caller was Ken Lurie in New York. He pressed the start button, talking through the headpiece worn against his short red curls. "Hey, *Ken.*"

"Hey, *Richard.* Just called up to talk about things."

"Listen, I hate to do this, but I have to make you wait. I'm in a zone and you know how *that* is. If you'll just quietly hang on for a few minutes, I'll be right back with you."

In his ear, Richard could hear Ken humming the old tune, "As Time Goes By." He smiled, picturing his handsome friend trying to distract him. But he was not about to be distracted. His bright blue eyes turned back to his work.

What lay beneath his hands was nearly done. It was a masterpiece, and he was going to sign it, just as if he were an Old Master. Actually, it was a huge arrangement, over four feet long and three feet wide, and meant to evoke the American native prairie in late summer. Its base was formed of lush native grasses growing in black dirt. In the back rose tall, tan, dried grasses twined with the clawlike seedpods—redolent of the early death of many plants by late summer. Rising above this mostly green expanse were poppies, coneflowers, and penstemon. Richard busily finished plugging them in.

Then he added his "signature," three dramatic blood red sunflowers, their stems wired for extra strength. Not minding that he was stressing the chunks of well-anchored oasis at their base, he forced the majestic flowers to lean a bit instead of standing straight, then gentled the delicate poppies below them into erotic curving positions that he hoped would evoke fantasies in the minds of both men and women. Richard firmly believed in the eroticism of flowers. He looked at his work and was pleased. The plants sprang so intuitively from this plane of grasses that an uninitiated person might swear, had it been September instead of December, that someone had *dug* this creation out of Nebraska and flown it intact to his Washington, D.C., shop.

Now that he was done, he turned his attention back to Ken. He could hear his friend's strained tenor approach the climactic moment of the classic love song—". . . *the fun—damental things apply, as—*"

Richard bluntly interrupted. "Beautiful, Ken, beautiful. I'm back. Sorry I had to put you on hold but I'm doing something special here."

"I know, you were in a zone. You're an arrogant *shit* when you're in a zone."

"Sorry, but I've been in one ever since Maud Anderson gave me the job. I'm doing a little practice arrangement right now."

"Huh. Filled with native plants, huh? I still can't believe the wife of a newly elected president would one-up her husband by throwing a party like that."

"It is strange, I guess," said Richard, finally done harassing the flowers. "The fellow hasn't even had a chance to name a cabinet. I just said to myself, though, 'A job is a job.' "

"I bet you did," said Ken in a sarcastic voice. "All this in the name of promoting native plants. That's not a new idea—Lady Bird Johnson did it thirty-five years ago. I suppose she thinks it's real hot, like organic food. On the other hand, it's a helluva lot better for us than if Maud Anderson'd decided that her favorite First Lady project was going to be mental *health*. That would have earned the two of us squat."

Richard laughed. Horticulture had been good to Ken, just as it had been to Richard. While Richard had come to rule as the nation's top florist, his New York–based friend made a fat living as a garden writer and magazine publisher, with a trendy new garden book coming out in less than two weeks. "That's what I like about you, Ken: you never forget the bottom line."

"So I hear this is a huge production—the flowers you're doing for the new First Lady."

"It *is* huge, Ken—you'll love it. But Gadsby's Tavern is an outlandish location, though it's very historic, I'll give it that. Being an insulated New Yorker the way you are, I don't suppose you've ever been to Old Town, Alexandria." Richard rattled on, not waiting for his friend's answer. "I went to check it out. The tavern and its hotel may have been the place to go back in the late 1700s, but, man, not today. It's going to be a nightmare. You go up these narrow, winding stairs to get to the ballroom, and naturally there's no elevator to carry up the *tons* of plants I'll be bringing there. Once you're there, the space is disastrously small for the grandiose plans Maud has in mind. To top it off, the joint stinks: it has a nose-tingling musty smell that makes you want to *puke*."

Ken laughed. "You've plenty of people to carry plants up a flight of stairs. And your nose always has been too sensitive. A little smell is nothing; the flowers will mask it."

"Maybe they will, since there'll be thousands of them—in contrast to the fact there'll only be about fifty guests. That makes, what? Two hundred, three hundred flowers per guest?"

"Sounds heavy-duty. I thought you were all booked up for inauguration events."

"Booked up to my eyeballs. Two inaugural balls, a dozen other bashes." His tone was calm, yet just listing all his obligations made his stomach churn, and he wished his antacids were handy. "This party comes first, however, and as Maud says, 'First must be best.' She wants me to turn that ballroom into a floral *bacchanalia,* with native plants front and center." He laughed hopelessly. "How I'm gonna do a bacchanalia with sickletop spleenwort, I haven't figured out yet. Right now, I'm fooling around with sunflowers, poppies, penstemon, and coneflower."

Ken laughed. "Don't try to get that by *me*—I know my native plants. That's sickletop *lousewort,* not spleenwort. Well, our new First Lady obviously knows that floral arrangements for rich people's parties have gone over the top. Besides, since the people invited to this affair are the country's top gardeners, she has to do something colossal. Once they're living in the White House, though, you won't get a dime's worth of business from her."

"Nope. The Park Service takes over then."

"I suppose rich Dems are paying the bill for this one," said Ken.

"You've nailed it. And I'll happily take their money." With one final touch to a coneflower, Richard stepped back, put his hands on his hips, and silently congratulated himself: he'd just consummated a love affair with six dozen flowers and twelve square feet of virgin grass. He emitted a long groan of pleasure. "Mmmm . . ."

"What are you moaning about?" Ken wanted to know. "What's *really* going on there?"

"I only wish you were here to see what I've just created. It's so good that I can't even describe it. I know—I'll shoot some photos and send them to you."

Richard blew out a breath, not wanting to bring up the subject with Ken, but feeling that he had to. "Uh, you're cool about Bunny coming to the party?"

Ken's voice was surly. "Sure, I'm cool. The limey slut isn't going to get to *me.*"

Richard recoiled slightly at the vehemence of the voice in his ear.

"On the other hand, why was *she* invited? Doesn't this Maud Anderson have any taste in people? Does she really think Bunny Bainfield *amounts* to something in the gardening world?"

"Calm down, buddy," soothed Richard, "it'll be all right."

But Ken fumed on. "I can see Bunny shoving her weight around, trying to dominate everything and everybody. She'll ruin the party. Well, she isn't invited to my book party at Trelage, you can bet on that."

"I don't blame you for hating her, Ken. You've had a rough go with that queen bitch of garden takeovers. She's after your body *and* your business."

"Richard, the woman's had the nerve to tell me that she'd drive me into bankruptcy if I didn't partner up with her. *Right.* I'd rather be dead."

"She just wants to acquire a thriving garden publishing venture," said the florist. "It would be another jewel in her crown."

"Well, Bunny ain't getting *my* jewel—or my *jewels,* either. Y'know what? I don't think Maud Anderson knows this woman at all; otherwise, she'd know people in the gardening industry walk on the other side of the street when they see her coming."

Richard shrugged his shoulders. "It's simply a

case where a million dollars of self-marketing pays off: the woman's landing on the White House 'A' list."

Ken lapsed into silence at the other end of the line. Then he said, "This party may not be any fun at all."

"If it's any comfort, you should know Bunny's been twisting me, too. It's that damned *bunny-bouquets.com.*"

"Same shit?"

"Same shit. She's gonna ruin me, too, she says, if I don't get in bed with her little Internet venture." He laughed. "I hope *I* can avoid her at this Christmas party. I'll just take cover in my flowers and native grasses. Ken, seriously, this is going to be a floral extravaganza that no one will ever forget!"

4

Bunny Bainfield tapped her long fingernails on her desktop and frowned faintly at a neatly stacked pile of papers sitting in front of her. "Anything urgent here, Peg?"

"Not much, really. Just what I put in your briefcase."

Bunny glanced sulkily at her assistant. Peg's elongated oval face reminded her of Matisse on a bad day, but that was just a detail; worst of all to deal with was her attitude. Peg had become a nosy, demanding, smothering woman. "Good," Bunny said, "because I'm *dead*." She leaned far back and rested her head on the chair top so that her platinum-colored sheath of hair fell loosely down behind her. Her damned neck felt as though it were in a vise; she'd spent the entire afternoon in a taping session in a TV studio in downtown Washington, demonstrating for the idiots who watched her gardening show how to make a bloody philodendron flourish. Only an idiot, she well realized, would need that information.

"Does it hurt, *kleiner Liebling*?" asked Peg.

Bunny sighed impatiently, causing her fawn-colored, deeply V-necked cashmere sweater to heave like a swell in the ocean. She didn't even want to look at her sycophantic companion right now, so she closed her eyes. Closed out the dark-haired, dark-eyed woman who wanted her so desperately. If she gave Peg even the tiniest encouragement, she would be all over Bunny, clawing at her body, massaging her tired neck, hoping they'd retire to the adjoining small lounge with its ample couch.

Bunny raised a graceful hand in a blocking motion, noticing how well her nails had weathered the gardening dirt she'd acquired while showing the demented how to repot houseplants. The nails were done in a rusty mahogany shade, a wonderful foil for her huge two-carat diamond ring. "No time for a neck rub, luv. I have to go to the house and have a drink with my sweetie."

Decoded, that meant spending a dull-as-dishwater evening with her impotent old husband, Bobby. But since Bunny'd ignored the man for most of the week, she knew it was time to pay homage to the fact that he'd created this little nursery empire in Frederick, Maryland. It was in the nursery's executive office that she now lounged. Once called Frederick Nursery, it was now enlarged and named in her honor, Bunnyland, which showed just how deeply Bobby cared for her.

Bunny divided the world into animal, vegetable, and mineral. Animal was what most men were. Vegetable was what had made her a millionaire, those acres of plants she sold in stores across the country. Mineral was the rocks she wore on her fingers, and occasionally around her neck: diamonds, sapphires, and rubies, all given to her by Bobby.

But it was important to throw a bone to Peg as well, for Peg had played her part in Bunny's rise to fame.

"I'm bloody exhausted, Peg. It took three hours to tape the program today. The *damnable* producer has the mind of an idiot. I'll have him sacked by month's end."

"He doesn't know how to show you off to your best advantage."

Bunny sniffed, "I wouldn't say *that.* Now, don't go off the deep end about every man in my life. If he doesn't know how to show me off well, how do you think my ratings are up so sharply?"

"Well—" Confusion. Peg was smart, but it was easy to confuse her. "Then why get him sacked?"

Bunny looked coolly at her assistant. "Lack of respect."

"*No!* How terrible. I had no idea, since I don't come with you to these tapings. What does he do? What does he say to you?"

"Nothing. Of *course* he says and does nothing untoward." She swiveled her head around to loosen the neck muscles, then sat up very straight, trying to imagine that her head was being drawn upward by a magnet to the ceiling. "It's the way he looks at me. He's a Princeton graduate, you know, just twenty-five or so, and he looks right through me as if he *knows* I didn't attend Cambridge or Oxford, or even *Leeds!* He thinks he's something quite special, but I'll show him he can't look at me that way. I just happen to have had my status elevated: I'm going to be the confidante of the First Lady of the United States after that garden party of hers."

"Oh, Bunny, are you sure we should go to that

party? There will be people there who don't like
you—"

"Yes, we are going, and you needn't try to drag
your feet, just because Fenimore Smith or Ken Lurie
will be there. They're my colleagues, after all."

"But, *Liebling*, they chase after you—"

Bunny swiveled around in her chair and
squarely faced Peg. "Let's get things clear, luv: I'm
leading my life the way I want, and I'm getting just
a bit ticked off at the way you're starting to inter-
fere." She narrowed her blue eyes. "Just remember, Peg, I *know* about you, I know every little
detail of your past. I'm going to live my life any
damned way I please, and I'll screw as many men
as I feel like, and you can sit and watch if you like,
but just keep your opinions to yourself. Otherwise,
I may be forced to do what *you're* so good at—
smearing your reputation so that, who knows? The
Feds might even be interested in deporting you!"

"Bunny," pleaded Peg, "you've misunderstood
me. I never intended—"

Bunny was uninterested in the whinings of this
woman. "Furthermore, we're going full speed ahead
with our research on native plants. By the time Maud
Anderson gets her campaign in gear, Bunnyland
will have the biggest and the sexiest supply of native plants in the whole damned country!"

"Of course we will," agreed Peg. "You know I've
been devoting all my efforts to that. Um, back to
the subject of your producer: how will you explain
wanting to get rid of him when the show is doing
so well?"

Bunny waved her hand airily. "It will be just like
one of those American divorces: I'll say we have 'ir-
reconcilable differences.' "

In a cautious voice, Peg said, "You'll be making
another enemy."

"He's *nothing*. Or he's nothing so far. Someday, I suppose he'll amount to something in the world of television, but a twit like that is no threat to *me*. The enemy *I* intend to make is much bigger—"

"Not Ken Lurie."

"Oh, but *yes,* Ken Lurie. There's a man who's going to get his just desserts." She exhaled an angry breath. "Nobody gets away with insulting me the way he has."

"Personally, or professionally?"

Bunny was annoyed again, Peg wanted to know too much. She could see the end of their relationship rapidly approaching. "If you must know, *both.*" She turned a steady gaze on her assistant. "I tried to make friends with him, you know that, but he's *afraid* to make friends with me." Bunny'd hit on Ken, and Peg knew it. Peg also knew and delighted in the fact that the egotistical lout had turned her down cold. Peg knew too much. "And he refuses even to *discuss* the possibility of a business merger. Well, he'll find out what little Bunny does when little Bunny's angry."

She slid her chair back and got up, noting Peg watching her every move. She slung her fawn-colored leather jacket fashionably over her shoulder and paused, as if posing for a fashion shot. "And now, I really have to run. Bobby's expecting me. Good old Bobby; he's the one man who's never given me an ounce of trouble." She looked meaningfully at Peg. "If only I could say the same thing of you." Then she strode out of the office, high-heeled boots tapping on the wooden parquet floor, hips switching a little in her tight leather pants because she knew the frustrated Peg was watching her all the way.

5

Gene Clendenin shuffled into his office on the fourth floor of the Agriculture Building and hung up his worn tweed jacket on a coat rack near the door. He pulled out his chair and settled in at his desk, resting his hands gently on the aged oak desktop. It was like settling in for a talk with an old friend. He loosened his tie and unbuttoned the top button of his shirt, then wiggled his neck to get the flesh sitting right. Only then did he address the work sitting before him.

First, he tackled the three-inch-high pile of pink telephone messages, shuffling them with stubby but deft fingers into the order of their importance. He set them alongside the stack of date-stamped, opened mail his secretary had prepared. It was six inches high, and already sorted in the order that she thought was most important.

What concerned him right now was the gilt-edged invitation propped up against his desk lamp. He'd not yet responded to it, though he'd received it more than a week ago; he had to do something about it today. He carefully reread it and scanned the lengthy insert that accompanied it, then propped it back against the lamp.

Annoyingly, his heart began to beat faster. That was the sign of anger building up, and he'd felt a lot of anger lately; he knew it was because he was ticked off at his wife for dying on him. He had to get a handle on it or he'd join her in the hereafter: his blood pressure had gone right through the roof.

He took a deep breath and tried to assess the situation without emotion. Clendenin was a bureaucrat, and proud of it. Bureaucrats were always having to handle problems such as the one presented by the material in that invitation. As chief of the USDA's Department of Natural Resources Conservation Service, he'd toiled for thirty years to make sense of man's crucial and perilous relation to the land. He guided the work of people in each of the fifty states who were trying desperately to do the right thing. They were some of the finest people he'd ever known, selfless, working with plant materials, both native and introduced, to make them more adaptable to the places in which they were being used.

Though not an ounce of sentiment flowed through his veins, Clendenin viewed this replenishing of pastures, roadsides, and native habitats as truly saving America the Beautiful and its most precious natural resource, the soil.

This damned invitation threw his work into jeopardy. Roughly shoving a few strands of silver hair over his balding head, he tilted his chair back and considered the problem. In fact, had he not recently given up tobacco, he would have lit up his pipe, just like Maigret in those Simenon mysteries.

Like Inspector Maigret, it had helped him think. Unfortunately, he now was on his own, sans nicotine, sans consoling wife.

The facts were these: an environmentally friendly president was coming into office, and that was a relief. But the man's wife was showing herself to be a wild card. She was going off half-cocked even before her husband was sworn in as chief executive.

Clendenin was a clever man, who along the years had known when to cover his ass and when to speak up. He was a good friend to others, and he'd built up plenty of sources in this snake-filled city of Washington. His sources told him why Maud Anderson was acting so precipitously: two of the worst characters in the gardening industry had gotten her ear. Bunny Bainfield and Bob Touhy had talked her into this glib "supporting native plants in America" program. It was not only redundant, it was a smoke screen for their own benefit.

Touhy, klutz that he was, only wanted power among his radical environmental set. But Bunny Bainfield was empire-building. He'd seen the woman only on television, hosting her ridiculous gardening show, breasts hanging out of her dress, silver hair dangling over her face. She was what his decent mother would have called a "tart."

As silly-looking as she was, the woman had to be taken seriously. She had already cut a swath through an industry that was worth billions annually; she couldn't be ignored. Now, she wanted to open a whole new market in a hot new field: native plants. What better mouthpiece for that than the First Lady of the United States?

What scared Clendenin was how Bainfield planned to fill the public demand for native plants. In her huge Maryland nursery, she was genetically tinkering with America's native stock—trying to make the flowers bigger, the leaves shinier, and the smell as much like the perfume of a French prostitute as her technicians could achieve. As far as he was concerned, that was going too goddamned far.

Few things did Clendenin deem holy, but one of them was America's native plant species, which he had worked for thirty years to cherish and preserve.

Now Maud Anderson wanted the top gardeners in America to rubber-stamp her idea—that was the sole reason for this fancy ball and conference. It was all he could do not to toss her invitation into the wastebasket.

He stared bleakly out the window of his office into the grayness of Independence Avenue. Since he'd recently lost the person who was at the very heart of his existence, he couldn't bear to lose any more.

He refused to jeopardize the work of his agency for this cockamamie scheme. Why, the states already struggled to find enough native plants and scarce native plant seed to serve the country's needs. The mischief this campaign could do was immeasurable. In addition to threatening plant resources and opening the door to irresponsible manipulation of native species, he could picture still another harmful result: American gardeners, lusting for these popular flowers, going into the wild and ripping out endangered species that his agency and others were trying so desperately to save!

This notion of Maud Anderson's had to be squelched. But how? He made it a policy never to fight frontally with people, and the wife of an incoming president was the last person he'd tilt swords with. But in some way he had to make an impact on the woman so that she would draw back and let people with some sense in their heads do their work.

Clendenin made his decision. He would attend the party and the conference; he couldn't leave the field to the barbarians.

He swiveled around in his chair to face his wall bookcase, and through his thick glasses peered at the titles of the reference volumes there, as if one of them would give him an answer. *Preserving Native Habitats in North America. Introduction of Beneficial Insects for Weed Control, and Their Unintended Consequences. Poisonous Plants in America. Land Use as a Philosophy.*

He often found his answers in books.

6

The subject of the new First Lady's party came up that night, when Louise Eldridge disclosed to her husband that she'd bought a new dress to wear—though she didn't disclose how much she paid for it.

Bill Eldridge suspended his fork over his plate. "By the way, isn't it a little odd for a person to hold a garden party in December?"

"Apparently the woman needs advice," said Louise. "Monday, after the ball in Gadsby's Tavern, she'll have an all-day meeting at The Federalist Hotel. She wants us experts to tell her whether she's on the right track with this native plant idea."

Bill said, "Well, is she?"

Louise, who since becoming hostess of a gardening show was expected to be an authority on all things horticultural, said, "Even I can see the downside, let's put it that way."

Her husband said, "I thought there were more

pressing issues for First Ladies. Oh, well. I suppose we were invited because you're on the National Environmental Commission."

"I suppose," said Louise, her mouth full of chicken and broccoli. The casserole, a recipe from her *Twenty-Minute Cookbook*, seemed to have suffered a little freezer burn.

Their seventeen-year-old daughter, Janie, flipped her long blond hair out of her face, stared at her mother, and said, "And you got appointed to that Environmental Commission because you found out the president had nominated a *murderer* to be a cabinet member." Her tone was angry, as if the matter had brought infamy to the Eldridge family. Regrettably, Louise's occasional involvement in solving crimes seemed to bother her daughter more as she grew older.

Louise looked over and saw that the seventeen-year-old was toying with her food with one hand, and playing with the cat with the other. Thank heavens for a distracting pet to soothe the resentment of the disgruntled teenager. Janie was delighted to have such a lively playmate, for although he was twelve, Hargrave still acted like a kitten. It wasn't as if they hadn't been warned, after a fashion: the friend in Connecticut who'd given them the cat had said guardedly that he had a "spirited approach to life." Hargrave also had dog qualities, for he liked to follow Louise around the house wherever she went. She was glad to have him around, since soon that beloved daughter sitting across the table would leave for college and she and Bill would be left with an empty nest. Maybe a meowing tabby would help to fill it.

Louise broke from her reverie and said, "Eat, Janie, and don't just play with the cat. You don't want to lose weight." Janie's hair had fallen back over one eye, further blurring the question of whether she was a potential anorexic, or whether she simply hated her dinner. Janie's hair, Louise realized, was like a door. When down over the eye, the door of communication was closed; when brushed back over the ear, the door was open.

Louise gave up on that for the moment and turned her attention to her husband. She pointed her fork at the little pile of papers Maud Anderson had sent, now in front of her on the table. "Darling, read that list of people who are coming to the con-ference—garden writers, nursery people, plant and tree experts, heads of botanical gardens and plant societies. You'll smile when you see the British-American Horticultural Society listed next to the Native Plant Society. What a combination that will be—elitist, British-style gardeners in the same room with muddy-booted environmentalists who like native plants."

"Gee whiz," said Janie sarcastically, "think of all those sitting ducks among that garden gang that you can sucker into appearing on your *program.*"

Louise gave her daughter a shrewd look. "Smart girl—you've read my mind."

Bill said, "I didn't think native plants were that big yet."

"Oh, but they are," said Louise. "Immigrants to America scorned them—thought they were too or-dinary to bother with: they liked those European plants they tucked into their trunks. But now na-tive plants are so *in;* that's why I wonder if this campaign to promote them is really necessary. But the meeting's going to be terrifically exciting for me, Bill—all those great garden figures gathered together, Theodore Van Sickle, Shelby Newcross, Nathaniel Poe—"

"I can hardly wait myself," he said whimsically.

"And then just going to a formal Christmas party will be fun, too. It's helping to get my mind off Christmas."

Her husband and daughter both looked at her silently. They already knew how she felt about Christmas, and why. Both sets of parents were coming to stay for the holiday, hers flying in from Chicago, Bill's driving in from Connecticut. That fact alone made her stomach clench. Bill's parents were Republicans, while hers were liberal Democrats. Politics and the related topic of the environment would have to be declared off-limits, for the last time they got together, Louise and her mother-in-law, Jean Eldridge, disagreed over whether there really *was* global warming. Jean thought it merely an environmentalist scare tactic. Being a fervent environmentalist herself, Louise was shocked into silence.

Jean not only didn't share her politics, she had little interest in gardening, and silently registered disapproval of her daughter-in-law's ventures into crime-solving. Still another problem was Louise's: she dreaded cooking a Christmas dinner under her mother-in-law's eye, for the woman was a chef of Julia Child proportions.

Her daughter's words interrupted her reverie. "So, lots of big shots coming to this party, huh? Why didn't you mention Bunny Bainfield? I bet she's coming, isn't she?"

"Well, yes, as a matter of fact, she is."

"The party won't be much fun with her there, will it?" continued Janie. "We've heard enough about how you hate Bunny Bainfield. You do hate her, don't you?"

"Janie, don't be silly." Louise had struggled enough today in that muck.

Her daughter was watching her closely. "I've seen her TV show once. She's quite a dish—I mean, if you like dyed platinum hair and boobs hanging halfway out of a dress."

"I think that's how she's made millions," said Louise primly. "But you have to give her credit— she's filled with energy and she's into everything you can think of, including those dot-com businesses. I can't go to a garden center without seeing a plant with a 'Bunny in Your Garden' tag, and her face grinning out at me. But I really don't hate her—I just think her approach to gardening is tacky."

Janie chortled. "Gee, Ma, what a surprise. 'Tacky' is the woman's M.O. I don't know why you bother to be jealous of her, though she has invaded your space, I guess."

Loftily, Louise said, "It makes me unhappy to think that someone like that could succeed so well on TV—though, of course, we don't compete for the same audience."

Janie lifted a skeptical eyebrow and said, "I thought gardeners were all the same."

Louise gave her daughter a sober look. "Not really, dear. There are gardeners and there are *gardeners*. . . ."

Bill smiled, as if she'd said something amusing. Then he said, "Janie's right about why Bunny's show's a hit. It's part of the new trend in TV. What could be better than a female garden show hostess with excess cleavage and a cockney accent?"

"Both phony, no doubt." Louise looked down at her inexpressibly plain self in drab gardening clothes and a sweatshirt that made her appear flat-chested.

"Now, seriously, Ma," said Janie, tucking her hair back of her ear again, "you need to follow the advice you gave me once when I had trouble with a kid at Groveton High. You said, 'Turn the other cheek and try to like the other person. In fact, *force* yourself to find something to like in the other person. The two of you might become friends.' "

The girl reached a slim hand out and rested it on her mother's arm. "Remember when you told me all that?"

Louise stared at her seventeen-year-old with curiosity. "Vaguely. Did it work?"

"Like a charm. So you go to this Christmas ball and you say to yourself, 'Can I stand this human being, and if I can't, what kind of a person does that make me?' You need to be really nice to her, and who knows, she might even be nice to you."

"The stories I've heard about Bunny Bainfield make me doubt that. But it does give me an idea—" She looked at her husband and said, "Since charity begins at home, maybe I should try the kill-her-with-kindness technique on your mother."

7

Sometimes Fenimore Smith had the entertaining idea that his wife Lily looked like the x-ray women Tom Wolfe had described in his book, *Bonfire of the Vanities.* Lily Smith wore a black, strapless dress that revealed her wide, bony shoulders, though her smooth pageboy hairdo and a swath of pearls on her long neck helped to soften the look.

Whatever his private opinions, he knew Lily liked a compliment from him before they entered a party; he usually tossed it to her at the very last moment.

They were now at the top of the creaky, circular staircase of Gadsby's Tavern. He cupped his hand around the bottom of her left buttock; she still had a good, round butt. "You look ravishing, my dear, have I told you that?"

"No, but thank you, darling, for the kind words." She looked coyly at him. "I hope your head is not turned tonight by anyone lovelier than me."

This was all talk, of course. Marital fidelity wasn't their top priority. Lily tolerated a certain level of straying on his part. Conversely, he never looked too deeply into her affairs, which occurred when she took an occasional vacation or weekend trip on her own.

What was important to both of them were his publishing career, her garden design career, their nursery business—and tonight's mission.

"*Attendez-vous,* Lily, *mon amour,*" he said, casting a quick look at the cocktail party crowd they'd just joined. "The gang's all here. Just remember: this is probably our last chance. We have to do it right, or we're going to lose everything. Do you have the nerve?"

Lily drew in a deep breath, and he saw her dark-painted lips tremble faintly. "I have the nerve, but please quit talking about it, will you? It just makes me more edgy. We've talked enough."

"I know, dear," said Fenimore. "Talk is tiresome. No more talk. Now's the time for action."

Louise and Bill ascended the circular staircase and stepped into a room full of people that, at first, they could barely see in the flickering candle-light.

"How wonderful," exclaimed Louise. "This must be what a party was like in colonial days."

"Tell me you see someone you know," Bill muttered, "if you can see at all."

"Our eyes will get adjusted soon," she assured him, tugging unobtrusively at the bodice of her strapless green silk dress. "In fact, I do make out some people I know—several of them."

They were in the smaller of the second-floor

ballrooms of the City Hotel, the hostelry attached to Gadsby's Tavern in the heart of historic Old Town, Alexandria, where the cocktail portion of Maud Anderson's Christmas party was in full swing. The old hotel and tavern had been a favorite stopping spot for Revolutionary-era soldiers and businessmen, when Alexandria was a busy port city. The incoming First Lady was giving it more attention than it had had in 200 years.

The guests milled noisily about in the centuries-old room whose light emanated from huge candelabra, but bolstered, as it turned out, by discreetly placed baseboard lights. Suspended across the high ceiling were ropes of flowers, giving the place the aspect of a hanging garden.

The lavish party was a familiar scene for Louise and Bill, since his job in the State Department, a cover for his actual job as an undercover CIA agent, had obliged them to attend interminable formal functions over the years, especially in the years when they were stationed at overseas posts. Louise thought of at least one reason for staging these parties—the salubrious "Cinderella's ball" effect. People, at least temporarily, were transformed, the men into handsome creatures by the simple act of putting on black jacket and tie, and the women into beauties by long gowns that concealed their figure flaws.

As at ease as she and Bill were in such situations, still it was comforting to see a few familiar faces; otherwise, they'd do a "cold circuit" of the room, as Bill described it. She waved at a couple of acquaintances, including a big, blond woman in a flowery gown, exuding bonhomie, or perhaps simple drunkenness. She was weaving through the crowd greeting first one and then another colleague. "There's Joanna Heath, for instance," Louise told Bill. "We'll have to go and talk with her. But first we'd better pay our respects to our hosts."

The couple was the focus of attention, greeting guests in a receiving line in front of a fireplace at the end of the historic room. Incoming president James Anderson was overshadowed by the dramatic-looking Maud, resplendent in red silk. Near them in the crowd, dark-suited Secret Service agents peered at every face in the crowd. They gave the party an added air of excitement, Louise decided, as did the presence of a roving photographer. He was a tense little man whose face she probably would never see, since the camera appeared to be glued to it.

As she and Bill approached the Andersons, Louise whispered, "Maud outshines her husband, don't you think?"

Bill whispered, "Don't be fooled by him. Under that faded hair and pasty face is a political genius. How else was he able to shake the dynastic son out of the White House?"

They strolled over to the receiving line and shuffled forward slowly. Finally, they stood in front of the president-elect and his wife. As they shook hands, Mrs. Anderson told Louise, "I'm sure you're going to have invaluable advice for me when we meet tomorrow—"

Before the woman could finish the sentence, the Eldridges were maneuvered away by tense Secret Service agents so that other guests in the crowded line could speak to the Andersons.

Bill's eyes were scanning the room. "Something's making the Secret Service edgy tonight." He was an authority on these things, having been in government for more than twenty years. "I'd guess it's all those giant candelabra, for who knows what kind of fire exits this old place has. And there are too many rooms to cover; there's a warren of little spaces attached to these ballrooms."

As they left the receiving line, they almost bumped into an older couple standing nearby, a white-haired woman in rose-colored lace, the man portly and dignified, with a white beard, both with that exhilarated look that descends on people's faces at successful parties. Louise and Bill were among their friends now.

Louise greeted them and said, "Dr. and Mrs. Van Sickle, this is my husband, Bill. Dr. Van Sickle's head of the National Horticultural Society; he's appeared on my show twice—"

"Louise," Van Sickle jovially complained, "by this time, you must call me Ted. What a wonderful *party* this is—and just to confirm it, I see another friend is here." A tall, very thin man had come up and clasped the elderly Van Sickle on the shoulder. "I want you and Bill to meet Dr. Shelby Newcross. I'm sure you've heard of him."

Louise's heart leaped with pleasure to be in the presence of the great British-American botanist, the discoverer of scores of remote plant species that had now become commonplace in people's gardens. She saw that he was a man who might make women wish they'd chosen a mate further along in years—strikingly handsome, with gray eyes, chiseled features, and a head of thick gray hair. One hardly noticed that his complexion was pale and yellowish. When she extended her hand to shake his, he took the hand and pressed it gently to his lips.

"Enchanted," he said.

She smiled and tried to think of something pithy to ask the great Dr. Newcross, but then their circle widened again, as two more men approached.

This removed the need to say anything, and she realized this party was one of those feverish affairs where there was no need to do much more than smile and drop a bon mot or two. People were moving and shifting like busy molecules under a microscope.

Shelby Newcross introduced the newcomers with courtly panache. "You may know Richard Ralston, Washington's preeminent florist, and Ken Lurie, our foremost garden writer, who has just been mentioned again, I see, in the national press."

"*Forget* Ken and those nasty New York book adventures for a minute," interrupted Ralston, with phony indignation. He was a stocky man with short red curly hair and round blue eyes that gave him a Kewpie doll look. "Please focus on the flowers. How d'ya like those fantastic ropes of blossoms? And what about the candelabra? I had them imported from France."

"Everything's beautiful, Richard," said Dr. Van Sickle. "It's as if we're standing in a bower."

The florist waved a hand. "Oh, but this is nothing. Wait until you go into the big room."

Louise said, "I read in the paper that you've done something special with native plants."

"My dear," Ralston drawled, giving her a wide-eyed stare, "it'll knock you out. I can honestly say it's the most excessive and the most enjoyable floral challenge of my career. And it's all *native* plants! And don't think it was easy: Secret Service agents have been on my tail all day, checking out every plant, flower, and tree that we dragged up these stairs, for weapons."

"I look forward to seeing your masterpiece," commented Shelby Newcross in his cultured English accent. "It sounds very expensive."

"It was," said Ralston. "Isn't it wonderful what

unlimited political donations can do for you? Shelby, you'll have to tell me whether I've gone over the top; you have *such* good taste. And just so you don't think this is a complete case of excess, let me assure you that Maud Anderson has decreed that all these floral numbers will be delivered tomorrow to worthy places like hospitals and nursing homes."

As Richard waxed on, Louise was observing Ken Lurie out of the corner of her eye. She could tell immediately how he had earned his reputation as glamour boy of the gardening industry. Not only was he a beautiful man, with his dark, wavy hair and golden brown eyes, but she could tell he had a winning way with women.

She turned slightly toward him, and could hear him conversing with the elderly Mrs. Van Sickle, complimenting her on her lacy gown, then prying out the fact that her first name was Jessie and that she'd been raised in a small farm town in the South. Soon he had her talking about her early life experiences, and how she'd met Theodore when both were students at the University of North Carolina at Chapel Hill. Mrs. Van Sickle flushed with the attention of the younger man.

The noted garden writer soon turned his charms on Louise. His discreet glance took her in from head to foot. "Louise *Eldridge*—so much more beautiful in the flesh than on TV. You make this party a special moment for me. I've watched your program, of course. I love it—and I especially love your humor." He took her hand in his and looked at it. "And these hands—you have gardener's hands. I love that, too."

"Oh, thanks," she told him, grateful that he appreciated her short, practical nails and skin that had taken a bottle of lotion and lots of rubbing to make smooth. "And your books, Ken—they're my favorites. I often use them as references." *Much more than a reference*, she thought guiltily. But, being professionals in the same field, they both knew using books for a "reference" was little more than a license to steal ideas.

Ken's gardening writing was popular. It was based on sound science, but his style was tinged with purple prose, detailing how sensuous and erotic was the whole world of flowers, plants, and bees.

Louise noticed that Ken maintained his body in a fashionable slouch. Was this natural, she wondered, or was it because the party photographer, who darted about the room like a low-flying bat, was hovering near?

Suddenly, the garden writer warned her, "Get ready," and clasped her around the waist and pulled her toward him. "Smile," he ordered. "You'll look good in the paper tomorrow morning." They both smiled and the flashbulb went off and blinded them. "Good job," he told her, then slowly removed his hand from her waist. Louise shared an amused glance with her husband from across the conversational circle.

Richard, who'd dominated the conversation, said, "Now that I've tooted my own horn, Ken, why don't you tell everyone about your notorious book launch. The important thing wasn't the brouhaha, it's the book," he said, smiling at Ken. *"The Sensory Gardener* is the name of it."

"I'll be glad to tell you the real story," said Ken, a sarcastic tone in his voice, "as opposed to the stories in the newspapers. There was a dynamite book party for me in New York Friday night, at Trelage. Or let's say that for *a while* it was a super party. Why, I can't tell you how much cheap wine was consumed, or how many votive candles were bumped onto the floor by drunk partiers." His face broke into a big smile, and a camera flash blinded them again as the photographer came in for another shot.

"Who *is* that photographer, someone from the *National Enquirer?*" complained Richard.

But Ken wasn't to be interrupted. "Drunkenness and rowdy behavior: that's a sure sign of a party's success, isn't it?"

"Ken did beautifully," chimed in Richard, "even when that wretch had the nerve to break in and attack him—"

Louise glanced up at Ken. "Who? Why would someone attack you?"

Ken scowled, which made him no less attractive. "It was Bunny Bainfield. I'm sure you know her."

Louise, who had been quietly obsessing on the woman for weeks, blushed. "I know *of* her—though I've not met her."

The Van Sickles frowned in concern. Jessie Van Sickle said, "How awful for that to have happened, Ken."

"That's because Bunny Bainfield is a terrible woman," declared Shelby Newcross. "There's little else one can say about her." Then his attention slid away, as he turned to talk to others.

Richard stepped closer to Louise and filled her in on the details. Bill, never known for his keen interest in gossip, put his hands in his pockets and stared at the worn pine floor that dated from 1760.

"Here's the situation, Louise," said Richard. "Now that Bunny's gained a stranglehold on the cut-rate retail nursery trade, she's reaching out to get Ken to let her buy into his publishing firm. He doesn't want her, of course, and certainly doesn't need her. So she shows up at this book party for the sole purpose of making a scene in front of everybody. When Ken politely tells her to leave—"

"She scoops a handful of votive candles off a credenza," continued Ken, "and sends them flying. Unfortunately, when Richard came to help, he and I and Bunny got tangled there for a moment. At that point she yells out, *This is assault and battery!*'" He shook his head in disgust. "My God, it was humiliating."

Richard said, "And now she's threatening to sue the both of us. Can you *believe* it?"

Louise's husband had regained interest in the conversation, and his face flooded with understanding. "Oh, yes—I read about that free-for-all in the *Post* this morning." Louise realized she'd been so busy beautifying herself for this party—a face-mask treatment at home, a trip to the beauty parlor to have her hair done—that she hadn't read the morning papers.

"Free-for-all is right," grumbled Ken. "First time, I think, that a party for a *garden* book has turned into a brawl."

"Or hit the gossip columns in Washington and New York," added Richard. "But Ken knows that it doesn't matter *what* they write about him as long as they mention his name."

Bill looked at Ken with newfound interest, and Louise could read the glance and realized that he wondered what kind of man would be opportunistic enough to crave publicity at any price.

"Bill," she said, sotto voce, "Ken didn't ask for a fight to break out at that book party."

Her husband nodded. "Of course not."

She reluctantly tore her mind away from the subject, for the great botanist had filtered back into the group and was in the midst of one of those general statements people make in order to draw a group together around a single topic. Newcross said, "Quite a distinguished mix of guests here tonight, wouldn't you say?"

Richard looked skeptical. "Who says they'll *mix*? All those foot-slogging native-plant people, like Gail over there, our rough and ready seed expert and Mother Earth figure, trying to mix with *you*, Shelby, so much her opposite, so patrician, so imbued with the English tradition—"

They all laughed at that.

"It's hard for me not to be imbued with the English tradition," said Newcross, "since I was born and educated there."

"Or mixing with Fenimore and Lily Smith," Richard continued, nodding his head at a very thin couple standing nearby. "Look at them: they're refinement personified. But *Wild Flower Farm*, what a wild misnomer *that* is. It evokes an organic, field-flower nursery, not one that specializes in lush English clivia plants." He took another sip of wine, getting into it now. "The Smiths, of course, are your prototypical American devotees of the British gardening tradition, David Austin roses and the whole bit."

Louise looked over at the couple and her curiosity was aroused. It was two years ago that she had met Smith, a successful New York book publisher who also owned Wild Flower Farm. She'd thought of Fenimore Smith as a perfect example of America's old aristocracy with his highbrow manners and lofty attitude toward gardening and life. Then, he'd seemed the unruffled sophisticate, acting as if the world was his oyster, with a casual "nothing really matters, my dear" aura about him as he looked at the world through lazy, hooded eyes. Now, something had changed. True, his flashy good looks were accented by his formal clothes, and yet he seemed thinner, and his body language indicated a man strangely ill at ease. Even his wife, in stylish black, looked uncomfortable, making small, nervous gestures as she talked.

Fortunately, the Smiths seemed unconscious of Louise's surveillance or the fact that their names and the reputation of their nursery were being bandied about.

In the background, the sound of the crowd suddenly hushed as a brilliantly clad woman ascended the stairs and emerged into the room. Her hair was as silver blond as a movie star's out of the 1930s. Her dress, embarrassingly enough, was the same as Louise's but done in candy-pink silk.

A woman followed her closely. She wore a long brown dress that might have looked dowdy to some, but which Louise suspected was an expensive Paris fashion. The woman's dark hair was like a helmet, her face harnessed with horn-rimmed glasses and adorned with just a touch of makeup. It was as if she were Bunny's doppelganger, the shadow of her brilliant-hued associate.

Since Bunny and the dark-haired woman were the last to arrive, they caused a stir in the room. Richard's smile vanished. He said, "This party was so *on*. But now we have Bunny, the great, self-invented Bunny."

Ken's eyes flashed with indignation. "Don't overlook that companion of hers," he muttered. "Peg Roggenstach. She's as bad as Bunny. There's *another* story."

Louise perked up. She recognized in Ken a man who liked to get to the bottom of things and didn't mind exchanging gossip to arrive at the truth. "The woman in brown?" she said. "Who is she, exactly?"

Since Newcross and the Van Sickles were engaged in a separate conversation, she and Richard and Ken could speculate at will. Bill could listen, or not.

"She's Bunny's business agent," explained Ken, "but more than that—she's her private investigator and industry spy."

"She snoops on Bunny's competitors?"

"Oh, more than that," said Ken. "She has gone so far as to hire a private detective to check out the competition, in one area or another. 'Spy and destroy,' that seems to be Bunny's motto, and Peg is her henchman. This puts the two of them in a class by themselves, because people in the gardening industry are not *like* that. Oh, they may be fiercely competitive at times, but they also are a generous lot who will do anything for each other. Because of their nasty habits, Bunny and Peg will never be accepted in the circle of professional gardeners."

"Peg looks foreign," said Louise.

"She's German. I've heard she has some history back in East Germany—"

"Yet the name 'Peg' doesn't sound German," Louise ventured.

He arched a handsome dark eyebrow. "Now, that's interesting, because it isn't. But East Germans, unlike the West Germans, were fascinated by Americanized names, did you know that? So there's a whole generation of Sallys, and Pegs, and Cathys. My guess is that Bunny *has* something on Peg. She acts like Bunny's body servant. Maybe that's to assure that whatever the secret is, it won't leak out."

Louise stepped closer to Ken and said, "How on earth did you learn all this?"

"Not in an ordinary way," said Ken, with a disarming smile. Louise was enjoying the company of these three diverting men, two of them, her husband

and Ken Lurie, being strikingly good-looking, and Richard's effervescent personality making up for whatever good looks he lacked. "I sensed it."

Louise's eyebrows shot up.

"Ask Richard," said Ken. "He'll confirm that I'm a psychic—"

Richard nodded. "It's true: he's a real Edgar Cayce."

"I psyched that out about Peg when I heard how she slipped out of East Germany in 1989." He stared openly at the plainly dressed, long-faced Peg. "I'd guess she was a black marketeer, only because a lot of the crime on the other side of the Wall was in selling verboten products." He shrugged broad shoulders. "And you have to admit the woman is smart: she has a business mind as sharp as a cobra's, and it's on account of her that Bunny's now worth millions."

Bill gave Ken a sharp look. "Maybe I'm naive about these things, Ken, but let me understand: you're not a private eye, are you? You're just guessing this, right? Why wouldn't you guess she was part of the *Stasi*? They were almost worse than the Gestapo. She might have decided to slip over to the West to evade prosecution after German reunification."

Ken blinked his brown eyes and remained silent for a minute. Then he said, "Now, you know, that's good, Bill. Except I came down on the black marketeer idea because I think she's more of a hard-line materialist than spy material. But then spies these days are pretty materialistic, too—they're all doing it for the money, aren't they? Whatever—I'm convinced that Bunny has *something* heavy on Peg; it's obvious in their lord-vassal relationship. Just like I know that Fenimore Smith—you've met Fenimore, haven't you?—and Bunny had it on sometime in the recent past."

"No!" said Louise. "Really?"

Richard nodded, as if approving of a protégé.

"*Oh*, yes," said Ken. "Everyone knows that Fenimore likes to flirt, especially with those nubile young editors in New York. Usually, that's all it comes to—flirting. But this time he scored, probably because Bunny called his bluff and dragged him into bed."

Ken nodded to a newly formed clique that included Fenimore and Lily Smith and Bunny Bainfield, with Peg Roggenstach lingering at the edge, as if she were lady-in-waiting to the queen. "See, there Bunny goes again; she isn't through with Fenimore yet, I guarantee."

It was true that Bunny was effusively hanging on the nursery owner's arm, but this didn't seem unusual at a cocktail party. Louise gave Ken an incredulous look: maybe she shouldn't believe this man. Her skeptical husband was studying the floorboards.

The garden writer raised that perfect eyebrow again and said, "You'll find I'm dead on target, Louise. It's the way Bunny is when she's in Fenimore's company. She has a way of telling *all* without saying a thing."

"How extraordinary," Louise said, amazed that a man could be such a complete gossip.

Ken Lurie's tall frame stiffened, and he leaned in closer to the little group. "Oh, oh," he said, "the witch approaches. Come, new friends and old, let's circle the wagons."

Ken pressed his lips together and looked at his companions in the constantly changing conversational circle. He hoped he hadn't gone too far. He especially hoped he hadn't clued in this Louise

Eldridge person, whom he heard had solved a few crimes and had a sense of the darker side of human beings.

He'd spent his life being charming, and it had never failed to pay dividends, until now. But this bitch, Bunny, had humiliated him in public and caused him to be a laughingstock across the country. It made his stomach churn to think of what happened at his own book party. But he'd retained his cool, even when the hussy had attacked him with her long fingernails, even when the cops came in and demanded that he explain things, as if he were somehow to blame—

Now his friends teased him for being a coward. What was he supposed to do, slug the bitch? He intended to give Bunny Bainfield her due, to blacken her name at every opportunity. He'd made a good start tonight.

But he was prepared to go even further, if the opportunity presented itself. The woman had to be stopped.

And now here she came. . . .

8

Bunny Bainfield, trailed by Peg, made her way purposefully across the room. When she arrived, she slid herself between Richard Ralston and Ken Lurie, who were forced to move apart to give her room. She gave the stocky florist a frigid look, then swung close to Lurie and whispered something in his ear. Louise heard the end of it: ". . . *dreadfully* sorry, darling—"

Peg, standing at Bunny's elbow, and apparently not to be introduced at all, did indeed act the part of a body servant. She fastened her glowing eyes on Louise and did not move her gaze. It was quite unsettling, and Louise wished she had a shawl to pull around her shoulders.

"*Friends,* all these *friends,*" Bunny was saying. "Do introduce me—" She looked expectantly at Louise. "I believe I recognize the PBS garden show hostess par *excellence*—"

"Really, Bunny," said Richard Ralston, "you do better with cockney than you do with French."

The glittering Bunny reached up and gave a hard pinch to his rosy cheek. "Now, now, Richard, behave yourself, why don't you, or I'll go to the ballroom and fiddle with your bouquets." She turned back to Louise and Bill and extended a diamond ring–bedecked hand to Louise. "I'm Bunny Bainfield. You're Louise, and"—her eye slid over Bill's graceful form— "*you* are certainly somebody very special."

"I'm Bill Eldridge," he said, smiling, "and in this crowd my only identity is as Louise's husband."

Bunny turned to Louise and said, "Well, my dear, your husband is simply dashing." Her glance moved down to Louise's dress and she fell speechless, seeing what Louise had recognized earlier—that they'd bought the same gown in different colors.

Louise, remembering her daughter Janie's provident advice, was determined to be nice, no matter what. She smiled. "It seems we have similar taste in clothes."

Bunny recovered quickly. "So we do. Louise, I'm so glad for this chance to meet you." The woman had an almost compassionate, I'm-so-sorry-for-you look in her eyes. "I wanted to make you understand that I didn't *want* to go head-to-head with you in this television garden show business. A television program, of course, is only one of my minor business pursuits. But I'm giving it my best, and I am just so astonished by the superb ratings. Now I know that you have quite a special *niche* audience, wouldn't you say?"

Louise felt her face coloring to about the shade of Bunny's gown. "It's true. I have a very discriminating audience," she said.

The woman clasped a firm hand on Louise's

arm and stared at her with sincere blue eyes. "Oh, I'm sure, my dear, your little band of viewers will remain loyal to you, though I, *too*, am piercing that organic gardening market you like to cater to so much."

Thankfully, Bunny released her grip on the arm. "As for me, all the experts tell me my ratings will probably break all records for a *garden* show."

The Van Sickles and Shelby Newcross had moved back into the circle in time to hear Bunny's remark. Dr. Van Sickle, known far and wide for his gracious manners, stroked his white beard and said, "Oh, Bunny, please, talk like that has such a negative effect. The world is ready for many kinds of garden shows. Louise's is a very popular program, and is in no way diminished by yours. She does a remarkable service to gardening."

"I could not agree more," said Newcross, with a cool smile.

"Nor can we," echoed Ken, apparently speaking both for himself and Richard.

Newcross continued: "And as we view and compare your show with Louise's, it's obvious the old adage remains true: '*Class will tell.*' "

Bunny shook her head and said, "Ah, Dr. Newcross, how typical of you. Always with that inflated Oxbridge attitude of yours." With that, she seemed to signal Peg with her eyes, and the two of them flounced away.

There was momentary silence, as if Bunny had poisoned the mood of this exuberant holiday party. Louise was about to thank her defenders, but they quickly melted away into the candlelight of the old room. Friends of Richard and Ken had come and claimed them, while others moved in to talk to the popular Van Sickles and Shelby Newcross. They united in new conversation groups, probably relieved to be freed from female TV garden hostess infighting.

Louise and Bill found themselves standing alone. Her enjoyment of the party had dropped sharply, and she wished she could slink out, drive home, and change into sweats.

"Bummer," she muttered.

"That was a very unfair attack on you," said Bill comfortingly. "Shall I go and get us a drink? I think we both need one to lift our spirits."

Louise restrained a sniff. "It's a myth that alcohol will lift our spirits. It'll do just the opposite. So make mine sparkling water."

He smiled. "My little judgmental Puritan."

Louise had never been a good drinker, and she was afraid to take even one exploratory cocktail tonight, just because someone had publicly insulted her. She touched the sleeve of her departing husband's coat. "Sorry for taking this out on you. Don't leave for a minute; I want you to meet Gail." She indicated a small woman with long, straight, sun-streaked hair who was rapidly approaching.

"Quick," Bill said, "tell me about her. Full name?"

"Gail Rohrig."

"She's the one they called our 'funky Mother Earth figure?' "

Louise smiled. "She's earthy, but nice. She's been on my program, and you won't believe it to talk to her, but she really can sound poetic when she talks about nature and gardening. She's very close to the soil, so to speak."

Bill smiled. "Another one of your many gardening contacts that I've never met. Does she accept or reject David Austin roses—which I gather are very fancy roses indeed—and by the way, which side are *we* on, vis a vis this rose question?"

"Very funny, dear. She runs 'Seeds in America.'

Concentrates on native seeds, as you might guess from that name. And she breeds horses. Think of her as a militant but balanced native plant type. She wouldn't plant a David Austin rose in *her* garden, but wouldn't have a fit if she saw one in ours, even if she did think we were misguided."

Gail arrived at her side, and when Louise introduced her, she said, "So *you're* that cool husband of Louise's." She gave him a brilliant smile. "I've heard about you; no wonder Louise never strays off the range."

Louise knew Gail was more nature child than woman, a nature child who was very charming one minute, but had a foul mouth the next. Her producer had had to extensively edit out her naturally flowing expletives in the tape. She had deeply tanned skin and yellow-green eyes, and wore no makeup. Her body was wiry and muscular and her breasts small, and she wore a long, blue, sleeveless sheath made of a South American weave and probably dyed with native dyes.

"I've been eavesdropping," Gail said, "and believe me, it wasn't hard—*I* heard the woman from halfway across the room."

"You mean Bunny?" asked Bill.

"Yeah," she told him. "This place has great acoustics, and she has a piercing voice. I only want to say, Louise, that your program will always be a thousand times better than any bullshit program that woman could dream up. She's a—" Gail flushed under her tan. "I was thinkin' to say somethin' *really* crude, but I guess I'm not in Santa Fe anymore. I don't want to shock your hubby by using five-letter words, so I'll just say, don't give the woman another friggin' thought."

Louise and Bill smiled a little at the crude language dropped down in the middle of the fancy party. She said, "Thanks for the vote of confidence. Do you realize I've never met the woman before? And yet I had a feeling she'd be like this. We were talking to Richard Ralston and Ken Lurie—"

"Two really great guys," interposed Gail.

Bill said, "They've had some hard times with Bunny Bainfield, according to what they were saying, what with that scene at the book party . . ."

"Do I know about that! Since I was comin' East anyway for this deal of the First Lady's, I stopped in New York for the party. It's a great reality check, bein' in the Big Apple." She laughed musically. "It always reaffirms my reasons for livin' in Santa Fe."

"You were there for the fireworks."

"Yeah, that asinine scene staged by Bunny. Great publicity for Ken's new title, but what kind of publicity? It makes him look like a chump. I woulda decked her, but then I'm a physical sort of a person."

"Why did she do it?"

"Publicity, Louise. Just a publicity stunt." There was no amusement in the gold-flecked eyes. "It was completely phony, her so-called fit of rage. She took a forearm to those votive candles and slammed them clear onto the floor of that restaurant. They should have arrested her. I told Ken to press charges."

"She's difficult, that's obvious," said Louise. "I hope I don't run into her much at the conference tomorrow."

Bill took Gail's drink order—a martini—and went to the bar. Gail looked at Louise and in a tough, Annie Oakley voice said, "Don't look so worried, girl. That woman *never* bothers me. You have to treat her like you do when you're breakin' a mare: you grab onto the reins, twist her rotten neck if you have to, and hold your own with the bitch."

The words jarred Louise. She said, "I'm not going to get down in the gutter with her and mud wrestle."

Gail gave Louise a measured look that took in the dangling rhinestone earrings, the elegant strapless gown, the perfect makeup and coiffure. "You're not? Of course you don't want to, because you're a lady. But be warned: *she's* no lady. Bunny fights like she's right out of the World Wrestling Federation."

A funky Christmas ball. A lot of people with their defenses down, because they were drinking and being fed like kings and queens. What a great time, thought Gail, for her to sneak attack.

Gail looked over at Louise Eldridge—a woman far too prissy to defend herself against the doyenne of bad taste, Bunny Bainfield. Gail was a different matter. She knew herself to have such a thick skin that she could do anything and still live with herself afterward.

Oh, yes, this upscale party was just the kind of opportunity she'd been looking for, and she couldn't blow it, or she'd be in the worst kind of trouble.

Bill Eldridge was coming back with a huge, V-shaped glass that contained her drink. A darling man, Bill, the kind who'd never cheat on his wife. Good for Louise, but bad for Gail. She put a hand on his sleeve and gave him a long, grateful glance, then took a huge sip of the martini. She'd need the anesthetizing effect of the gin as the evening wore on, for she intended to strike Bunny just when the dumb broad thought she was at the top of her game.

9

Richard Ralston, a small man puffed up with understandable pride, stood beside his Christmas garden like a parent displaying a new offspring.

Louise was impressed: this was more than just an array of plants and flowers. It was a miniature botanical world, a two-story-high display that filled almost a third of the eighteenth-century ballroom and evoked a veritable gardening cosmos, with its small forest of trees and evergreens, wetland, minuscule frosted winter garden, open plains, and jungle with lianas, ferns, and palms—all set in handsome grasses and mosses. Out of this miniworld spilled flowers and shrubs and trees of many kinds, froths of small ones and medium ones, and huge varieties of orchid, canna, and hibiscus. Leaves and limbs gently moved, as from a hidden breeze, and Louise guessed that a fan was blowing in the garden universe's hidden depths, just as she knew hidden scaffolding held the higher plants and trees in place.

This lavish garden had a path winding through it, so guests could momentarily experience walking among native plants plucked from one coast to another, and Alaska and Hawaii as well.

And it smelled wonderful, suffusing the big ballroom with the odors of plants from every region in the fifty states, spicy sage smells mixing with the heavier perfumes of orchids and lilies, flowering tree odors mingling with the pungent scents of eucalyptus and pine.

Louise could see that the garden was the star of the Christmas ball, and all else came second, including the guests. They were to be packed in at dinner tables crowded into the remaining space in the room.

Richard, as creator of it all, was reveling in the effect his masterpiece was having on spectators. In a carrying voice, he gave out a little spiel to passing guests as they started down the path. "As you can see, there are native plant varieties from virtually *every* region in the fifty states—including, of course, Hawaii and Alaska."

Louise exchanged a meaningful glance with Bill. "No wonder he had to do it," she said in her spouse's ear.

"Had to do what?"

"Take shortcuts—"

She didn't finish explaining, for they were approaching Richard. She leaned forward in puzzlement to examine a brilliant clump of plants in the "high plains." Surrounded by waving prairie grasses, they looked out of place, with their inch-wide lush flowers in gaudy pink. Louise had never laid eyes on them before, and surely no flower that lush grew in the dry plains, as far as she knew.

"Richard, what are these magnificent things?"

He paused to wipe his sweaty brow with his handkerchief. Then he gave Louise a wink that was so quick she wasn't even sure it had happened. He said, "They represent the western penstemon, of course."

He came closer to her side and barely mouthed the words. "They're not strictly native, of course; they're a water-loving variety. I couldn't resist; I had them flown in specially from England." He made a motion with his fingers, as if locking his lips.

"Of course," said Louise, as she restrained a smile, "we won't breathe a word."

The height of the flowers carried Louise's gaze up the teal-colored walls to a nearby musician's balcony, done in ivory and gold gilt. She nudged her husband. "Look at that." Against an incongruous door set in the high wall a quintet sat on gilt chairs and played Mozart.

"That balcony's not accessible except by a ladder in the outside hall," said Bill, "and it's another source of ulcers for the Secret Service team."

"What kind of trouble could musicians cause? I'm sure they were searched on the way in, just like us."

"Just the same, it's a great place from which to take a potshot at someone."

As the crowd filled the room, people congregated by the stunning flower arrangement. Bill told Louise, "We're getting a logjam here." Just as he spoke, two Secret Service agents stepped forward, organizing people into a line and admonishing them to take a look at the flora and then go directly to the table to which they'd been assigned.

"Incredible," said Louise, as they made their way to their seats. "Richard Ralston is a genius. I have to get him on my show."

Her more cynical husband said, "I thought the theme here was native plants. That arrangement's a tribute to the South American jungle."

"That's what I meant by shortcutting. Richard obviously had a challenge. Mrs. Anderson asked him to create a huge, dramatic display like this with a month's notice. Ordinary native flowers weren't prolific enough or possibly even available to do the job, so he had to rely on plants from our tropical zones—southern Florida, California, and Hawaii— to make it look lush. That's perfectly okay, I guess, but what about the ethics of flying plants in from England? On the other hand, we have to keep in mind that plants from Britain may have *originated* from America centuries ago." She gave her husband an inquisitive glance. "Is that confusing to you?"

He grinned. "You better believe it."

"What happened is that plants were trotted back and forth across the Atlantic. Europeans coming to settle tucked them into their luggage, and ships returning to England had American native plants strapped to the decks."

"I'm beginning to see the real issue," Bill said with a laugh. "The question is just what you gardeners mean by a native plant."

She slipped her arm around his. "Darling, you may not be much of a gardener, but you are so smart: you have just put your finger on the whole problem." As they came in sight of their table, he tightened his grip on her arm, as if to caution her. Louise saw why. A tense-faced Peg Roggenstach was already seated at the round table, her salad sitting in splendor before her, empty seats on either side of her.

The woman with the cloche-style hair turned her head slowly and watched the Eldridges while they found their place cards and settled in their seats.

They introduced themselves. The woman leaned forward in her chair and said to Louise, "Aren't you the woman who does detecting?"

Louise, who hadn't expected to have her crime-solving exploits raised at a party like this, said, "Not as a career. Usually it's something I've stumbled into."

Peg sniffed, as if in making light of the matter Louise had given the wrong answer. "In Germany, I, too, dealt with criminals, but I never stumbled." Maybe Bill had guessed right about the woman working for East Germany's Secret Police. Before Louise could prolong the conversation, the woman ended it by turning away to stare at someone else.

Louise looked at her husband and shrugged. "Don't say we didn't try," she said. She examined the place card at the seat next to hers and discovered it belonged to Dr. Nathaniel Poe. This guaranteed that their dinner conversation would be interesting. Still, she was dismayed to see that Bunny would be at her table. At least she was placed next to Bill. Louise was glad of that, for she knew that her husband, more than some of the others here, could be counted on not to be rude to the gardening celebrity.

With a disconcerting thump of the heart, she wondered just why she was being so concerned about Bunny. She was the most obnoxious woman Louise had ever met. Maybe it was because of her daughter Janie's challenge: *Can you stand this human being, and if you can't, what kind of a person does that make you?*

There were three people she knew seated on the other side of the table, three that she and Bill hadn't connected with during cocktail hour. It was difficult to see them through Richard Ralston's inspired centerpiece design, a three-tiered epergne laden with floating flowers in low crystal bowls, from which glittering streamers fell like cascading water. Fenimore and Lily Smith were talking with Joanna Heath, who owned Creekside Gardens Nursery in North Carolina.

On a large woman like Joanna, floral-patterned chiffon, a headful of intricate blond curls, and very red lips looked good. But she seemed to have mislaid her party spirit, and was almost combative as she sat and verbally sparred with the handsome Fenimore.

Louise gave them a friendly wave, but they paused only long enough to dodge their heads around the streamers and return the greeting. She clued her husband in: "Joanna runs the biggest nursery on the East Coast—or at least she did until Bunny Bainfield's 'Bunnyland' doubled in size."

Up went one of Bill's eyebrows. "Tell me I didn't hear right. *Bunnyland?*"

Louise stifled a giggle. "Yes. Part of Bunny's success is the advertising genius who invented that, as well as her 'Bunny in the Garden' slogan that appears on all her plant labels."

Bill smiled mischievously. "I've seen those. I like it that someone with platinum hair and big breasts is pictured on plant labels."

She gave him a reproving glance. "But don't think Joanna's going to let Bunny take over as number one nursery without a fight."

Her spouse surreptitiously examined Joanna. "She looks like she could put up a good fight."

"She knows how to market. She sponsors a traveling garden show that visits botanical gardens all over the country each spring. That tour makes Creekside a household name. Joanna's good buddies with all the top horticulturalists, including Dr. Van Sickle and Shelby Newcross."

Bill said, "And how does *Joanna* stand on David Austin roses?"

Louise laughed and explained, "Just like Fenimore Smith, she loves them and sells lots of them."

She noticed a new man strolling toward their table. He stopped and bent over solicitously and chatted with Peg. The woman had remained isolated from table talk both by the empty seats on either side of her, and by the cold expression in her eyes, which practically shouted, *Don't bother me!* Her expression softened a little after this brief encounter.

The man slipped into the seat next to Louise. He was Nathaniel Poe, the most distinguished garden professor in the United States. Instantly, she was in awe, just as she'd been in awe of certain teachers when she was in college.

Peg Roggenstach felt frozen. Her gaze traveled about the room, noting where the figure in pink was at all times. Bunny never completely escaped her surveillance. Peg had been trained to observe, and found it hard to let it go and just relax.

Besides, Bunny was such a part of her life that she could not bear to take her gaze from her. But eventually she did, looking across the table at Fenimore Smith. Her eyes bored in on him. She knew all about the man, his successful New York book business, his frightfully botched nursery business, his innumerable affairs, often with girls young enough to be his daughter. The man was ruthless, not caring who was hurt.

How anyone could be attracted to him, she didn't understand, but Bunny was. Peg didn't bother to mask the hatred in her heart for Smith, and knew it was probably mirrored in her face.

Two other attractive men at the table might grab Bunny's attention: Bill Eldridge, sitting next to her, and the curiously kind Nathaniel Poe—though he was a bit old for Bunny's tastes.

She felt a sour dread in her stomach and realized her situation was hopeless. She couldn't let it happen again—she couldn't bear it. And yet Bunny was beginning to hate Peg for her jealousy and intense devotion, even threatening to disclose her past if Peg did not stand aside and let her pursue her wanton ways with men.

Peg had to do something, and soon.

10

Louise turned to look into one of the most engaging faces she'd ever seen, young in expression, and with interesting forehead wrinkles. He shot out a hand for her to shake and said, "Poe. Nathaniel Poe. Penn State—I teach design."

An unneeded introduction, she thought, for one of the country's leading educators in landscape design, the effervescent teacher who had to turn away scores of overflow students from his popular classes. She guessed he was in his mid-sixties. His amused eyes were partially hidden behind wire-rimmed spectacles, and his thinning hair fell boyishly over his forehead. His face was familiar from his long-running PBS series, *Land in America*.

Poe leaned over and shook Bill's hand, then said, "And do you know Peg?" They assured him that they had met Peg.

Even the charming Poe had a hard time breaking up what appeared to be a business meeting in progress across the table, though he knew them all: "Hello, Joanna, Lily, Fenimore. How very nice to see you."

Joanna and Lily gave him a distracted nod. Fenimore, at least, had the good grace to raise a hand, as if to say that their little confab would soon be over.

"Not a social lot, are they, at the moment?" Poe said. Apparently satisfied he had played host long enough, he settled back in his chair and stuck his thumbs under his coat as if searching out a vest, but found none. He turned amiably to Louise. "Quite some group we have here, don't you think? People eyeing each other over that great divide between gardening and environmentalism. Nurserymen. Botanists. Ecologists. Garden designers. Garden editors. Garden writers. People from the Agricultural Research Service and Department of Natural Resources Conservation Service. Tree and seed experts. TV personalities." With this final mention, a graceful nod of the head toward Louise.

"And environmentalists, of course," he continued, warmed up now to his topic, "environmentalists who think with their hearts, others who think with their heads. Environmentalists of *many* stripes—many, many stripes." He rolled his eyes in a comic way, a perfect wrap-up to the little monologue.

She could imagine that his students at Penn State remained riveted during his lectures, for his delivery was as eloquent as an actor's.

"You make environmentalists sound as bad as lawyers, Dr. Poe."

"I'm *one* of them, of course, so maybe they are. And drop the 'doctor,' would you? I have no medical bag, you know, no scalpel, no scissors, just a sharp tongue. Now, as I was saying, there are so many subspecies of environmentalists these days, *too* many. They're fragmented, going in all directions, sort of like the Bolsheviks after 1917, don't y'know." He burst into laughter over his own little joke.

"I'm sure you know more about that than I do," she said. "I know some of them—Gail Rohrig, for instance. I know she has strong feelings on the subject."

"There's a very radical example at the next table over." As if he'd heard his name mentioned, a huge, dark-haired man got up from his chair and sauntered his way over to their table. He leaned down and proffered a hand to the professor. "Dr. Poe," he said, in a low-pitched, almost boring voice, "I'm Bob Touhy. We've met a couple of times before—"

Poe nodded graciously. "I remember, Bob. I see you've become part of the select few to advise the incoming First Lady on her forthcoming project. But let me introduce the Eldridges."

Touhy mechanically accepted the introductions, but his intense eyes were focused only on the professor. "You know, Dr. Poe, ever since the First Lady first tapped me to help her, I've worked twenty-four seven on this native plant program of hers. I have some *dynamite* ideas for her, but I need to talk them over with you first. Could you slice out some time for me tomorrow?"

The professor assured him that they could spend a few minutes together. Louise noted that Touhy, using his size to his advantage, seemed to be trying to John-Wayne it through life. Big man. Straight talk. Sincere manner. She was relieved when he returned to his own table.

Poe quietly said, "I don't know Gail Rohrig, but I hope she has a more reasonable stance on issues than Mr. Touhy." Assured that Bill also was heeding his words, he said, "In my opinion, Bob's quite the extremist. Others think so, too. He's earned an ominous moniker: he's known as a native Nazi." A gentle chuckle from the famous landscaper, perhaps in hopes of taking some of the sting out of his words.

While Louise digested this alarming description, Poe said, "Bob *fears* imported plants, as one might fear the introduction of the mad cow disease in the United States. He's on one far end of the spectrum. Clinton's presidential order a few years ago only encouraged him and the other zealots to believe that we should get rid of all plants that have been introduced to America."

"Leaving only the natives?"

"Absolutely. As you can imagine, this would be a radical move, rather like some of the thinking back in the Vietnam War. Remember when the military explained they had to *destroy* a Vietcong village in order to save it? Well, Bob doesn't care how much herbicide it takes to do it, either, but he wants to rid the country of a heck of a lot of plants we all grow in our backyards."

Bill said, "It sounds like what's happening in Colombia—"

Poe nodded in agreement. "Yes, a desecration, really, our drug policy there. We help the Colombians eradicate coca plants, and in some places have managed to kill all living flora. That's why we must be careful with our own environmental policies, to be sure they do not go off in wild directions."

"I'd heard some environmentalists are like that," said Louise, "but I haven't met one yet."

"Now's your chance, my dear. Then, on a more pleasant note, we have the sober-looking gentleman at the next table, the one with the thick glasses who's seated next to Shelby Newcross. That's Gene Clendenin—he's wonderful."

Louise looked over to see a crusty-looking little man with balding head and a poorly executed black tie. "Actually," said Poe, "I should go over and say hello to Gene and offer condolences. The man just lost his wife. Do excuse me." And with that he leapt from his seat and bounced over to the adjoining table and hugged his friend unabashedly. The solemn little man broke into a smile.

Bill arched an eyebrow. "His friend looks as if he's slept in his formal clothes for a week. I bet he's an interesting fellow. Sometimes I think a man's attractiveness is in inverse proportion to his sartorial splendor."

"That makes bums the most interesting people of all, then, doesn't it?"

Bill looked at her drolly. "Bums have interesting lives, Louise."

Professor Poe came back to his seat, a big grin covering his face. He said, "Gene heads the USDA's Natural Resources Conservation Service; he's probably the most sensible environmentalist of the whole bunch here. Sitting with him are a group from the ARS, the Agricultural Research Service. Gene's job, or rather, his agency's job, is to make all plants, native or 'foreign,' more adaptable to the environment."

"How does Mr. Clendenin like the First Lady's native plant project?"

"Not much, I'm afraid. He thinks Maud's scheme is dangerous, that it may lead to genetically altering native plants. It's also bound to draw resources away from the good things his agency's trying to do. He privately thinks Maud Anderson is a bit naive."

Poe leaned forward and placed a hand on Louise's arm. "Of course, this is off the record, you know; being a public official, Gene doesn't like to publicly insult anyone. But Mrs. Anderson, from what we can learn, unfortunately is under the influence of misguided individuals as widely disparate as Bob Touhy on the one hand and Bunny Bainfield on the other." He looked at Peg, whose attention was focused across the room, and lowered his voice. "Do you know of Bunny Bainfield?"

Louise smiled ruefully. "I know *of* her. Bill and I met her for the first time tonight. She certainly has the room buzzing."

"The woman generates lots of controversy. I hear she and Touhy are fighting like cocks for first place in Maud's esteem."

"She's advising Maud Anderson on *native* plants?"

"Incredible, isn't it, especially that combination. Touhy's like the mad environmentalist, his spray of herbicide in hand, chasing after every non-native plant in the land. Bunny is learning to talk the conservation–native plant talk quite well, but do you realize her main sellers are water-hogging varieties that are in no way native? Some think she's tried to cloak herself as an environmental champion when she's—I hate to say it—quite the opposite."

"I wonder who *will* like Maud's idea."

The professor sat back in his chair again. "Bunny Bainfield and nativists like Bob Touhy, of course." He nodded over at the trio across the table. "And they will, the nursery operators; they like any idea that fattens their profits."

Louise noted that the Smiths and Joanna had broken out of their cocoon and were now talking to a passing guest. Joanna Heath, perhaps suspecting that the three of them had been rather rude, rose from her chair, and made her way around the table toward them.

"The trouble is that once the First Lady gives people a new thirst for native plants, nursery owners'll have difficulty meeting the demand," said Poe. "These nurserymen are struggling in an industry that's rapidly consolidating—with the big guys getting bigger, and the smaller guys in trouble and in need of big-profit items to sell."

Bill spoke up. "I've heard that native plants aren't always that showy."

The professor gave Bill an admiring look. "You've hit on the problem, my good fellow. I wasn't aware that you, too, were a gardener. It's *not* shy little natives that attract masses of customers."

He looked up as Joanna Heath placed one hand on his shoulder, and gazed down at him. Bending down, she planted a kiss on Poe's cheek. "Nate, honey, hello."

He put a hand up and touched hers. "Joanna, my dear. Joanna knows—"

"What am I supposed to know?" she said.

"We're talking about what sells best. I say it's big plants with sixty buds on them ready to burst into bloom—"

She nodded enthusiastically. "That's *exactly* what sells best. Plants born and bred to be big and opulent. They pop right off the shelves into customer's hands. Now, you dear people, I have to run off, but I'll be back in a minute."

Poe leaned forward and continued. "The fact that natives are shy little devils is the rationale for Bunny Bainfield and others to step in with genetic alterations. They want to make those little blooms larger and the small leaves fatter, all with the aim of appealing to a broader market."

"That's disturbing." Louise thought of the inappropriateness of the gigantic version of the penstemon plant, native to western states, that Richard had imported from England to jazz up his plant extravaganza.

"Bunny's hurting the mail-order people a lot," continued Poe. "Take the experience of my fine-looking friend, Fenimore Smith, over there. He and Lily are in trouble with their mostly mail-order nursery business: they're selling out. It doesn't matter financially to Fenimore—just *psychically*. He makes his real money as a New York publisher. He's a weekend nurseryman, but that nursery is his pet project. He loves it."

"He's selling Wild Flower Farm?" said Louise.

"To Joanna Heath. That's why they've had their heads together. It must just *kill* Fenimore to have to do this." Poe shook his head slowly and made a clucking sound. "I feel sorry for him."

A short silence and Poe leaned back in his chair. "But back to your question, Louise: you asked who else will like the First Lady's idea. The garden writers and editors will. For instance, that redhead over there."

He pointed to a bejewelled woman in black chiffon sitting at the next table with what looked to Louise like dreadlocks falling around her face.

"Nice hairdo," said Bill. "Reminds me of Medusa."

"That it does," said Poe. "Only in New York or Milan, perhaps, would you see fantastic hair like that. That's Mardi Lischer, the eminent editor of *Horticulture Today*. She'll delight in stories about a native plant renaissance. But that's writers for you."

He cast another disarming smile on Louise and Bill. "I know this well because I often put on a writer's hat. Quite naturally, garden writers will jump on the bandwagon when it comes along, because essentially they are news people and have a nose for the latest breaking story. They'll discourse endlessly about native plants simply because the spotlight's been turned on them by a charismatic new First Lady."

"It does have news value, I guess," said Louise, thinking of Charlie Hurd, the newshound from hell, who'd dogged her footsteps for years. She'd been dodging Charlie's recent phone calls wanting information from her on Maud Anderson's project.

"And then we need to gossip a bit about the people who run the five hundred or so botanical gardens in the United States," Poe said. "There's one thing certain about them—they love plants, and they're gluttons." He laughed again, and his forelock fell on his brow, giving him a rakish appearance. Louise was slightly alarmed at this blunt description of botanical garden directors.

"You make them sound unattractive," she said.

"Oh no, not unattractive, I wouldn't say, just *human*. They seek big endowments to support their gardens, and that means creating garden displays that appeal to their rather affluent patrons. Actually, they aren't much different than your ordinary backyard gardener, that man or woman who becomes possessed when the growing season sets in and goes to the garden shops and doesn't come home until he's spent a couple hundred dollars on bedding plants and perennials."

Louise realized the professor was describing *her.*

"What botanical garden directors have is an insatiable need for plants," he said, "and they can indulge that need with other people's money. They may seem to be approaching this for a noble reason—that is, to educate the general public—but when you pare it all down, it's a guy who has to have everything, every single plant that grows in the whole world. And he'll often travel the world to find the ones he's missing."

"But I've seen plenty of native plant displays in botanical gardens. They always feature them."

"Of course they do," agreed Poe, with a wide sweep of his hand. "They pay their dues: they'll have gardens of native varieties scattered around and about—but don't think they don't have another agenda as well. They like getting credit for the exotics that they search out and import from Africa or Asia. I know because I go on field trips with them. Sometimes, to avoid political problems of whether it's a native or an import, they simply bring them in and give them Americanized names."

He gave her a sober glance. "The fact that one of these plants could get into the wild and become another imported troublemaker like the kudzu vine is sometimes not foremost in their thinking, and that's one of the things that environmentalists complain about."

"What about you?" Louise challenged. "What's your attitude toward exotic plants?"

He flapped his hand in the air again. "Call them what you will—'foreign,' 'exotic,' 'introduced'—these are plants that have come over to America over the decades by ship, plane, and by birds and wind as well. Plants *move.*" His eyes crinkled in another smile. "The answer is, I don't discriminate, Louise. They're all native to Mother Earth. Actually, I've never met a plant I didn't like."

She could see his alert eyes, which had seen many plant species over the years, examining three human species that were now approaching the table. "Aha, and here, at last, is the remainder of our table."

* * *

The situation was perfect. A crowded ballroom. A jam of guests distracted by the holiday gaiety. The over-the-top floral decorations, distracting and titillating everyone. Even the Mozart music was distracting, and people would soon be shocked and surprised when the musical program changed up there in that little gilt balcony. Secret Service people were lurking in every corner, but they only seemed interested in the First Couple, not the rest of the people. After all, everyone had been frisked and found free of weapons.

There wouldn't be another opportunity like this, ever. Was it Henry V who said, "The game's afoot . . ."?

11

When nearly everyone was seated, Nathaniel Poe resumed his role as host and began to introduce the newcomers. Michael Sandoveld, they learned, was director of the Greater St. Louis Botanical Gardens, a man of about fifty. His wife, Laura, floating in on a sea of aqua chiffon, leaned heavily on his arm. Bunny Bainfield, her shocking-pink dress a beacon as bright as a headlight, flounced into the seat next to Bill.

Bunny interrupted the professor's introduction. "Nate," she said, and she batted her blue-eyeshadowed eyes at him, "if I may be allowed to call you Nate, I know everyone here, and everyone knows me." As far as Louise was concerned, she was a pink, disquieting presence.

"Fine," said Poe, turning his attention to his salad and rubbing his hands together in anticipation. "Now we can dig into our food. I've been on a train all afternoon, and I'm simply starved."

It was evident that Bunny was more interested in drinking wine than eating the food. She took over the conversation, effusing at length over the floral arrangements of a man whom, Louise had observed earlier, she despised.

"How very talented Richard Ralston is—a veritable genius. I've *told* him how lucrative it would be for him to join forces with me in my *bunnybouquets.com,* which is simply soaring."

From the other side of the table, Joanna Heath shoved her ample shoulders forward, taking on the look of a football lineman. She pushed back her hair from her forehead, smiled, and drawled in a North Carolina accent, "Maybe he can get along without you, Bunny, did you ever think of that?"

Louise, seated two places from Bunny, could see the woman's face tightening around a mouth already tight, Louise was sure, from a recent face-lift. But then Bunny smiled. "Most people have found it easier to join me than to fight me, sweetie," she purred.

Nathaniel Poe shifted his gaze between the two women and asked Bunny, "I hear you've entered another selling agreement, this time with Wal-Mart. How will you keep up with the enormous demand for plants you'll create?"

Bunny looked at Poe, a grateful expression on her face. Louise felt a tug of guilt for thinking so badly of this flamboyant woman. She might be troublesome, but she still had feelings.

Just as these compassionate thoughts crossed Louise's mind, Bunny spoiled the moment by bragging, "Darling Nate, do you know what I've done? I've filled almost every segment of the garden market. Isn't that so, Peg?" And she turned to the woman beside her and pressed her brightly manicured nails into the arm of Peg's brown dress. Peg nodded obediently, her dark eyes locked on her employer. Bunny slugged down the remainder of her glass of wine and demanded a waiter keep her glass refilled.

"I raise and sell *plants*," continued Bunny, with an extravagant gesture of her hands, as if to indicate the hordes of plants she'd sent to market, "thousands raised through micropropagation alone." A pause, and a deep breath that Louise noticed caused her sizable bosom to heave in her low-cut dress. Louise glanced at Bill, who was also focused on Bunny's bosom. She nudged him with her knee under the table, and he grinned.

Bunny shot the people at the table a reckless look. "Let's face it, *luvs*," she said, reverting to her Cockney accent, " 'plant' business is 'show' business. Plants change as quickly as the latest fashions." She tipped her nose up at them, as if daring someone to object. "And why not? *Fashion* designers have their annual fall preview shows. *Plant* designers have their special spring introductions. *I* play this fashion-plant game for all its worth, and I'm not ashamed of it. The tag in my plants with my picture and slogan, 'Bunny in Your Garden,' is like a garment label by Versace. . . ."

She punched out the next phrases: "I sell garden *designs* through the Internet. I sell *floral* designs through the Internet. I sell garden *art* through the Internet. And soon, I hope, I'll be publishing my own garden magazine—maybe with Ken Lurie's touch as editor. If not, I'll be publishing without him, and who knows what will happen to *his* rag?"

Unperturbed by her bragging and threats, Poe said, "Even with micropropagation, how will you supply Wal-Mart?"

"Darling, it's not a problem—I'm opening up

two regional nurseries to augment my plant supply. I assure you that gardening will turn larger profits than ever before in history. And what benefits me has a ripple effect through the industry." She looked around the table to meet the glances of the others and then continued more quietly, "I can only hope that I get some credit for it."

"If that's what you'll do," said the professor, "surely we'll all give you credit." He looked around to see less than enthusiastic expressions on other faces. "Won't we, folks?"

After a moment of numbing silence, the director of the Greater St. Louis Botanical Gardens spoke up. Louise was surprised to hear a deep baritone voice emerge from the mild-looking Michael Sandoveld. "One must make distinctions, Nate," he said. Everyone paid him rapt attention. A person with a voice like that had to be saying worthwhile things. "We can grow the industry in quantity, but we also have to consider quality. Laura here, for instance, is a prize-winning horticultural artist." Sandoveld's large frame seemed to bend in tribute to the slight, sandy-haired woman beside him.

"Of course," said Louise, "I've seen your books of garden art, Mrs. Sandoveld. They are simply beautiful."

Laura, whose violet eyes were ringed with puffy circles that even makeup could not conceal, gave Louise a wan smile. "Thank you so much."

Sandoveld put a proprietary hand on his wife's arm. "The point is that there has to be a market left for quality work such as Laura's."

"Just as there has to be a source of quality plants for people to buy for their gardens," added the debonair Fenimore Smith.

"And a source for original and quality garden

designs such as mine," said Lily Smith. Lily also had a strong voice for one so thin.

"I say amen to all of that," piped up Joanna Heath, with a toss of her unruly curls.

"And just what are you saying to *me?*" asked Bunny querulously. "What are you all bloody *inferring?*"

Fenimore Smith patted his mouth with his napkin and said, "I believe you mean *implying,* Bunny."

Bunny stared at Fenimore and cried, "*Et tu,* Fenimore—I can't believe it. . . . How you have the audacity to insult me, after—"

"Oh, Bunny, my dear," interrupted Lily Smith, fingering the ropes of pearls on her long neck, "you really must not get your feelings ruffled. Fenimore would not insult you deliberately. You know he's fond of you. He's just correcting a small error in usage, as he might correct an offspring. He's *forever* correcting my usage."

As the infuriated Bunny continued to glare, Lily smiled coolly and shrugged her bony shoulders. "I'm only trying to help you understand."

Bunny's mouth started to open, and Louise could practically see a new outburst forming on her lips. Louise looked quickly from Nathaniel Poe to her husband Bill, eyes pleading that they step up and quiet the troubled waters.

Then it came, a distraction. But not from Bill or Nathaniel Poe. In the musician's balcony a raucous horn broke into the melodious Mozart. A lone trumpet blared out the Dixieland favorite, "When the Saints Go Marching In."

12

The upbeat song had a strange, chilling effect. Conversations halted in mid-sentence. All eyes turned to the gilded balcony.

"Bill, what on earth's going on?" asked Louise.

Her husband gripped her arm as they watched Secret Service agents begin to move in different directions. A ring of dark-suited agents hustled President-elect and Mrs. Anderson out of the ballroom.

Four agents stationed themselves under the balcony, guns drawn. Two of the men clambered up the scaffolding hidden inside Richard Ralston's garden.

Louise could see the horn player. He looked young, like a college student, she thought. He had long, dark brown hair and wore rimless glasses. As the Secret Service agents climbed higher, the trumpeter continued to play, as though leading troops into battle.

This persistent blowing of the horn was terrifying. What might happen next—a bomb, an outbreak of gunfire?

Louise stood near the table, Bill still clutching her arm. The tuxedo-clad men moved about in nervous confusion like excited penguins. The women moved awkwardly, as their gowns became entangled in chair and table legs. Gasps were heard as the agents ruthlessly toppled flower containers to the floor and dashed toward the horn player.

People jockeyed for position around the flower garden, their necks craned upward. The agents finally reached the musician. A voice shouted at him to stop playing and put his hands in the air.

"Goddamn!" cursed Gail Rohrig, as she tripped over Mardi Lischer's trailing dress, and fell against the chairs at the other side of the dinner table. A cluster of men, Shelby Newcross, Gene Clendenin, Ken Lurie, and Bob Touhy, were there to catch her and set her on her feet. Joanna Heath, who was mingling with the others, shook her head and plopped down in the nearest chair at the table, Peg Roggenstach's.

Nathaniel Poe was standing nearby with Newcross, the rumpled Clendenin, and the two ARS officials. Louise could hear the famous landscaper commenting, "I'd not like to be that young man. Wonder what possessed him?"

"Just what I was thinking," growled Clendenin. "What kind of a young fool does a thing like that with a president-elect in the room, unless—"

Louise missed the rest of Clendenin's comment, for she had to step aside quickly so that the huge Bob Touhy could pass by without smashing into her.

Joanna Heath got up from the chair she'd occupied and joined the group just as the Smiths wandered over. Joanna's eyes were bright and excited. "Have you ever been to a dinner party with this many fireworks?"

"Never," said Fenimore with a sniff. "Anything that comes after this from our new First Lady about the future of native plants will be a complete denouement."

Lily Smith commented drily, "It was bound to be a bust, interruptions or not. I fear Maud Anderson's native plant project is going to fall like a soufflé left out of the oven too long."

"Not because of native plants," grumped Gene Clendenin. "It's because her whole proposed strategy is flawed."

Louise said, "I've been glad to hear Mrs. Anderson speak out on things like global warming and the depletion of the ozone layer. But this native plant idea—"

She didn't know quite what to say about it. But Lily Smith did. "Her plan is nonsense. It's redundant. Been there, done that. I wouldn't be surprised if somebody who disagreed with Maud Anderson hadn't *hired* that young man. And of course, look what's happening: Richard's arrangement is ruined." They watched as the two agents awkwardly guided the musician down to ground level, while flower containers continued to teeter and fall.

The sanguine Nathaniel Poe, who up to now had seemed to see good in everything, even Bunny Bainfield, had to admit the incident had thrown a pall on the party.

Yet the room gradually regained the party din, though it was not as happy a sound as before, for guests were put off by the delay in serving dinner, and by the dishevelled appearance of the Christmas garden. It looked as if it had been caught in a tornado, and a white-faced Richard Ralston stood by, poised to rush in and save his flowers as soon as the Secret Service gave him the nod.

Guests were stirring restlessly by the time Louise heard a tapping on the microphone. It was Maud Anderson, a graceful figure in red, standing on the podium on the far side of the room. But before she began to speak, she reached down and took the hand of a woman in bright pink at the base of the podium. It was a gesture of gratitude.

Louise exchanged a look with Bill. "We know what Bunny Bainfield is doing over there: scoring points."

Her husband stifled a smile. "Marketing herself; it's what she does best."

Maud Anderson spoke to them in a mellifluous voice. "Friends," said the First Lady-To-Be, "what a *cruel* interruption, when we were just about to enjoy our dinners! And what a surprise, to have a young man like Bryan Keller serenade us so *mischievously* and so *unexpectedly*. But Bryan—the young man you saw in the balcony giving us a very spirited rendition of 'When the Saints Go Marching In'—has explained himself. He *voted* for my husband, and on a dare from a friend, he tooted out his joy over the results of the election."

Louise could see her unwavering smile from across the room. "And we all know how very close an election it *was*. But, I fear our diligent and wonderful Secret Service contingent wants to have a little talk with Bryan, so we'll have a quartet from now on this evening."

The guests laughed appreciatively. Bill murmured in Louise's ear, "A little talk, hell; he's going to be questioned all night long."

The new First Lady's gracious voice continued, "And now, I beg you all to be seated so that the salad course can be removed and the main course served. I will forgo any pleadings for my cause of Native Plants for America until after dessert. And even then, it will be a brief talk, so that we have plenty of time for dancing in our Christmas garden, in the very room where our first president, George Washington, and his wife Martha came and danced."

There was scattered applause at these comforting remarks, and guests obediently resumed their places. Even Bunny came back, though she had strayed farther afield than anyone else, explaining, as if she were part of the force protecting the new First Couple, "I had to be sure that Maud was all right."

From the looks on people's faces, Louise could tell that many people viewed Bunny as an opportunist of the first stripe, who by the end of the party and the garden conference would be even closer to the wife of the new president. Maud must be naive, she thought, to become so easily beguiled by a person like Bunny Bainfield.

Bunny now added insult to injury: "Of course, anyone who's British will tell you that the Brits would have handled this situation much more efficiently—"

"Give us a *break*," Louise heard someone mutter.

Bunny glared at Fenimore. "Oh, but *yes*, Fenimore—they would have managed everything with complete grace, and without all those vicious firearms brandished about!"

"Isn't that too bad," declared Michael Sandoveld, in the baritone voice that was impossible to ignore. "What a pity that you don't like our police methods. But it's over, and I say, let's drop the subject."

* * *

Bob Touhy sat tall in his chair and kept a sharp eye on things in the ballroom. He was perfectly comfortable in the nation's capital, having come here dozens of times to testify before congressional subcommittees about the perils of invasive plants in America. Tonight, he was out of his element, but he could handle it—he was handling it.

He had two women to contend with, Maud Anderson at one end of the room, and Bunny at the next table. Maud may have landed in the White House, but he'd known her when thirty years ago they'd both landed in jail for protesting logging the vicious but effective way—by driving huge nails into trees marked for cutting.

And then there was Bunny, who was as cunning as a she-wolf. The two women were dominating his life at the moment. Bad enough to have any woman dominating him, but two was way too many. One must go, and it wouldn't be Maud. He noisily exhaled. Not one to mince about with things like this, he needed to act, and act swiftly.

After that, he would be in the catbird seat. He'd be right by the side of the incoming First Lady when she decided how to run her native plant program. That would catapult him right to the top of the competitive little world in which he always knew he'd be a star.

13

Finally, the crisis appeared to be over. Order had been magically restored. Music resumed—a little less full-bodied, of course, but pleasant. Waiters streamed in quickly, serving dinner plates with steam covers, popping them off to the "oohs" and "aahs" of the guests to reveal huge lobster tails, accompanied by risotto cakes studded with raisins, and tender asparagus with hollandaise sauce.

As Louise took up knife and fork, she could feel the salivary juices forming in her mouth. The excitement had left her starved.

Still, things hadn't completely settled down. Bob Touhy took this moment to hop over to their table, leaning over Bunny Bainfield and whispering in her ear for what seemed to Louise like an interminable minute or two. The man filled up so much physical space that he jarred her. Bunny and Bob smiled conspiratorially before he returned to the adjoining table where he belonged.

Richard Ralston, she noticed, wouldn't be eating for quite awhile. Having divested himself of his black jacket, the sturdy little man stood in the middle of the enormous Christmas garden in his dress shirt and directed his crew in restoring the garden colossus to its former beauty. They worked with such adroitness that she suspected they'd erase every trace of the rough tramplings of the Secret Service men.

Then there was another delay, as Nathaniel Poe proposed a toast. Reluctantly putting down her silverware, Louise picked up her wineglass, and all ten at the table raised their glasses together. "Let us drink to all of our good healths," said Poe, "and to a friendly dinner together."

No "hear, hears" or amendments to the toast, just the tipping up of the glasses and the drinking of the wine. Then there was that moment of delighted murmurs and rustling silverware as people prepared to take their first bite of a magnificent dinner.

Bunny had settled in her seat and turned her undivided attention on Bill. "Too much excitement, isn't there, luvy?" she asked him. And with that she picked up her wineglass and gulped the contents down. Suddenly she jerked to her feet, scraped her chair back, and dropped the goblet onto the table, crashing it into her water glass and sending shards of glass flying.

Both of her hands went to her throat, and she hoarsely cried out, "*Goddamn*—one of you bloody sods *poisoned* me!"

As one, the occupants of the table scrambled to their feet. They stared in horror as Bunny Bainfield staggered a few steps toward Richard Ralston's floral masterpiece and then began to droop like a parched flower.

In an instant Peg was by her side and had the slumping figure in her arms. She cried, *"Liebling,* no, it can't be—" The German woman looked around wildly at the others and bellowed, "Someone help her!"

Bill quickly supported Bunny's other side, but the woman was now moaning and trembling.

"Louise," barked her husband, "get the Secret Service, quickly. . . ."

Before she could scan the room, a Secret Service agent reached the table, still busily signaling others on his walkie-talkie. He shoved Peg aside, and he and Bill stretched Bunny out on the floor. She was immediately ringed with gawking guests. Louise watched in horror as foaming green liquid flowed from her mouth. Bunny was choking so violently that people nearby automatically brought their hands to their mouths, as though to stop the horror.

Louise pulled in her breath and clenched her fists. Her strongest feeling was not helplessness or fright, but a deep desire to register everything and remember it.

Three people from the next table, the Van Sickles and Shelby Newcross, were standing apart, looking grave as death itself, obviously not wanting to intrude on this intimate moment of human tragedy. Not so Bob Touhy, Joanna Heath, Fenimore and Lily Smith, and even the amiable Nathaniel Poe: they had all pushed forward to get a better view. Michael and Laura Sandoveld had quietly resumed their seats at the table.

The disheveled Gene Clendenin, his hands shoved deep in his pockets, his face emotionless, also strolled over to gaze at the scene; it was as if he understood quite well what was happening to Bunny. Louise looked around for Gail Rohrig; where had she gone?

Finally she turned back to where Bunny lay, catching only glimpses through the crowd of the writhing body in bright pink. Two people, one on either side of the prone woman, tried to keep Bunny's head from slamming into the floor. Even though partially restrained, that platinum-haired head tossed back and forth like a fish on a hook, frantically trying to cheat death.

Louise stared off into space, needing to remove herself from the ghastly here and now. But that only took her into long-buried memories of another poisoning.

Just three years ago she watched a person die before her very eyes, and now it was happening again. Suddenly she felt the room begin to spin, and she feared she would fall to the ancient pine floor, as if she were conjoining herself with the dying woman's plight.

A Secret Service man noticed just in time to grab her in his arms.

Gail could pretty much guess what was going to happen next to Bunny Bainfield. No rescue worker was going to give her mouth-to-mouth with that green stuff sluicing down her chin, that was for sure. And by the time the resuscitating machines were dragged in from the emergency vehicles, the woman would be dead.

It was time for Gail to get the hell out of there. The lady's room would be a perfect excuse. All she had to do was to stick her finger down her throat and she'd vomit with complete veracity. That would take her out of the limelight, which at any cost she couldn't afford to be in at the moment.

14

"Louise," said Bill, who had taken her from the Secret Service man's arms, "sit down." He helped her to a chair. For a moment it was as if the world had been frozen in a frame. Dark-clad Secret Service agents were rushing President-elect and Mrs. Anderson out of the ballroom. People wandered nervously about, trying to figure out what was happening.

Louise had missed only a couple of beats of life.

"You went out there for a minute," said her husband.

"How's Bunny—is someone helping her?"

His lips were parted slightly, as if he were thinking of a kind answer. "They're doing all they can. The medics are here."

"Oh, Bill—" Her voice broke. "She's been poisoned, we both know. It's just like it was with Madeleine—"

Her husband smoothed her hair with his hand.

"I knew you were thinking of that. It's easier for me to say and harder for you to do, but try not to dwell on that right now."

A Secret Service man with a nervous voice came to the microphone. "Ladies and gentlemen," he said, "one of our guests has fallen ill. Please move out of the ballroom, down the hall, and into the adjoining ballroom. This is necessary if we are to provide her proper air and emergency medical help. Do not try to leave the Gadsby's Tavern complex. I stress, do not leave the building."

Grumbles filled the room as Secret Service agents slowly herded the guests toward the door. After all, they were plied with drink and tempted with lobster, only to leave it on their plates because of another emergency.

Bill started to help Louise to her feet, but she said, "Thanks, but I'm all right now." Nevertheless, he insisted on holding an arm around her waist as they moved toward the door with the others, then waited for some bottleneck to clear.

Joanna Heath, walking next to them with the Smiths, passed a loud aside to Fenimore Smith. "They're calling Bunny a victim. I'd never have thought of her as victim. It's other people who are *her* victims."

Smith frowned disapprovingly. "It's not only inappropriate, Joanna, but dangerous to make a remark like that. After all, it looks as if someone poisoned that woman. The police are going to want to know who and why."

By word of mouth the story had spread, and if it hadn't, the arrival of the police would have told them this was more than someone stricken with a heart attack or food poisoning. The crowd became quieter. Even without an official announcement, Louise knew Bunny Bainfield was dead.

Like a magnet to north, Louise's gaze went to the other end of the room. She could see Bunny in her pink dress now, since the medics had stood up with an air of tired resignation and walked away to pack up their equipment.

It was a bizarre scene. The lavish floral background, Richard Ralston's greatest creation, looked like a huge pagan altar arrangement. The dead body of America's premier gardening impresario laid out in front of it resembled a sacrifice to the gods.

15

Charlie Hurd was a master at getting into places where people didn't want him. Tonight, his approach was simplicity itself. He'd thoughtfully filched a clipboard from the *Washington Post* newsroom for this very purpose. So it was the clipboard tucked under his arm, combined with the look and the walk: as good a disguise as a super-spy's.

His self-assured look and strutting walk alone had gained him entrance to amazingly difficult places. It said to people, *I belong here.*

He slid right by the police and upstairs into the Gadsby's Tavern ballroom, following closely on the heels of an EMT crew. Obviously the cops thought he was one of those important aides who came along not to take pulses but rather to jot down officious notes that might be used later for some obscure bureaucratic purpose. He'd had an intuition that this party of Maud Anderson's would yield a good story. He rubbed his hands, happy to be standing in the warmth of the ballroom after spending almost two hours outside Gadsby's Tavern in the chilly December night, checking off and identifying all who entered. When the police started rushing into the building, he knew something had happened, and he was in business.

He scanned the big space, noting an outlandish gardening display that hogged probably a quarter of the room and a woman laid out in front of it. It took only a moment to understand the situation. Those unhappy big-shot guests shuffling out were leaving uneaten dinners behind. The stricken woman was laid out like a corpse—and that was because she *was* a corpse; had the woman in pink still been alive, she would have been carted off to the hospital by now. And he knew who she was, the notorious garden superstar, Bunny Bainfield.

The reporter could practically smell and taste it: the woman on the floor didn't croak from anything natural, like a stroke. She had been murdered.

With a grunt of dismay, he recognized the man who was directing the swarm of police. It was a man Charlie knew and didn't like, Ron Goheen. He was tall and muscular, with black wavy hair and a swarthy complexion. A black Irishman, and head of Alexandria's detective bureau. When Charlie and Goheen had locked horns on a murder case last year, Charlie had unfortunately taunted the man, saying that he needed to smile more because otherwise he looked like witnesses' descriptions of the killer himself.

The dry, humorless son of a bitch had shoved him out of the office. But it didn't make a hell of a lot of difference, for Goheen was the kind of police official who didn't care about good press anyway. He was the worst kind of source, even if you were nice to him.

The reporter was ready to go into action. He swiftly crossed the twenty feet to where Goheen was doing his thing. Tapping him on the arm, Charlie said, "Sir. I have to speak to you."

The man looked down at Charlie through oval-shaped wire-rimmed glasses, eyes cold as Alaska. "What the hell do *you* want?"

Charlie swiftly flashed his press card. "Hurd of the *Washington Post*, in case you don't remember me, sir. And though you may not think I belong here, I have something to offer you."

The man took a step back and looked at him as if he were some kind of annoying insect, which Charlie didn't like at all.

"Oh, yeah. I recognize you. *Charlie* Hurd, right? What do you have to offer, especially since you're trespassing?"

Charlie cocked his head at the woman on the floor. "I see something pretty tragic has happened here"—he took a big leap—"a death by poison. Well, I just happen to have some information that you might appreciate knowing about." He had edged close enough to the prone figure to spy the green goo that had slid out of the woman's mouth. He'd guessed right: it *was* a death by poisoning. "Look, Mr. Goheen—"

"*Captain* Goheen to you, Charlie."

"Captain Goheen, then. I've got the goods on some of these people because I *prepped* for the new First Lady's party." He resisted the temptation to poke a finger into the detective's muscular abs. "I'd be willing to trade that expertise for an exclusive story for my paper. What you've got here might be a plot right out of *Murder on the Orient Express!*"

"What the *hell* are you talking about?" Goheen's brown eyes moved restlessly around the room as if to assure that everybody was following his orders.

"And make it fast; I have no time to waste with you." The detective captain was hustling him toward the exit door, and Charlie knew his time was limited.

"What I'm saying, Captain, is that practically everybody here had a motive to off Bunny Bainfield. Maybe they *all* murdered her, what do you think of that? A conspiracy of gardeners. Or, on the other hand, it could have been just one perp."

"How are you so sure she was murdered, when we don't know that at all?" asked Goheen, who now had Charlie's elbow clamped in an iron grip.

"Look, I'm not dumb. I know. I can see the damned poison slathered all over the corpse's face—"

Goheen's slightly pock-marked face hardened. "That's enough; you're not supposed to be in here, and now you're leaving. Let's go."

They were abreast of the people filing out of the ballroom. Charlie broke free from the detective captain's grasp and pointed to one of them. "Look, there's Fenimore Smith. And there's Joanna Heath. I checked them out; they both have nursery businesses suffering big time from Bunny's takeover of the market."

He didn't welcome the frosty stares of the two nursery owners, but kept talking anyway. "That woman in green, that's Louise Eldridge. D'you know her story? She's a TV garden show host, just like Bunny Bainfield was. And Bunny was *cleaning* her *clock*—taking her audience away from her. I hear they were gonna replace her with a cooking show—"

Charlie saw Louise stare at him with anger in her eyes. Her husband Bill looked even more pissed.

Goheen stuck his hands in the pockets of his

gray wool pants and looked hard at the three people Charlie had mentioned.

Charlie saw the sliver of an opening. He stopped in his tracks, and so did the detective captain. "So you see," he said, "I've got the scoop on practically everybody here. Don't you *want* it?"

Goheen looked down at him without smiling. "Go downstairs and wait for me in the bar, Charlie, and in a few minutes you can share some of that expertise. Now, get out of here—I've got work to do. And don't plan to come back tomorrow, either."

"*Tomorrow?*" asked Charlie hopefully. "You mean, the garden conference is still going on tomorrow at The Federalist?"

"That's right." His eyes were averted from Charlie's, and Charlie knew a lie was coming. "The conference will go on as scheduled, in a manner of speaking, in spite of the unfortunate death of Ms. Bunny Bainfield, due to causes unknown at the moment."

Charlie smirked. "I get it. Having the conference go ahead is a way for you to keep these out-of-town people around longer for questioning."

"Why don't you quit speculating and just go. And remember, security at The Federalist is going to be twice as thick as it is here, so don't bother to try and get in. Another illegal entry like this and I'll throw you right in Alexandria's fine city jail."

Charlie sidled quickly by Fenimore Smith and his skinny wife, then nearly collided with Louise and her husband.

"Hi, there, Louise," he called out. "Look, I'd love to talk to you. Want to meet downstairs in the bar?"

She shook her head, her eyes wide, her mouth tight. Bill Eldridge's eyes were dangerous slits. As if making a joke of it, Charlie raised his clipboard like a shield and said, "I guess you must have heard me talking about you. Now, don't take it personally, you two. I was just making the point that every last living person here—"

Bill Eldridge approached from one side, and Goheen from the other, so he knew it was really time to get the hell out of this ballroom. He swung around, bumping hips with the big blonde, Joanna Heath, then eased his way out of the place. He felt lucky to escape without getting punched in the nose.

He was happy; once he gave Goheen all the background he had on these gardening characters, he'd be in like Flynn with the lead detective. And even if the guy told him nothing, he already had a hot story, including that green goo.

Louise and Bill were the last people in the line that made its way slowly into the small ballroom. There, light from wall sconces had replaced the romantic cocktail party candlelight from the big candelabras. They were snuffed out now and looked like faded wallflowers after a dance.

Once in the smaller room, they found out what the holdup was: the police were signing everyone out and demanding phone numbers and addresses. "I wonder how Charlie Hurd sneaked into this place?" she asked her husband.

"That's Charlie for you," said Bill drily, "the unstoppable reporter. I couldn't believe the way he was badmouthing you."

"He was lying. My show's ratings may be down slightly, but nobody's told me they're replacing it with a *cooking* show!"

"He was dealing the dirt on Fenimore Smith and Joanna Heath, too—he must be desperate to get in good with that Alexandria detective."

She gasped. "Look who's here now." Tramping wearily up the circular staircase was a large man with a shock of white, curly hair, and wearing a worn brown suit. Fairfax County Detective Mike Geraghty, who worked out of the county's Mount Vernon District Station south of the city of Alexandria, was a man they knew well. Louise had been involved in helping clear up three murder cases in the Fairfax County jurisdiction. She and Geraghty were friends, when they weren't adversaries.

Geraghty looked at them, shook his head as if to say, "I might have known you'd be at the site of a murder," then walked directly over to the muscular, bad-complected man who appeared to be in charge of things. The two men stood at the doorway, conversing, their heads close together.

"I guess our friend Geraghty is going to help with this investigation," observed Bill, "though why, I don't know. I'm sure the city of Alexandria will run it."

After a moment, the two policemen looked curiously over at Louise. There was nothing friendly in their attitude. Geraghty looked big and formidable.

The meaning of it all dawned on Louise. She turned to her husband and said, "You heard what Charlie was saying to that detective: he was laying out the reasons why I might have wanted to kill Bunny. And now Mike Geraghty is over there and they're rehashing it. Bill, I'm just another suspect."

16

December 16

Louise's eyes fluttered open, saw only darkness, and closed again. She was snuggled against Bill, spoon-style, and felt as warm and cozy as a caterpillar must feel inside its chrysalis. He was snoring gently, so she knew he wasn't ready to get up. Neither was she. She could lie this way, cuddled against her husband, for an eternity. Maybe after a while, she'd turn into a beautiful swallowtail butterfly. . . .

She was almost back to sleep when an unpleasant thought seeped into her consciousness as stealthily as poison dropped into a liquid.

Something was terribly wrong. In this moment of half-sleep she couldn't remember what it was. And besides, the bed wasn't right—it didn't have that slight dip in the middle, so it couldn't be *their* bed—

She sat up with a jolt and looked around in the dim hotel room. *"Bill*—we're not home."

Startled into wakefulness, he gave a little snort, then rolled over and said languidly, "You mean you're not in Kansas anymore, Dorothy?"

"Very funny. I love a man who can wake up with a joke on his lips."

Then it all came back to her. Bunny's poisoning. The interminable questioning by the police. The search of their hotel room and luggage. Finally going to bed, exhausted, at four in the morning.

"I remember everything now," muttered Louise in a somber voice. "We're at The Federalist, and Bunny's dead."

"Are you asking me to decide which is worse?"

"Bill, that's not very respectful—"

"I know, of either Bunny *or* The Federalist. Just give me a chance to wake up, Louise, and maybe I can do better. What time is it?" He struggled up from the covers and sat on the edge of the bed and peered at the big red numbers on the night table that said it was eight. "We've only had four hours' sleep," he said.

She stared at the pale light that came through the crevices in the silk double drapes, wishing that she were at home in Sylvan Valley and didn't have to face what she'd have to face today. This place might be posh, but it didn't matter: it was as discomfiting as a cheap motel.

Bill came around the bed, turned on the bedside light, and sat beside her. "Are you going to be all right, honey? I didn't mean to joke about what happened last night—it was monstrous the way Bunny died. Will you be okay if I leave you here while I go to work? I'll pick you up at four, when your so-called conference is supposed to be over."

"I hate the idea of having to stay in this place all day."

"And I know you aren't fond of Ron Goheen."

Louise and the Alexandria detective captain had become well acquainted when he interrogated her for more than an hour last night. It had not mattered that Detective Mike Geraghty had been on the hotel premises—he wasn't allowed in on the interview. Goheen obviously wanted to handle her without some erstwhile police friend in attendance.

"But we didn't do badly, when you think about it," said Bill. "I pitied those half dozen people left till last, your pal Gail among them. Funny thing about her—"

"What do you mean?"

"Did you notice that she disappeared from sight after Bunny collapsed?"

"But she was here at The Federalist when we arrived. She didn't like Bunny, but are you saying she'd *murder* her? I can't believe Gail'd ruin her own life by doing that."

"Listen to us, will you," remarked Bill. "Bunny this, and Bunny that. It's as if we're talking about an old friend, when she was anything but."

Louise was silent a moment, and then admitted, "I didn't like her much. Did you?"

"No. Too egocentric for my tastes, but I certainly didn't wish her dead."

Louise sat slump-shouldered. "That's just the trouble—some of those people did."

Bill was on his feet now, wide awake, and in his usual organized way was heading for the bathroom. "Louise, maybe you'd better get ready for your conference. As for me, I have a meeting this morning at State, so I need to get out of here, too."

Tripping over a big orange throw pillow on the floor, Louise trailed him into the sleek, taupe-tiled bathroom. He had turned on the shower, and she took off her nightie so that she would be ready to step in right after him. No joint shower this morning; she was too sleepy.

He called out to her, "At least this time I'm glad to see you're not going to be the police's little helper."

"No way," said Louise, putting the taupe-colored toilet seat lid down and sitting on it. "In the first place, I'm just as much of a suspect right now as everyone else. And I wouldn't want to be involved, anyway—it's too gruesome and it could involve a colleague."

He poked his head out of the steam, looking quite different with his hair wet against his head. "I know a way to find the murderer," he said, lathering up. "They call it the mass-interview technique."

"What's that?" she asked dully.

"I'll tell you in a second," he said. When he came out of the shower, he gave her bottom a gentle touch as she slipped by him. Once she'd finished and was rubbing herself dry, he was lathered up for a shave and ready to continue his explanation.

"A mass interview is just what it sounds like. You question lots of people at one time, asking them essentially to reenact an event. Sam Marshall—you know, the Army historian—used to do it. It's how he got the materials for his war books, sitting soldiers down after a big battle and getting them to tell what they thought went on during combat."

"It sounds familiar."

Bill drew the razor smoothly up his cheek. "It's a very accurate way to get information about complex situations. One soldier would challenge what another said, and so forth, until Marshall finally decided he'd come to the truth of the matter—or as true as anyone can come about battles involving hundreds, maybe thousands, of men."

Louise had a dawning realization: she knew all about this stuff. She watched as her husband carefully covered all the whiskered ground on his cheeks and chin. Bill Eldridge would never arrive at his job in Foggy Bottom to help solve the problems of the world without being clean-shaven.

"I know this technique."

"You do?" he asked in surprise.

"Sure. I just never call it a reenactment. Hercule Poirot uses that method all the time. The only difference is that it isn't soldiers, but guests at an English country mansion."

"I thought Poirot assembled the guests after he knew who the murderer was, and not to find the murderer."

She finished rubbing her hair dry with her towel, then folded it neatly and put it over the shower rack. "I think you're right about that. Anyway, it's all academic. I'm not the least bit interested in getting involved in this mess."

"Good. Then I won't have to worry about you. And since the hotel is loaded with police, I doubt anyone's in much danger today."

17

Louise opened the door of their hotel room before she remembered she had left her purse inside. Leaving the door ajar, she went to the table by the window, where she checked to be sure everything she needed was there—pen, notebook, makeup case, wallet—and slung it over her shoulder. Once back at the door, she froze in place.

Across the hall a door had opened, and in the doorway stood Fenimore Smith and Joanna Heath. Smith was in a traditional suit, but Joanna wore a silk bathrobe, her hair uncombed and blowsy.

Louise wondered if she should just forge ahead or wait until the two finished their conversation. She heard Fenimore say, in an intimate voice, "Don't worry, my dear friend, we'll work it out." He bent down and held Joanna's face in a gentle hand, and brushed his lips against her hair. It was a proprietary gesture, as if this man knew and understood her well.

Suddenly looking up and seeing Louise standing there, Joanna gave her a transfixed, almost bucolic look. Was this the assertive businesswoman she knew?

Smith turned to see what Joanna was staring at, and said casually, "Good morning, Louise. Joanna, Lily, and I are planning a breakfast rendezvous. I hope you and your husband slept well in spite of the events of last night." Then without waiting for her reply, he turned back to Joanna and quietly said, "Lily and I will expect you in, say, fifteen minutes?"

Joanna nodded obediently. Louise walked quickly toward the exit signs, idly wondering if a woman in Joanna's state of dishabille could pull herself together in fifteen minutes. Louise was sure that *she* couldn't.

The elevator was coated in panels of mirror and brushed aluminum, but Louise kept her eyes on the floor. She was loath to examine herself too closely after having had only four hours of sleep; though she'd carefully covered the rings under her eyes with makeup, even after a good brushing she'd barely been able to tame her long brown hair. Peevishly, she reflected on the folly of men who put mirrors in elevators in the first place. She was sure that she looked almost as bad as Joanna.

The encounter in the hallway a moment ago made her wonder what was going on between Joanna and Fenimore Smith. She didn't know any male friends of hers and Bill's who would treat *her* in that way, but then, as she'd often found out, people were a lot looser in their views of things than she sometimes was.

* * *

The lobby doors of the elevator silently opened, and Charlie Hurd couldn't believe his good luck. Louise Eldridge, looking about six feet tall, stepped off and practically fell into his arms. The *Washington Post* reporter wished he were a little taller. The woman was formidable in her striped wool business suit and three-inch heels.

"What are *you* doing here, you—you little *gossip!*" Slinging her leather shoulder bag back out of the way, she put her hands on her hips, and for a minute fear ran through him. He was reminded of Xena the Warrior Princess, ready to attack.

Off to a real bad start, thought Charlie, looking around nervously and hoping no one had heard her. The lobby was almost empty, with policemen far off near the hotel entrance. He put out a hand in a placating gesture. "Now, Louise," he said quietly, "calm down. Be a sport and take what happened last night in stride. *Please* don't tip my hand."

She looked down at the lapel of his stylishly cut suit; he was wearing his cleverly obtained convention badge. It read, *Charles Hurd*—GARDENS ALIVE MAGAZINE.

"Of all the bloody nerve," she said, "making yourself out to be some *garden* expert—"

He hurriedly shushed her. "Please, I need your help. I can get a story here, Louise, that will really *rock* Washington and the new administration. You know me: *I* know how to get to the bottom of a murder like this."

She turned away and started quickly across the lobby. He was right beside her, keeping pace. He intended to be as persistent as a barnacle attached to the bottom of a boat, for he'd found that worked well with recalcitrant people like Louise.

She looked down at him in distaste, and he

could see loathing in her eyes. This made him sad, since the two of them once almost had been buddies. She said, "You're *such* a good crime solver, especially if someone else does all the work beforehand and endangers their life to do so. Then you come in like a vulture and scavenge a story out of it."

He kept striding along beside her, unabashed at her harsh words. "Louise, just because you think I didn't do you right, that time out on the island—"

"When I was going to be weighted down and pitched into the *Potomac*—"

"I had the situation *totally* in hand."

"You made me suffer longer than I had to at the hands of that man. I can't forget or forgive you. You let me twist slowly in the wind, so to speak, just so you could get a bigger story for your newspaper. And last night was the last straw, Charlie. I heard you spilling your guts to that Ron Goheen, trying to make me out to be a suspect in Bunny's murder. *You*, Charlie, are the pits; you would sell your own mother to get a good story—" she stopped to glare at him "—and in your case that is not a cliché, it's the utter truth!" Then she started walking again.

He quickly fell into step with her. "But, Louise, at least answer just one question, a kind of academic question. This big party and conference is all about those weedy little native plants, right?"

"Right," she snapped.

"I have my ideas on this, but why the hell do *you* think someone would kill over weedy little plants?"

She laughed derisively at him. "Weedy little native plants, my ignorant friend, are very hot these days in gardening. *Gardening* is very hot. I know you've never dipped a spade in the soil in your life, but real people, Charlie, spend billions on plants and trees and shrubs these days, on flamingos and urns and gazing balls, on watering systems and hoses—" she stopped for a breath "—and on those beautiful little native plants that you think are weeds."

She'd stopped now to look him square in the eyes. He warily moved back a step. "I've answered your one question. Now leave me alone. I'm starved and I'm going to eat."

She turned and headed toward the entrance to the hotel restaurant. Charlie stood there, wondering if he should pursue her further. He didn't want a scene in the damned restaurant.

Then he saw trouble. Approaching Louise diagonally across the lobby was that shabby Fairfax detective, Mike Geraghty, who looked like a cat dragged him in. Last night, he saw that Geraghty'd finagled himself in on the interrogations conducted by the Alexandria police. The man might or might not recognize him.

Hurd moved to the side of the lobby and tried to blend in with the poinsettia plants. Geraghty was talking to Louise, and she probably was going to squeal on him. But before she could even get the words out, the fat old detective's eye scanned the lobby, and he was caught.

The detective lumbered across the room as fast as a big grizzly, and in three strides he was hovering over him. "Who have we here? Is that you again, Charlie? Whatcha doing, posing as a designer or somethin'?"

He laughed when he read Charlie's badge; at least he wasn't as hard-assed as Captain Ron Goheen. Geraghty beckoned to one of the policeman at the door of the hotel, who quickly came over. "Kindly escort this gentleman out of here, and while you're at it, confiscate that phony ID badge."

"Look, Detective Geraghty," Charlie said, "if you want an accurate story for the people of Washington to read—"

"You'll just have to wait on that, Charlie, maybe until tomorrow." The reporter turned back and watched as the detective walked off with Louise Eldridge.

Damn, he thought. That woman would hear all about Bunny Bainfield's murder. And here he was, shut off completely.

18

"So much for your security system," said Louise. "It's pretty good," said Detective Geraghty. "It's just that Charlie Hurd is the most devious con man I ever met who wasn't a real criminal."

"I suppose you're helping out with the investigation."

"Yeah. Ron Goheen's asked me to stay on board. I have to go and see what he needs me to do next."

"Well, I'm going to breakfast. Are you interested?"

Geraghty looked around to see who was watching. "Sure. But let's not eat here—I don't exactly want folks to know I'm breakin' bread with you."

With a weak laugh, she said, "That's because I'm just one of your suspects. I could tell, because Goheen spent so much time questioning me last night."

He gave her a sheepish look. "Hell, I know you didn't do it, Louise. But Alexandria police have to investigate their way; Goheen felt you'd have a good read on what happened." He cocked his head toward a side exit to the hotel. "Let's go out that door. You won't need your coat. Follow after me in a minute. I'll instruct the officer there to let you through."

Outside was a small garden delineated in boxwood. They walked the short distance to a small, historic Old Town breakfast joint, both of them tired, neither one of them with much to say.

Louise had polished off a full cup of coffee before her synapses seemed ready to connect. She sat back and looked knowingly at the big detective. "The reason we're here today is not for a garden conference. The police only want to have us handy for questioning."

"That's it," admitted Geraghty. "Still, you'll have a couple of meetings to talk over the First Lady's ideas; I hear she hasn't given up on her pet project just because someone was murdered at her garden party."

"Why doesn't the Alexandria police department call the FBI in on this? After all, the president-elect was there last night."

Geraghty shrugged. "That he was, but his presence doesn't seem related to the crime. I'm sure the bureau would have sent over a few men if they'd requested it, as additional support, but this is the Alexandria police's baby—a capital crime in their jurisdiction. Goheen *is* sending the physical evidence to the FBI forensic lab." He leaned forward. "Look, this is a nightmare case, don't think it isn't: almost fifty suspects. Usually we'll have two, or three, maybe four. And Goheen's under additional pressure because some of these people are kind of highfalutin', y'know."

"All the more reason to get FBI help, isn't it?"

Geraghty laughed. "I think the Alexandria police can handle this case. After all, they had Aldrich Ames, the big master CIA spy, and Robert Hanssen, the FBI spy, right there in the Alexandria jail."

"That must prove something," she said dubiously.

"Goheen's doin' fine, Louise. He's doin' second interviews with certain folks already. He'll reinterview someone six times, if that's what it's goin' to take. The man knows his stuff."

She remembered Bill's idea of having a group interview. "What about talking to everyone together—for instance, everyone at Bunny's table? Let people reenact what happened, who was where, when—that sort of thing."

"Huh," said Geraghty in a grunt of dismissal, "no way Goheen would do that." The Irish cop unabashedly stared at her. She reflexively put a hand up to straighten her tousled hair. "Look, Louise, I know how you like to operate; in kindergarten, you probably were the kind of kid who colored outside the lines of the pictures."

She smiled. "That's how I garden, too."

"Yeah, but when you're investigatin' crimes, it's different. Police don't work that way: they have orderly procedures for doin' things. And you'd be surprised how successful it can be to just keep pressin' individual suspects."

"Do you think group interviews have no value?"

"I'm not sayin' that, exactly. I suppose it might indicate some level of innocence on the part of those who participated. But police think they get more information separatin' people."

"Has Captain Goheen learned anything so far?"

He glanced around, checking to be sure no one was listening. "I don't know that it will hurt to tell you this. But keep it to yourself. He's thinkin' the poisoning had to be done by one of the people who sat at your table."

She thought of that party scene. "I'm not so sure of that. When the trumpet started blaring, there was a great deal of confusion, people milling about—"

"True, and the neighboring table was situated pretty close. There are at least a couple of individuals sittin' there who he's lookin' at real close."

"Who would they be?" she asked.

Geraghty hunched over and frowned. "Louise, you're not in on this, you know; we don't need your help—"

She put up a hand, as if to block his words. "Believe me, Mike, I'm much too tired. Anyway, I'm not that interested." She looked down at the Formica-topped table. "Well, maybe I'm *curious*, but I don't intend to do anything about it."

"Gene Clendenin is one. Do you know him?"

"I didn't have a chance to meet him."

"He's a very direct man. He says it flat out and says it rather harshly: *he* thinks Bunny put the First Lady up to this native plant project just so Bunny could get a toehold in the native plant market. She'd already started"—the detective consulted a small notebook—"to do work on genetically altering native plants to make them look like exotic plants."

"I heard a rumor to that effect," said Louise.

The detective looked puzzled. "Louise, just what *are* exotic plants? You mean orchids and stuff?"

Louise smiled. "Any plant imported into the United States is called exotic, or 'introduced.' Some orchids, by the way, are native to America. Lots more aren't. That would be an interesting motive, because lots of true believers would hate the idea of tinkering with native species. But I certainly can't believe the head of a federal agency murdered Bunny."

"Why not, if he's such a goldarned plant freak? Look, there weren't any unimportant people at that affair last night unless you count the service people. As you would expect, Goheen's thoroughly checked out the waiters and waitresses, the maître d'hotel, and the manager, and he's tracing that wine all the way back to the winery it came from. And the musician, of course, *especially* the musician. That's one track of the investigation. The other is those guests. *Some* big shot very well may have done it. Why, among those people, you're probably the one with the least—"

"Least what? Credentials?"

The natural red of his face deepened to maroon. "I didn't mean that the way it came out."

She roughly shoved her hair back from her face. She guessed the hostess of a Saturday morning PBS garden show didn't have the same clout as botanists, horticulturalists, environmentalists, professors, landscapers, or even garden writers. "No offense taken, Mike. I think I know what you're trying to say. As for Clendenin, I heard he didn't like the native plant project *or* Bunny Bainfield. But it doesn't mean anything. Lots of people slammed Bunny Bainfield last night. It was like a celebrity roast without the good jokes."

Geraghty's big marblelike eyes looked haunted. He hunched farther down over his coffee. "That's what Ron Goheen's afraid of: there are going to be way too many suspects. At least he got the cooperation of every guest for a search of bags and rooms."

Their breakfasts had arrived, and Louise felt better just looking at her big plate with one egg over easy, bacon, sourdough toast, and a small pile of fruit. She dug in.

After she'd polished off her egg and a couple of pieces of toast, she said, "And who else is Goheen interested in?"

"Your tablemates, the Smiths and Joanna Heath."

"That's only natural," said Louise. "They were Bunny's direct competitors. I suppose you'll narrow the list, too, by eliminating people like Nathaniel Poe, and Dr. and Mrs. Van Sickle, and Shelby Newcross."

"Why?" asked Geraghty. "Because they're too old?"

"Poe can't be more than sixty-five. The others are in their seventies. But it's not their age. They don't have motives, do they?"

"They don't?"

"Van Sickle and Newcross both disapproved of Bunny, that was clear, but they voice their disapproval from these lofty scientific heights, Ted Van Sickle's heights being a little higher, I guess you'd say, than Shelby Newcross's. As for Poe, he was one of the few people who didn't seem to have any gripe with Bunny."

"You sure of that?" he asked, flipping through his notes.

"Pretty sure, but it's your business, not mine." When she asked her next question, she tried to sound casual, as if she didn't really care. "Who's the second person at the adjoining table?"

"Gail Rohrig." The detective picked up his fork and resumed shoveling in his food, not looking at Louise. "That's *some* woman—a mouth like a stevedore, and an attitude like a witch—"

He looked up and saw Louise's concerned face. "Oh, oh—is she a friend?"

"I know her pretty well. She's been on my program."

"She couldn't explain satisfactorily where she went after the poisoning. *Claims* she was in the ladies' room barfing her brains out. Nobody can corroborate that for us."

"Why would she sneak out if she *had* poisoned Bunny? That would only make people suspicious."

"Maybe to flush an excess poison supply down the toilet, maybe because she couldn't face seeing what was going to happen to Bunny down on that floor. I hear the scene was terrible."

Louise had set that memory aside, but now it came raging back. The heat of the ballroom, the almost sickly fragrance of hundreds of flowers exuding from Richard Ralston's extravagant arrangement, the glamorously clad woman wiggling on the floor as if trying to escape from the devil himself—

She closed her eyes for an instant. "Let's not talk about that right now. I'd rather hold on to my breakfast than lose it. And by the way—"

"Yes?"

"There probably are a few more people from that adjoining table you might want to check out."

"Who?"

"Bob Touhy, for instance. He and Bunny were rivals for the attentions of Maud Anderson, in gardening matters, that is."

Geraghty looked blank.

She looked at him curiously. "You mean you don't remember the big man with the thinning black hair and the droning voice?"

"Yeah, vaguely. Didn't sit in on every interview, that's for sure. Who else are you talkin' about?"

"I hate to mention them. Richard Ralston. Ken Lurie. You should know everything about them so that you don't suddenly begin to suspect them."

"Ralston, the florist? And Ken Lurie, that fellow that writes garden books?"

She nodded again. She'd been quick to cast a cloud on the rude Bob Touhy, but loath to do the same to Richard and Ken. Yet honesty required it of her, and anyway, they'd soon hear stories about the two, and they should have a chance to counter those stories with the facts.

"From what I hear, all three of them had trouble with Bunny." She gave Mike Geraghty a sad smile. "Touhy looks like the killer type, while Ken Lurie's more of a lover," she flushed, "—and Richard's a—"

"What?" asked a sarcastic Geraghty. "A little sweetheart?"

"I'm just telling you this because you're bound to hear it anyway from more than one source. In spite of their problems with her, no one would ever think that Richard or Ken could kill a flea."

Immediately, Louise lowered her gaze. Despite those mitigating words at the end, she knew she had implicated her new friends. She wasn't supposed to be helping the police, but suddenly she felt like the ultimate snitch. It was a dirty business, tattling on nice people who'd trusted her.

19

Louise and Geraghty walked the short distance back to the side door of The Federalist. As they parted, the detective said, "Thanks for that tip, Louise. I appreciate it. You're an observant person, you know that? Now do yourself a favor and just relax, and I'm sure Captain Goheen will allow you all to go home this afternoon."

She sighed. "I wish I were home right now."

With a nod at the patrolman, the detective left her there to slip in and rejoin the others. By this time, she knew, they would be assembling—grumpy, probably, from sleep deprivation and the stress of witnessing a murder.

She headed quickly for the women's lounge, for she had a strong desire to get clean again. To splash cold water on her face, perhaps wash her hands just like Pontius Pilate, and rid them of the guilt of betrayal.

She passed from the main lobby through a smaller

lobby, off which lay the men's and women's rooms. For the first time she paid close attention to the decorations of this highly touted new hotel, wondering why it depressed her to look at it.

The overall color scheme was a rather tiresome mauve and gray, with stone-colored carpeting and actual stone and marble inlays in the floors. Thank heavens for the near arrival of Christmas, Louise thought, for huge vermilion-colored poinsettia plants had been placed about and helped relieve the gloom. Bright red would have been better, but at least it was a move away from total drabness.

In spite of the name of the place, there was only a token nod to the federalist style, and that was in the hotel entrance, and in the wainscoting that appeared on almost every wall.

The bedrooms, on the other hand, though they also featured wainscoted walls, were much lighter, like romantic berths for illicit trysts. Off-white walls with golden trim and golden light sconces were played down with dim lighting and carpeting, bedspread, and drapes in shades of taupe, then played up again with a clutch of dramatic throw pillows in magenta and burnt orange.

She'd had a brief glimpse of Joanna's bedroom this morning. It looked exactly like hers and Bill's.

As much as she didn't like hotel living, The Federalist had two advantages: good art from many periods scattered through the rooms, and newness, which meant it didn't have that enclosed smell that hostelries picked up after a period of use. The smells of *people,* she supposed, which wouldn't go away even after the cleaning crews had done their best with vacuums and mops and polish and brooms. She only hoped the day would go fast, since the walls were already closing in on her.

She pushed through the door marked WOMEN

and entered the lounge, where a small figure sat in an upholstered chair, holding the front section of the *Washington Post* in front of her face.

The tooled boots and dashing denim skirt tipped off Louise. Gail Rohrig was the only one at this conference who'd wear an outfit like that. "Gail, is that you behind the front page?"

Gail lowered the paper and grinned weakly, looking pale under her healthy tan. She wore a short, fringed jeans jacket with beaded embroidery to complete her Girl-of-the-Golden-West outfit. "Hi, Louise. I'm reading about what happened to Bunny." Gail was on the jump page, so Louise could see the front page: the two-line headline reached across several columns.

NOTED GARDEN FIGURE IS MURDERED
AT PRESIDENT-ELECT'S PARTY

Louise had been so distracted, first by Charlie Hurd and then by Mike Geraghty, that she hadn't even picked up a copy. She knew the story would carry the byline of Charlie Hurd. "So what did they say about it?"

Gail turned back to the story. "Did you know Bunny has six brothers and sisters in England, and that she was generous with them, and they all 'loved her dearly.' Isn't that just too sweet? Or that her husband, that old fogy Maryland nurseryman she married for his nursery, is still alive, but retired and sick, so that Bunny heads the business? I didn't know the husband was still alive."

"Gail, what's wrong with you? You look pale."

The tawny-haired woman gave Louise one look and collapsed the paper in her lap. For a moment her face looked like it, too, would collapse into tears, but this was only for a moment. She recovered, and with chin thrust out said, "You mean, I don't look so good—"

"I didn't mean just that—"

"Well you don't look so good either, friend, if you want the truth, with those dark circles under your eyes."

Louise gave up trying to explain herself. "I know," she said. "What a drag this has been, staying up half the night."

Gail swung her long, gold-highlighted hair back from her face, like a woman who was about to get down to business. "And I'm pissed, Louise, royally pissed. The police have somehow got suspicious of me, and so it's only natural that I'm damned nervous. Questioned last night, questioned again this morning by that guy who thinks he's such hot stuff. So how am I? I'm pissed and I'm nervous."

"You were up late. We saw you going into the interrogation room as we were leaving."

"For an hour, from four till five," she said indignantly, "and then another thirty minutes just now. I told Goheen the truth, that I hated Bunny Bainfield for moving in on the native seed business which *I*, almost alone, originated. Native seeds, Louise, in case you don't know it, are very hot. Why, suppliers are even *stealing* stuff from each other, or did you hear about that case in Oregon? *Bunny*"— Gail sneered out the name—"wanted to make her mark in the seed industry in the worst way, especially when she discovered the profit potential, that Indian Paintbrush seed, for instance, goes for $500 a pound. I know her: she would have charged five dollars a throw for a little package holding a dozen seeds whereas I'd only charge four. But the sin of it all is that she'd do her damndest to corner the seed market on this plant—it's like a splash of color from God's paint set—and try to make a killin' on it."

She tossed her long hair and said, "They think that just because we squabbled over stuff like that, that I might have killed her." A self-pitying expression covered her face, as if she'd just remembered she was supposed to be pathetic and sick. "Besides, Louise, I feel really rotten; I threw up on and off all night long."

"So that's why you left the ballroom last night?"

"You mean even you thought I had something to do with killing that woman?" The yellow-green eyes blazed with anger. "I wouldn't give her the satisfaction of serving jail time by taking a good-for-nothin' life like hers!"

Louise sat on an adjoining down couch, which had a pattern of white roses against a purplish background. "I'm sorry you felt ill—and sorry they've given you a hard time. So you missed everything?"

"Yes, I missed the diva's death scene on the floor. Of course I've heard all about it from Ken and Richard." Gail screwed her mouth into a semblance of a smile. "She'd never have chosen such a crummy floor to die on if she'd had a choice."

Louise fell silent, partly to let Gail know she disapproved of her brazen attitude, partly because she'd noticed something when Gail smiled that made her heart skip a beat. The paleness in Gail's face was not from being ill: it came from a heavy application of light-colored make-up. Why, she wondered, was Gail deliberately lying about being ill?

It seemed useless to pursue this point with her defensive companion, so she said, "Who do you think would have the nerve to poison Bunny right there in the middle of a crowd?"

Gail gave a strained laugh. "Glad you put it that way. We both know lots of people would *want* to off that obnoxious chick, but it had to be someone with the balls to step up and actually do it."

Louise winced and shook her head. "Gail, maybe you shouldn't be so blunt."

"What difference does it make? Everybody knows how I feel—my friends, my enemies, my analyst. Just kiddin'; I'm not *in* analysis."

Experimentally, Louise slid her legs onto the couch, and found it wonderful to stretch out her tired body. Good, as long as she didn't yield to the temptation to fall fast asleep. "So what's your take on all this?"

Gail shrugged. "Take your pick, Louise. It could have been Touhy. That big asshole was competing like mad with Bunny for the attention of the divine Mrs. Anderson."

"I heard that from Poe. And he acts like a rough kind of man. But who else?"

Gail was warming to the subject, and no amount of pale makeup would convince others that this strong little woman was ill. "Think nursery competition. Take Joanna Heath, for instance, our round-heeled friend from North Carolina. After Joanna agreed to buy out Fenimore Smith, she and Bunny were going to be the two big frogs in the pond, that is, the pond that is the huge Eastern Seaboard garden market."

"Maybe she thought there ought to be only one big frog in the pond. I bet this whole thing was hard for the Smiths to take, losing Wild Flower Farm."

"Hard isn't the word; it was downright *humiliating* for that prick. And all traceable back to Bunny's aggressive marketing." She shook a finger at Louise. "Never underestimate the egotism and general shittiness of Fenimore Smith. True, he may make his big bucks in publishing, but Wild Flower Farm was his love. He would do anything for his little family nursery business. Losing it is a big insult to his, you know, gonads: his family heritage and all that shit."

"I don't know the Smiths well, just well enough to know they have a lot of pride." She was silent a moment and then asked, "What do you think of Gene Clendenin as a possibility?"

Gail flipped a hand up as if dispatching an annoying insect. "No way. He didn't bad-mouth Bunny any more than the rest of the people there, probably less." She stared off into the space of the lounge. "My worst fear is that the police latch on to Ken, or maybe Richard. I'd hate it if they got accused of doing Bunny in, though either one of them had good reason. She was leanin' on both of them pretty hard."

Louise's heart thumped, as she thought of her Judas performance with Mike Geraghty.

Gail leaned back in her chair and stretched. "Sorry if I'm bitchy, but it's all the shit that's been handed to me by Captain *Goheen*. There's another scenario, you know, Louise. Forget garden industry market shares and stuff like that. How about straight-out sex?"

"I heard some rumor about that. You mean Bunny's affairs?"

"Not rumor, Louise," said Gail, flipping her hair back again. "What you heard was fact. Bunny got it on with Fenimore Smith last summer; I heard all about it. So how about that anorexic wife of his for a suspect? Or how about Joanna Heath, who was jealous as hell of our platinum-haired beauty? Joanna thinks of herself as the love goddess of the garden industry."

She grinned, as if knowing in advance she was going to shock Louise. "Her motto was, 'Screw a nursery man whenever you can.' So think of how pissed she was when another goddess, Ms. Bainfield, came on the scene with those big boobs of hers and lured away all the eligible adulterers."

"Good heavens, who could be jealous of—"

Gail leaned forward and gave Louise a steady look with her catlike eyes. "Why can't you believe that? What about *you*, my friend? Those big boobs of hers were attracting lots of garden-show audience share, weren't they? And it didn't help that your program and hers both ran on Saturdays, did it? You had a reason to kill, just like a lot of other people."

Louise sat up a little straighter on the couch, and her face slowly colored, knowing that in her darkest heart she had disliked Bunny simply for her blatant sex appeal. It had seemed an unfair advantage for a garden show hostess to have.

But Gail was happily off on another tangent, her eyes lit up and her body perched forward in her chair. "Here's the sleuthiest scenario of them all: wonder if a green-eyed Peg Roggenstach administered that fatal potion?"

"Peg jealous, but why? You don't mean Peg and Bunny—"

Gail arched a golden eyebrow and twitched a tanned finger in the air. "Oh yes I do. Bunny swung from both sides of the plate. Her manager was also her lover; I have that from good authority. So how did it sit with Peg when Bunny went to bed with Fenimore?"

"Wow," said Louise. She felt sorry for Ron Goheen. It was just as Mike Geraghty had said: there were too many suspects, too many motives.

The door to the lounge slowly opened, and a

white-haired woman poked her head in. Louise immediately swung her legs off the comfy couch and onto the floor.

"Hello, my dears," said Jessie Van Sickle in a comforting, musical voice. "I'm glad I found you. Ted is looking for everyone. Actually, he's out in the lobby with his list, taking a head count. He wants to start the morning session if you ladies are up to it."

This morning, Dr. Van Sickle's wife wore a blue woolen dress with a golden locket suspended from a chain. She was the picture of clear-eyed good health. *Naturally, she looks fresh,* thought Louise. *No one interrogated this nice lady into the wee hours of the night.*

"Of course," said Louise, springing up from the couch.

"Here we come," drawled Gail. She got up from her chair with a swirl of her denim skirt, and neatly scooped up her newspaper and tucked it under her arm. "C'mon, Louise," she murmured. "Now we have to join all the other suspects and bicker about native plants."

"Bicker?"

"Or maybe fight, who knows."

20

"Ah, wonderful," cried Theodore Van Sickle, eyeing the approach of Louise and Gail. "We're almost all accounted for now—except for the Smiths." Then Fenimore and Lily emerged from separate sides of the registration desk across the room. Behind it were the offices used by the police for interrogations. The entire group realized the couple had been called in again for separate interviews. But they walked as proudly as if they were royalty.

How serene they appeared today, thought Louise, in contrast to their high-strung behavior last night during the party.

Ted Van Sickle welcomed them and said, "Now our entire family of gardeners is here." Like a shepherd with his sheep, he stood in the midst of the crowd, his white-bearded head held high so everyone could see him. "That makes forty-six of us. I understand, Louise, your husband, Bill, has been allowed to go back to work. And, under the circumstances, of course, Mrs. Anderson has been advised not to attend. Now we need to go one floor down to the ballroom level and the Thomas Jefferson Conference Room." He beckoned them with a big sweep of his arm. "Just follow me down the escalator."

Gail clung to Louise's side as if afraid of being nabbed again by the authorities. She grinned. "Too bad your big, beautiful hubby isn't joining us." Louise gave her a sidelong look. She'd wished she could have taken notes when Gail was revealing all those juicy tidbits.

But why should she have taken notes? Geraghty had made it clear that the police didn't need her input; he didn't even want to be seen talking to her, for, nominally, she was still a suspect herself. Still, he might have been interested in how much this western woman—supposedly out of the mainstream—knew about people in the garden industry. Her remark about the fight for dominance in the Eastern Seaboard garden market rang a bell. Money had often been a motive for murder.

Or could it be something quite different, like the conflict between the European-leaning gardeners and the muddy-booted environmentalists?

As they seated themselves, Louise saw that minicoalitions had formed: Ken Lurie and Richard Ralston were hunkered together, Ken as attractive as ever, Richard as puckish as ever, but both looking tired; they'd been among the last of the crowd questioned last night by Ron Goheen and his fellow investigators. They sat next to the flamboyant editor Mardi Lischer.

Just in front of Louise sat the prestigious and dignified trio, Shelby Newcross, Nathaniel Poe, and Gene Clendenin. They were in order of size, from largest to smallest, with Newcross probably topping six feet four, Poe at six feet, and Clendenin somewhat shorter. The nursery people also tended to cluster, the oversized Joanna Heath leaning over deep in conversation again with Fenimore and Lily Smith. Seated with them was a clutch of people she recognized as West Coast growers.

Bob Touhy, his big body twisting this way and that, was holding the attention of a group from the state Native Plant Societies. Reginald Farraday, the director of the British-American Horticultural Society, sat aloofly with several wealthy owners of America's most prestigious public estate gardens, and with Michael Sandoveld and his wife Laura.

Dr. Van Sickle rapped for attention on the small podium, and the crowd quieted. He led off with a tribute to the fallen Bunny. Louise knew he was a deeply religious man, and she herself felt the spiritual affront that Bunny's murder represented. She bowed her head even before he called for it. "I want us to have a moment of silent prayer to remember our unfortunate colleague," said the horticulturalist. "Bunny was a vibrant member of the garden community—"

Out of the corner of her eye Louise saw a movement as Gail turned her powdered face toward her. She whispered, "Isn't it great—the murderer has to be among us. I wonder what he's praying—that he'll beat this rap?"

Louise closed her eyes tightly and tried to shut out Gail, think good thoughts about Bunny, and wish her well in the afterlife. In truth, however, her mind was full of the racy new scenarios that Gail had laid out.

A jealous Peg Roggenstach as the lesbian killer? Or Joanna Heath, since it turned out she had not one but *two* motives—loss of market share and loss

of her position as the garden industry's femme fa-
tale? Or Lily Smith, finally fed up with her husband's infidelities?

The motive for all three women would be not
money, but sex. Or in Joanna's case, money *and*
sex. Louise was not surprised at this, since money
or sex seemed to underlay most of the murders
with which she'd had personal contact.

Dr. Van Sickle delicately harrumphed, signaling
the end of prayer time. He took up another awk-
ward housekeeping duty, explaining Maud Anderson's absence. "Our incoming First Lady very
much regrets she can't be here at our little conference to present her ideas on native plants," he said
with a diffident glance at the audience. "But you
can understand that circumstances have kept her
away."

Gail turned to Louise again and, holding a hand
in front of her mouth, muttered, "Oh, yeah, let's
face it: Maud can't afford to risk being poisoned
herself by one of us."

Louise looked at Gail and realized it was useless
to chide her further.

Van Sickle told them the police wanted them to
stay until about four o'clock, and by that time he
hoped they would be able to accomplish a great
deal in the two short business meetings, one in the
morning and one in the afternoon.

He briefly outlined Maud Anderson's native plant
project, saying, "Mrs. Anderson wants the whole
country to first *educate* itself about what *is* a native
plant, and then, secondly, to use these plants as
fortuitously as possible in our communities and in
our home gardens."

He tiptoed cautiously around the merits of the
plan, that is, why native plants should be promoted
when they were already the hottest thing in gar-

dening. Van Sickle said, "We understand well that this trend already exists in the United States. Our incoming First Lady only hopes to accelerate it."

Ken Lurie spoke up next. "We garden writers have always paid our due respect to natives—and we'll naturally increase the amount of space we devote to these plants if there's some national campaign for their use. Wouldn't you agree, Mardi?"

He turned to Mardi Lischer, who this morning was wearing an emerald-colored suit with her auburn corkscrew hairdo. Incredibly enough, this brilliant effect was upstaged by black-mascaraed eyes, bronze-rouged cheeks, and mahogany lipstick.

The woman had a lovely contralto. "We *love* the First Lady's idea," said the editor, "and intend to focus a whole new section in the magazine to native plants and their uses." Seconds were heard from other editors and publishers in the room. *Good,* thought Louise. *At least some people are jumping on Maud Anderson's bandwagon.*

The nursery owners were next. They applauded the idea, but saw a dark cloud on the gardening horizon—a shortage of native plant stock created by new demand.

"After all," said Joanna Heath, with a shake of her curly head, "if we can't get native plants in big enough supplies, we can't slap big color photos of them in our catalogs. That's the long and the short of it. And I think that if Bunny Bainfield proved nothing else to us nursery operators, she's proved that *hype* sells." She looked around defensively at her colleagues and added, "I, for one, am going to take a big leaf from her book."

Then Bob Touhy got the nod from Dr. Van Sickle, and Louise could almost see in the way he slowly rose to his feet that this big man was ready to fight. "Look, Ted," he droned, "Maud Anderson is right on target. We've got to support her a thousand percent. Trouble is that half the people in this room are on the wrong track, the nursery owners and botanical garden directors being the worst, their main focus being *ornamental* gardens."

Touhy made the word, "ornamental," sound profane. "They're willing to import *anything* into this country, as long as they can make a buck off it—"

Fenimore Smith jumped to his feet, his usual cultured demeanor gone. "What are you saying, Touhy? I resent those words, and I don't think you know what the hell you're talking about. Are you saying that we have no responsibility to the environment? That we're louts who introduce scourges like kudzu into the environment? That's wrong, and it's grossly unfair."

"Why, I bet you'd even sell tamarix, Fenimore," cried Touhy. "Harmless, is it? Its roots go down fifty feet into waterways. It *is* a scourge, just like loosestrife and lots of other plants I know you're selling—"

Looking alarmed, Ted Van Sickle pounded the gavel, but now Gail sprang to her feet, eyes blazing. "Fenimore, Bob's makin' sense. Don't jump down his throat because you want to deny everything. The First Lady's on the right track—you folks are livin' in the past, and on the *wrong* continent. We all know how you favor Europe—"

Gail stopped, and looked around and grinned in a vain attempt to soften her words. "Aw, look, we love you all, but admit it: you're confirmed Anglophiles. The English cottage garden of Gertrude Jekyll is imprinted on your psyches." She spread her hands wide, like a preacher. "You've never fully accepted the beauty, the purity of American native gardens, but now you need to get with the program!"

Another voice, that of a Native Plant Society member, was heard from the rear: "It *is* true that great Irish gardener Helen Dillon is sick of the traditional English garden. She's going to tear hers apart and totally do it over—says she's tired of what she calls 'rosy-posy, foxglovy, honeysuckly kinds of gardens.' "

Van Sickle, apparently feeling the nativists had had the floor long enough, beckoned next to Michael Sandoveld. The botanical garden director turned to Gail, and in his sonorous baritone said, "Pardon me, my dear lady, if I say that you and Mr. Touhy sound like Puritans out of Salem, Massachusetts."

A communal gasp came from the audience. Yet Sandoveld's tone was so gentlemanly that it didn't sound like an outright insult to the seed expert and the radical environmentalist.

"You must understand," Sandoveld told her, "that horticulture is a form of artistic expression. When we hear remarks like the ones you and Mr. Touhy just made, it makes us think you want to erase much plant life from the country, everything but so-called 'natives.' It is no wonder we're inclined to think you're self-righteous zealots. People who love gardening as an art form want to use the many plants that God and nature have provided the earth, with care and prudence. We don't want to be limited by the thoughtless discrimination of shortsighted people who have no real sense of the meaning of horticulture." As he sat down, his wife Laura reached out and clasped his hand.

Now Shelby Newcross unfolded his tall, thin body and rose, leaning both hands on the chair in front of him. "I agree with Michael Sandoveld. Some, I fear, have a mental fixation, believing that certain plants are bad. That's why we in the United States now have our 'white list' of invasive plants that, frankly, contains some that I cherish very much." He paused to smile. "Rather like the pope's list of condemned books, don't you think? Since when did a plant become all good or all bad? Even weeds can live to have their day."

He paused for a smile. "You know what they say: 'A weed is a plant that we haven't learned to love yet.' We have to look critically at this burgeoning environmental-industrial complex that preaches that every non-native must be wiped from the face of the earth. I believe it is insanity. We must address the question, *what constitutes a native plant?* Some think such plants must date back to a couple centuries ago, while others have much looser standards."

Newcross's gray-eyed gaze traveled around the room, and he said, "I want to quote my friend Nathaniel Poe, who has always said, 'I never met a plant I didn't like.' I agree; I find very few totally objectionable. Let's take some time and at least clarify the basic question of what we're talking about by saying *native.*"

A frowning Gene Clendenin spoke up next. He was just as rumpled in his tweed suit today as he had been in his black-tie outfit last night at the party. Unconsciously, he shoved back a piece of thin, straggling hair and said, "I have a slightly different take on this, my friends. Mrs. Anderson's goals are wonderful in principle. Of course I, too, prefer native plants. My agency promotes them far and wide across the fifty states, each of which has a Plant Materials Center to carefully manage the plants in that region. However, just as Ted Van

Sickle implied, Mrs. Anderson's idea is redundant: it's already being done. There are hundreds of state programs already in place.

"I fear this new one will simply suck away resources from the good things that the Department of Natural Resources is already doing. We must remember that there is a finite supply of seeds; we don't want to compromise plant material by creating too great a demand. Beyond that, I strongly oppose any effort to genetically alter native plants in the laboratory just so they'll have more popular appeal. We already have established programs for selecting plants for their drought resistance and seed vigor. Speeding up the process through genetic engineering could cause us to lose these important qualities."

Clendenin's frown deepened. "To breed for mere beauty is egregious, akin to something as unholy as human cloning."

"Hear, hear," echoed Newcross.

Bob Touhy turned to Clendenin with an ingenuous look that Louise had trouble believing was real. "Who said *that* was in the cards?"

"I've heard from very reliable sources that this was to be part of Mrs. Anderson's program," said Clendenin in his no-nonsense voice. "I believe it's an idea that originated with, um, the deceased, Bunny Bainfield. The trouble is, native plants are *not* big-faced impatiens, nor should they resemble such. So we needn't shoot genes into them in an attempt to make them so; they should remain in their natural state." With an abrupt clearing of his throat, he sat down.

A new voice was heard as Professor Nathaniel Poe rose to join the debate. First, he shoved his thumbs into his tweed vest, something Louise guessed he did before he led off any speech, large or small. In his usual amicable tone, he said, "You can see that we have some colliding views in this room. I suggest, Ted, that we adjourn now and talk some of these things out. Some of you adversaries might help by getting together over lunch."

As if advising a roomful of unruly students, he chuckled and put up an avuncular hand. "No rough stuff, of course—let's keep this civil if we can. Then, when we return for the afternoon session, we can work out our differences."

As Van Sickle quickly wound up the meeting, Gail Rohrig muttered loudly to Louise, "That'll be the day. We'll never get together on this. Maud Anderson invited too many people."

"You mean some of them aren't the right people?" asked Louise with a smile. She was reminded suddenly of the snobbish Foreign Service couple she'd met in England who used the term "NOCD." It stood for "Not Our Class, Darling" and described people who were too lowbrow to be associated with. She was dismayed to realize that Gail was just as snobbish as that Foreign Service couple.

"You bet I mean that," said Gail. "Eastern snobs—except for the reasonable ones like Ken and Richard—shouldn't be here. Then we could reach consensus."

Louise was amazed at Gail's outspoken demeanor; she realized why police were suspicious of her.

Just as the crowd was about to disperse, an officer slipped in and beckoned to Ken Lurie and Richard Ralston. They followed the man out, their eyes cast down. Louise felt hollow and desperate; her tip to Geraghty had to be the reason the two were being questioned again. Somehow she had to make it up to her two new friends.

As people filed from the conference room, the

juxtaposition at the crowded doorway couldn't have had a worse result. For Louise, it cast a little light on Gene Clendenin's personality. Clendenin tried to exit at the same time as Bob Touhy and was accidentally thrown against him.

"I'm terribly sorry," said Clendenin, as he regained his balance.

Touhy looked down on the shorter, older man with a malevolent eye. "Still trying to make your point, Clendenin?" he groused.

"Son," said the federal official, "I've been making my points rather well in my thirty years as a government employee. I don't intend to yield now to imprudent plans that threaten the whole future of plant materials in America."

"Oh, my, aren't you virtuous," said Touhy. "Does that mean you'd do anything in the name of your sacred Natural Resources agenda?" He raised a hand, perhaps in a gesture, perhaps to strike the older man, but friends in the Native Plant Society pulled him back a couple of steps.

"Bob," said one, "this is not a war. This is a native *plant* conference."

21

Louise put a hand under her chin and stood looking at the figures of Shelby Newcross, Nathaniel Poe, and Gene Clendenin as they retreated down the mauve and stone-colored hallway. It was a huge, luxurious hallway but did not escape being somber and tunnel-like, as all this hotel's hallways appeared to Louise.

Like horses heading toward the barn and the food trough, the three scientists hurried toward the escalator that would lead to the dining room and lunch. Up until now, Bunny Bainfield's murder had totally distracted her from this private mission. But now she viewed the retreating figures as potential guests on *Gardening with Nature*. As her daughter, Janie, had said, *"Think of all those sitting ducks you can sucker into appearing on your program."*

Newcross would be the most distinguished guest she'd ever interviewed. He would represent a high point in her television career. But could she get him? Her associate producer had already tried and failed; he'd be a tough sell. The cameras would love Nathaniel Poe, a famous man whom she'd never even thought of inviting on the program. And Clendenin, frumpy, rumpled, and grumpy though he appeared, was a man whose probing ideas about use of natural resources would be perfect for her audience.

She practically ran down the hall and fell into step with them. Newcross and Poe greeted her cordially, but Clendenin looked at her without recognition. In the confusion last night in the ballroom, they had never met. When she began her pitch for them to appear on her program, it turned out he was also unfamiliar with her television show.

"You mean," said Clendenin, "that you focus on organic gardening?"

She smiled. "Yes. We could bring our camera crew out and visit a plant materials center to see what you do there." She looked at Newcross and Poe. "I'm hoping to convince the two of you to come on the show, too."

Clendenin cleared his throat. "I don't see why I couldn't. Just give me a call at the office."

"Thanks, Dr. Clendenin."

He squinted at her. "Just call me Gene."

Nathaniel Poe also agreed to be interviewed, on the topic of land use in America.

The only holdout was Newcross. The tall botanist sniffed in dismissal. "I don't think I'm of great interest to your viewers."

She said, "That isn't true at all, Dr. Newcross. You'd be simply wonderful—you'd be inspirational."

He said, "Kind words, my dear Louise. Well, let me think about it."

Hardly able to contain a smile, she accompanied them back to the lobby. "Will you join us for lunch?" asked Poe. "It's the best we can offer you, since these police don't intend to let us get outdoors even to stretch our legs for a bit."

Louise declined, having the sense that the three old friends would like to lunch on their own. Besides, an idea was slowly percolating in her mind. She recalled the conversation with Bill about reenactments. Surely, there'd be no harm if she were to set up a reenactment this afternoon. A casual replay of the events of last night, something to break the monotony of the day until the police allowed them to go home. Why, Mike Geraghty had even implied that those who took part in such a group interview might be considered innocent. . . .

But she was kidding herself. She knew her real motive wouldn't be to relieve boredom. She needed to do a little sleuthing on her own. The things she'd heard this morning, from Gail, from Fenimore Smith, and Joanna Heath, and even from Gene Clendenin, had concerned her.

She'd do nothing big, nothing intrusive that would offend the police, just a little coloring outside the lines. Just a playacting exercise that might help her uncover that kernel of truth that would solve Bunny's murder.

How, without arousing their suspicions, could she convince people to replay that ghastly scene in Gadsby's Tavern? Judging from her own growing boredom, she guessed a little reenactment might come as a needed reprieve to the tedium of hotel living. And she also would do some name-dropping.

She went into the dining room, lit by dim chandeliers done in modern style, with eighteenth-century echoes. Her eyes searched out the people she would need the most: the Smiths and Joanna Heath. As she expected, they were seated together, already sipping wine. She gave them no opportunity to say no; she just plopped down in the fourth chair at their table.

"I'm starved," she said, pulling her napkin into her lap. "How about you?" Surely they couldn't run her off now that she had a napkin in her lap. She kept a big smile on her face although she was sweating like a pig in her woolen suit, having hurried down a couple of football lengths of hall and up the escalator in high heels.

"Louise, honey," said Joanna in a patronizing tone, as she leaned her ample frame forward, "we love you and your show, but the three of us need to talk privately."

Suddenly Louise realized just how to convince them to sit down and be part of her murder revival. "Joanna, Fenimore, Lily"—she opened her eyes dramatically—"I need you. And you need me. I'm sure that, like me, each of you would like to get off the hook as a suspect in the poisoning of Bunny Bainbridge."

Fenimore and Lily Smith looked at her warily. From under her fabulous blond curls Joanna Heath stared at Louise with new interest. "Now you're talking. But just what are you saying?"

Louise was bent over her spinach salad, thinking fast, realizing she was talking to three hard-boiled pros, people who'd been around and might not believe her thin story. But she had to give it her best shot.

"Well, you see, I know this local detective, and he hinted that a replay of the evening might be a good idea." This lie had probably brought color to her face, but she was already so overheated that she was sure it didn't matter. "What we'll do is just sit down together and reprise that little bit of time from the bugle song to the murder. Uh, maybe I'll invite a couple of people from the next table, too."

She smiled. "Would that be okay? At least it will help us forget we're virtual prisoners in this hotel."

Fenimore Smith's hooded eyes now covered half of his eyeballs. "Why didn't the Alexandria police do this instead of leaving it to you?"

Louise shrugged. "Oh, it's too primitive a technique for them."

Smith made a casual gesture with his hand. "Doesn't matter to me; I'll be part of your little game. How about you, Lily?"

Like Louise, Lily Smith also had made the wrong choice of wool for trekking around an overheated hotel. But unlike Louise, she'd not lost her cool, perhaps because her suit was thin white basket-weave wool, not charcoal-striped serge. "It's quite all right with me, especially if it stops the incessant police questioning."

"Well, I don't guarantee *that*—" Louise started to say.

Joanna interrupted her. "I don't *like* stuff like reenactments. Reminds me of touchy-feely groups I was in during the seventies, when we were supposed to spill our guts about everything we did and felt. But maybe it's okay if it will take the heat off us innocent people." Then she turned her attention to her chicken cobb salad, but before she took a forkful, she asked, "Who from the next table will be joining us?"

"Oh, just Bob Touhy, whom I'm sure you know, and Ken Lurie and Richard Ralston."

Joanna gave a relieved little laugh. "Well, that's a suspicious bunch! I've always thought there was a killer among them." And she ate her bite of salad.

Having fulfilled her mission here, Louise hurriedly finished her salad, left some money for her portion of the bill, and begged to be excused. "I need to line up the others," she explained.

Life was beginning to be more interesting, now that she'd embarked upon her own private investigation of the death of Bunny Bainfield. With a quick glance at her watch, she saw she had little time to buttonhole people before they went off in all directions.

It was no trouble convincing Michael and Laura Sandoveld, who sat by themselves at a table in the corner. As she left them, Nathaniel Poe was passing by on his way to the men's room. He, too, was easily enlisted in what he called her "game."

"I've heard about you, Louise," said the professor. "Aren't you some kind of undercover investigator?"

She shook her head vehemently. "Oh no. Believe me, this is just something Detective Geraghty mentioned as a way to clarify the facts."

Poe smiled enigmatically. "Methinks you protest too much." Then he walked away.

Across the lobby Louise spied Peg Roggenstach staring out the front windows of the hotel. She approached the woman cautiously, not wanting to startle her, but Peg turned suddenly, and there was terror in her big eyes.

"Oh," she said, with a sharp intake of breath, "it's only you."

"Yes, it's only me. Peg, would you sit down with me for a minute?" They settled in two overstuffed chairs done in antelope-colored leather. The lobby was almost empty, and Louise realized Bunny's murder and news that the suspects were all holed up at The Federalist might have turned business away.

"What do you want from me, Louise?" said Peg in a somber voice.

She told Bunny's assistant about her plan to reenact last evening. "I know how you must be grieving, and I'm terribly sorry and I hope this isn't too much for you. But it might just help sort things out, and at least take us off the hook as suspects."

They sat next to each other on the large chairs, and Louise was discomfited when Peg swung her knees around until they almost touched hers. And yet the woman, with her long face, her dark helmet of hair, and dark gray sheath dress, was the picture of a woman in mourning. Big tears began to fall down the rather horselike face. Louise almost felt like reaching over and patting her hand, but she kept her hands clasped together in her lap.

"I was more than Bunny's business agent, but you wouldn't know that. She was everything to me—" The sorrowful eyes looked up into the anonymity of the lobby, hoping perhaps to see a vision of the beloved Bunny.

"You've been with her for years, I heard."

"Since 1989, when I came from East Germany." Her mouth bitterly turned down. "People gossip about me, about how I was a black marketeer, or a spy, or something worse—but that wasn't true; I was very clever, and with a partner I found a source of valuable *guano*—"

Had Louise heard right, and if so, was the woman serious? Wasn't this part of the plot of some movie she'd seen? But Peg's face was sincerity itself.

"You mean . . . bat guano?"

Peg nodded, as if talking to the already converted. "Yes, and being a farmer's daughter, I knew how valuable it was. My partner and I—what would you say?—touted it, cleverly promoted it, and sold it for a fortune in what I like to think of as the gray market." She smiled. "It was not verboten, you know, to sell *merde*, as it was to sell butter, or cigarettes. It was not a large fortune, of course, but enough to get me out of East Germany. I met Bunny, and she was very kind to me—and since I had money and business experience, I was very kind to her."

"That's where the money came from, to bankroll Bunny?"

"Yes. And I *investigated* for her." The dark eyes looked resentful again. "That's created gossip here in America."

"You were an industrial spy for Bunny."

Peg looked appreciatively at her. "You understand. And there's nothing wrong, and there's nothing illegal, about industrial spying. In fact, I hear it's how many Americans have become millionaires, checking out the competition, buying out competitors for the bottom price. Look at Bill Gates." She threw her head back proudly. "I could probably get a job with Microsoft simply on the basis of my special abilities to generate information about other companies."

She waited, as if to see whether Louise accepted what she'd just said.

"I'm not judging you, Peg. I just want to get you to take part in my little—dramatization."

Peg's eyes grew stormier. "I will take part, provided you do me a favor. There are others, you know, besides the people at our table who might have poisoned my—Bunny. I want you to invite Robert Touhy and Ken Lurie to come, too."

Louise was curious to see that Peg had the same instincts as she did. "You think they might remember something."

"No," said Peg coldly. Whatever genuine sorrow the woman had shown was now encased in icy anger. "I think one of them is the murderer."

* * *

Joanna surreptitiously popped a tranquilizer into her mouth and washed it down with the dregs of her second glass of wine. If she doped herself enough with pills and alcohol, maybe she'd live through this ghastly afternoon.

Last night, she'd been numb as she watched Bunny go through her death dance. Not regretting it a moment, but trying not to revel in it, of course. Only Fenimore had recognized how uncaring she was about the woman's suffering.

Today was harder for her. Too many police questions, too much thinking about it, and now she walked around with the truth hanging on her like the albatross that had hung around the neck of the Ancient Mariner in that damned high school poem.

How was she supposed to handle this? What could she do now, just pretend Bunny's death hadn't happened? She was such a forthright person, and it wasn't like her to dissemble and lie, not for herself or for anyone.

If only she could get through the next two or three hours, she'd be all right and she could think more clearly. But now that busybody, Louise, wanted to restage the crime scene. Damn her, anyway! That in itself could reveal the whole truth.

Joanna's gaze fell on the wine bottle, and she saw that there was still some left. Not even looking at Lily and Fenimore to see if they wanted a drop, she took the bottle and poured the remainder into her own glass and slugged it down.

22

As she left Peg, Louise realized with sinking heart that this could be the reenactment from hell. She strode on, refusing to dwell on this ugly possibility, and instead counted up her numbers. She had eight of the eleven participants lined up, with only Richard Ralston, Ken Lurie, and Bob Touhy left to go. She didn't dare invite Gene Clendenin if she invited Bob Touhy; otherwise, she'd have a fight on her hands. She would try to talk to the federal official later, one on one, just to see if the police were right in suspecting he had a motive to kill.

This little playacting exercise might be tough to sell to these last three, especially the rude-appearing Touhy. She walked into the dining room far enough to see that none of them were there, then entered the cozy dusk of the nearby bar-restaurant. Here, she realized, a body could relax in an atmosphere where the only illumination came from dim sidelights done in burnished chrome, table candles with mauve shades, and the reflections off shiny surfaces.

Richard and Ken were huddled over drinks at the end of the burnished chrome bar. They looked up suspiciously as she approached.

"It's only me," she said, sounding like a broken record.

"Sit down and join us, Louise," said Ken. "We're pounding down a few brews, trying to ignore the fact that the cops suspect us."

"I saw you leaving the meeting with the police. So they questioned you again."

"Yeah. We think it's because of all that publicity about the book party."

"That's the reason they think you might have poisoned her, because Bunny became angry with you at a party? That doesn't make sense."

Ken smiled the languid smile of the drunk. "Maybe it's that my new book is too hot," he said, in a slurred voice. "I make the point that flowers *excite* people sensually, and inadvertently draw them close—like they do the bees—and get the people, like the bees, to do their bidding."

He looked at Louise and waggled an eyebrow for emphasis. "So we, like the bee, cooperate in the flower's evolutionary game of prolonging its life. We plant it and we propagate it. Let's face it, folks," he plodded on, "and Richard knows this well: flowers give people more erotic pleasure than anything with the possible exception of porno flicks. I mean, what's more erotic than a flower, with all those blatant sexual parts sticking out—"

"My *God*, Ken," observed Richard, "you're *smashed*. What a maudlin, low-down book analysis that is! By the time you're done, Louise'll think you've written a dirty book."

"God knows I tried," muttered Ken, and Louise watched him lower his head to the bar as if he might take a little nap.

Looking vexed, Richard rubbed a hand through his disheveled short curls. "I like the way Ken's worried about himself, but *nobody's* worried about me but *me*. Are those police really naive enough to think that I'd jeopardize everything I've worked for, for twenty-five years, by offing a slut like Bunny?" He gave Louise a hurt look.

Ken perked up a little at these words and turned to his friend. "Maybe you did it, Richard, just because you have the balls to do it, and somebody had to—"

Before one or the other of them either confessed or drowned in a sea of alcohol, Louise made a quick pitch for them to join her reenactment. It seemed to make them both more alert.

"*Cool,*" exclaimed Richard, "a reprise of the crime. You're a regular Mrs. Poirot, Mrs. Eldridge. I'm game, especially if it might put us in good with the cops."

Ken stared deeply into his beer glass, looking like the despondent hero out of an Ernest Hemingway novel—a hero, perhaps, who'd had his private parts shot off in the Big War and couldn't consummate his true love. . . .

Bunny Bainfield hadn't beaten Ken Lurie into submission when she was alive, but she seemed to have accomplished it by her death.

"It isn't going to help me," said the garden writer, "but I'll come anyway. It'll be better than just sitting here getting even more stinkin' drunk."

Louise felt somewhat responsible for the plight of her new friends. "Um, maybe now's not a good time," she said, "but would either of you consider appearing on my television program? You're both so talented."

The invitation seemed to cheer Richard a little. "*I* would. You name the time, and we'll do it." He clapped his friend Ken on the back. "Ken'll do it, too."

"I can see it now," she said excitedly. "We'll tour a garden you're writing about, Ken, and—"

"But don't pin him down right now," warned Richard, slumping back on his bar stool. "Believe me, he's too bummed out by Goheen and his questions."

Ken gave her a helpless smile. His eyes, she noticed, were the color of his beer.

"That's true, Louise. You might say I'm wallowing in self-pity."

What would he do, she wondered, without his stronger friend, Richard? But his sense of survival had not vanished completely; he looked at the bartender and said, "Better give us a couple of cups of coffee, old man. The two of us have got parts in a play."

She slipped away from her morose companions and crossed the lobby again, feeling sweatier than ever. She wondered if she would last the afternoon, with little sleep, a light salad for lunch, and no exercise. What she needed was a pool. There had to be a good health center in this fancy place.

Investigating could wait; she was going to take a swim. Louise didn't go anywhere, even for a mere overnight visit, without packing her swimsuit. She hurried into an elevator and went to her room.

Because of the extreme circumstances, The Federalist was giving the garden conference participants until four o'clock to check out of their rooms. Her and Bill's quarters had not been touched, and its taupe and gold aura did not disguise the fact that it had that same level of dishabille that it had had when she left here four hours ago.

She tossed the orange throw pillow onto the unmade bed, undressed, and put on her bathing suit and robe. She went to the Health Center on the eighth floor, a cool, quiet maze of rooms and corridors with young, fit attendants at the desk and in the exercise room. They looked bored, probably since they had a paucity of guests today.

Soon Louise was in the water, and magically she began to feel like a real person again. She stroked swiftly down the lap lane and reached the deep end. As she turned quickly to return the way she came, she saw two figures clinging to the edge of the pool and stopped in mid-stroke.

"Lily. Fenimore."

Fenimore Smith, his salt-and-pepper hair plastered to his well-sculpted head, smiled at her. "We're the only three smart people here." Lily looked equally relaxed, a gaunt Nefertiti, her dark, long hair securely cinched inside a tight bathing cap, unlike Louise's hair, which flowed free.

Louise smiled. "I agree. Well, off I go." She resumed her laps, marveling at how the muscles of her body rejoiced in being used again for some purpose beyond strutting around in high heels in the hotel's claustrophobic spaces. She ceased thinking, and simply moved in the soft water, uniting herself with those amphibious ancestors of millennia past who existed primarily in water. She wondered what was better in this life than swimming. Perhaps only holding Bill in her arms.

Finally she pulled herself up the ladder and headed for the hot tub, where she spied the Smiths' heads in the swirling mist. It didn't take long for them to get on the subject of Bunny's death, for that was the overriding reality that had tarnished all of their lives for the past sixteen hours.

"I suppose you know we've been targeted, so to speak, by the police," said Smith. "It's because they believe I held Bunny responsible for my troubles with Wild Flower Farm."

"I—I hadn't known."

"Oh, yes," said Fenimore, closing his eyes, so his head looked as if it were floating independently on the 104-degree water, "they realize the trauma I'd suffered—a cherished family business for two generations, almost lost—" He laughed bitterly. "My writer friends, who have little sensitivity, were giving me a very hard time about selling out. You know it is the tradition of some of New York's finest authors to contribute to our garden catalogs."

"Yes, I knew that," said Louise. "What a shame this has happened."

He gave his wife a smug look. "Or that it almost happened."

Lily said, "It's foolish, of course, to think of that as a motive to kill, especially for Fenimore, a man who made the second biggest profit in publishing last year."

"Oh, and how did you do that?" said Louise, laughing. "Or can such an accomplishment be described quickly enough so that we don't all roast in here?"

Fenimore's hooded eyes opened and stared coolly at her. "It's Business Administration one-oh-one, my dear. You must reduce overhead. Get rid of midlist writers who earn little or nothing for you, divest oneself of unnecessary and expensive real estate, downsize the editorial staff . . ."

Louise was glad she wasn't working for him. But there was nothing unfeeling in these words for Lily Smith, who just chatted on: "Ron Goheen doesn't even realize that *I* had just as much reason as Fenimore to resent Bunny. And I don't intend to educate him on this point. She *ruined* garden design businesses like mine, just drained business away with those prosaic Internet garden designs of hers."

"I hadn't realized that."

"That's the trouble," said Lily. "People didn't realize what a glutton Bunny really was, waging those colossal advertising campaigns and hogging every market she set foot in."

Louise closed her eyes and set her back against the rough, pulsating water of the hot tub. Even as she reveled in this pressure against her tired back, she was aware that she was in the company of two people who'd hated Bunny Bainfield enough to plan her demise.

She pulled herself up and slowly climbed the steps from the tub. "Have a great soak," she said, "and see you soon."

Back in her room, Louise hurriedly packed, first selecting a fresh blouse to replace the sweaty one she had started out with that morning. Bill had taken his bag with him. She brought her bag and her coat down with her to the lobby and gave them to a desk clerk, noticing that Bob Touhy and the Smiths were also going through the early checkout procedure.

She walked over and waited until Touhy had finished talking to the clerk. "Hi," she said, "Louise Eldridge. We met briefly last night, but haven't had a chance to talk. And here we'll soon be going home—"

"Yeah," he said, without a smile but with an appreciative glance at her long legs, "that's how it goes. You win some, you lose some." That John Wayne droning voice again; what a bore, she thought. But as obnoxious as Touhy was, she needed him.

She filled him in on her plan to replay last night's events.

"Is that Clendenin guy going to be a part of this?"

"Actually, no."

"Well then, fine," said Touhy. "I'm game for anything, it's so damned boring in this hotel. I'm beginning to suffer from oxygen deprivation, too. And if it will show we're cooperating with the cops, so much the better. See you in ten, then."

He strode away, a man who looked as if he had nothing at all weighing on his conscience.

23

It took a hotel employee a few minutes to pull eleven chairs from the fifty in the conference room and arrange them to Louise's liking. The coffee and cookies she'd ordered sat on a nearby banquette.

She poured herself a cup of coffee and sat down in one of the chairs, feeling herself heating up again after that nice swim. *Calm down, Hercule—you've got a job to do,* she told herself.

She had barely finished the coffee and pulled out her little notepad and a pen when her "reenactors," as Nathaniel Poe had jokingly called them, started to arrive.

"Take a seat anywhere," said Louise. They helped themselves at the refreshment table and sat down. It took a while, but Louise noted everyone gradually realized there were more people here than were sitting at Bunny's table last night. "We asked three from the adjoining table, just because they might have seen something that could help."

So far, so good, thought Louise. Everyone looked as if they could get along, except for Peg Roggenstach. Peg glowered at three of the other participants, Bob Touhy, Ken Lurie, and Richard Ralston, but since she habitually wore a scowl, Louise doubted that anyone besides herself noticed.

She smiled in what she hoped was her most disarming manner. "Remember, I'm just trying to help all of us deal with this messy situation. The final meeting of the conference starts in half an hour, so we'll move quickly. What we want to do is to share what we remember about last night."

"Not the whole evening, surely," said Professor Poe with a smile. "Some of us don't have memories like computers."

"Let me restate that," she said. "Let's focus on the period between the blowing of the horn and Bunny's cry that she was poisoned." She held her pen at the ready above her notebook and asked Joanna to start. Mistake number one, for the owner of Creekside Gardens Nursery balked.

Her full, round face was flushed below her disarranged curls. "Don't start with me, Louise, because I'm like Nate: I can't remember that well. Start with someone else."

Poe good-naturedly went first, talking about how many people left their chairs when the musician interrupted Mozart with a Dixieland tune. "There was a great deal of confusion after that."

"Laura and I were about to get up," said Michael Sandoveld, "but then immediately decided the best thing was to sit down again. So that's what we did."

Louise nodded; she remembered that.

"But the rest of us got kind of tangled up," said Ken, who was still bleary-eyed from his drinking bout in the bar, but nevertheless very earnest. Here was a man anxious to deflect suspicion from himself.

Richard, alert as ever, said, "That's because Mardi Lischer was wearing some crazy Lucretia Borgia dress with a little train, and Gail tripped on it. I saw that much—"

Joanna said crossly, "All of you remember what happened. The men were trying to help her back up—Ken, Shelby, Gene Clendenin, maybe someone else as well—"

Louise had a vague memory that the "someone else" was Gail's table companion, Bob Touhy. She busily recorded it all on her pad.

Joanna continued. "I sat down in a chair for a while, I remember, to get away from the confusion. I hate confusion almost as much as I hate reenactments."

Louise gave her a quick look and Joanna glared back at her, looking defensive.

Peg Roggenstach pointed a long finger at the nursery owner. "You sat down in *my* chair at the table."

"I did?" said Joanna. "I don't remember. And why do you butt in when Louise is supposed to be running this thing? Why does it matter anyway exactly where I sat down?"

"It *all* matters. It was the chair next to Bunny's chair."

"Let's turn the tables," said Fenimore Smith. "Just where were you, Peg, during all this?"

Her dark, haunted gaze moved over to Smith. "I was with Bunny for a moment, but then I left."

"Bunny had to run over and comfort the First

Lady," said Lily, restraining a smile. "Peg was right there with the rest of us. Do you remember, Peg?"

The woman seemed to have retreated a little. "I was just standing there, watching, like the rest of you."

Nathaniel Poe said, "I do recall that we were all in a group on the side of the table nearest the flowers. It was great *theater* watching those Secret Service agents clambering up that magnificent floral structure."

"Agonizing was what it was," groaned Richard, rolling his bright eyes heavenward. "If you only knew how I felt at that moment: hundreds of flowers and plants, weeks of planning and hard work, and all about to be destroyed."

"Back to that moment, Nate," said Louise. "Do you recall who was in the vicinity?"

"Oh, everybody now present except the Sandovelds. Plus Gene, Shelby, Mardi, and Gail."

There was a few seconds' pause while the import of this became apparent. That was the side of the table nearest Bunny's seat and Bunny's recently refilled wine goblet. No one was off the hook except Michael and Laura Sandoveld.

Peg Roggenstach, in a voice of doom that matched her long, drawn face, spoke again. "You've forgotten Bob Touhy. He was there, too."

Poe politely said, "I believe I stated, 'everyone present except the Sandovelds'—and that, of course, includes Bob." He gave Touhy a smile.

The native plant zealot didn't bat an eye but merely sat, looking huge. "Of *course* I was there. We were *all* there, confined by the layout of the place to one small area. So *what?* That doesn't mean we reached over and dropped poison in Bunny's glass."

Louise had been writing quickly, and trying to

think just as quickly. This exercise had excluded the Sandovelds from suspicion; they could safely be ruled out as the poisoners. And it ruled into the mix a half dozen people from the neighboring table.

She wondered if the police already knew what she knew.

Looking up from her notes, she saw that everyone was staring at her. She drew herself up a little and was about to adjourn the meeting when she thought of something else.

"One more question. Once we were seated again and served our dinners, do any of you recall visitors to the table?"

Joanna grimaced in frustration. "Oh *God*, when are we getting out of here?"

"In just a couple of minutes, I assure you," said Louise.

Peg fixed her glance on Touhy again. "I remember one visitor. Robert Touhy came over and put his arms around Bunny and whispered something in her ear."

Touhy reared his body forward in the chair impatiently, and Louise felt herself pulling back instinctively to stay out of his space. "Holy *hell!* I was just informing Bunny that we should try to schedule a little private meeting with—" He seemed reluctant to continue.

"With Maud Anderson?" accused Peg, as if this would have been a betrayal of her relationship with Bunny.

"Yes, in fact. I was only there an *instant.*"

"Thanks, Bob," said Louise. "I've noted that down." Smiling her most public smile, she said, "As we say in the television business, 'That's a wrap.' You all were great, and I hope it at least broke the afternoon's boredom. Just coming here shows your willingness to help the police."

Richard said drily, "Let's hope it keeps us out of the gas chamber."

Joanna got up and made a beeline for the door, calling out huffily as she left, "I doubt it sincerely."

24

It was time for a little fence mending. Louise was surprised that Joanna Heath was upset by the get-together that afternoon. She had thought that Peg Roggenstach, Bunny's close companion and lover, might have broken down during the session, or that Bob Touhy might have seen fit to lose his temper and chew them all out. Instead, it was a woman nursery operator known for her tough but pleasant disposition who was left in a shambles.

Just why, Louise could not even imagine, unless Joanna was riddled with guilt. But over what? Joanna hadn't seemed upset last night after Bunny's dramatic departure from this life. She had even made a nasty crack to Fenimore Smith about the deceased woman not more than ten minutes after she died.

She caught up with Joanna in the hall outside the conference room and plucked on her sleeve. "Can we talk for a minute?"

Louise was tall, five foot eleven with her three-inch heels, but Joanna was even taller, and much heavier. She wore a bright-figured dress that made her look even larger. Louise had never seen the woman before at such a disadvantage, with her face a conflict of emotions. Resentment and a huge sadness were fighting to gain control.

"Louise," said Joanna, "don't ever ask me to do a thing like that again. Rehashing events that were horrid the first time, and sickening the second time. That Goheen fellow is conducting this investigation, and I think you're just meddling in police affairs, trying to gain attention for yourself." Her lips drew tightly together.

"Oh, Joanna, *please*. What stake could I have in this? I only thought I could help myself and some of the people whom I've always considered my friends."

The nursery owner exhaled a deep breath. "All right. I guess I'll have to take you at your word. It's just that I have other things pressing on me, some heavy-duty things that I don't even want to talk about." Her eyes now had a pleading look. "Don't expect me to be myself today."

Louise reached out and took one of the woman's big hands, which, unlike the woman's beauty-spa–modified body, were plain and work-worn. The owners of large nurseries did not escape hard work, as difficult and physical as any that a pioneer hardscrabble farmer had experienced. "I don't expect anything of you. I know how terrible this has been for everyone."

The touch of another's hand seemed to soften the woman. "Thanks, Louise. I wish I could get my mind on something else, that's all."

"As a matter of fact, Joanna, there is something off the subject that I intended to talk about with you at the conference. I wanted to ask if my *Gardening with Nature* crew could come down to Creekside and do a spring show."

Joanna shook her frazzled golden curls and gave Louise a warm look. Even her cheerful Southern accent became more pronounced now that she'd relaxed a little. "Forgive me for being a big grouch. Of course, I'd *love* for you to do another show. And if I do that for you, just remember, Louise, you'll owe *me* a favor." She looked nervously down the vast hall space. "And now I have to go get something settled for good and all, before that darned meeting starts."

It was so close to three o'clock, Dr. Van Sickle's designated time to open the second meeting of the day, that Louise decided to simply return to the conference room and stay there and straighten out her notes.

Using them as a guide, she drew a layout of the end of the ballroom that included the Christmas garden, the balcony, and the two tables situated in the area. Then she plotted the movements of people as best she could, using little arrows and initials for names.

People reaching in and over and under, people tripping, people bumping into other people: the diagram was like the stage directions for a play. At least she knew now who all the players were, though she still had no idea of who was the villain.

She closed her notebook and put it away in her big leather purse. Without her having noticed, the crowd had started arriving for the second session of Maud Anderson's seriously crippled native plant conference.

Perhaps from weariness and delayed shock resulting from Bunny's murder, the garden experts were lethargic. Dr. Van Sickle had to urge people to raise their hands and make suggestions about how to proceed.

Michael Sandoveld rose to his feet and in his grand baritone declaimed, "The morning session showed us that we can't reach a solution during this meeting. We have grievous differences, the gardeners on one tack, the environmentalists on another. What might be useful to the incoming First Lady is a standing committee that would meet periodically, and in some reasonable length of time come up with a recommendation."

Van Sickle asked for discussion, and there was a reprise of some of the arguments of the morning. Finally, the horticulturalist asked Sandoveld to put his idea in the form of a motion.

With this done and seconded, the group voted unanimously for the idea, which included the proviso that Van Sickle himself, the most benevolent garden expert in the country, should name the committee.

Louise sat back happily. This was a reasonable outcome of a sticky situation. Now, soon, she could go home with Bill.

As she passed for possibly the last time through the immense and desperately lonely downstairs hall, Louise chatted amiably with her fellow gardeners. She realized that despite their resentments—for instance, of who authored the lead article in *Horticulture Today*, who received a cream-puff job in garden design, or who was picked for the director job of a prestigious botanical garden—they were mostly generous, hardworking people who'd do anything for one of their colleagues.

The murderer, Louise realized, might have

thought that he or she was doing a favor to the industry. Justifiable homicide, so to speak. But in the process, the killer destroyed a woman whom others loved dearly, people like Peg Roggenstach, her mother, all those siblings she so generously supported, and Bunny's aged husband.

It was nearing the end of a day filled with talk and not much else, and Louise felt an unnatural thirst. She turned to Nathaniel Poe, who was walking slightly behind her. "I think I need a double Scotch," she said.

"*Oh,* you must be a real drinker."

"Actually, I'm just joking. It's something my husband says. He'd even follow through. Not me; I'm a virtual teetotaler, simply because I regret it so much when I do drink."

The professor looked at her curiously, as if trying to imagine the awful results, and his face broke into a smile again. "Well, let's go to the bar," he said, "and you can have a Shirley Temple. It looks inviting in there, and what else is there to do for diversion in this place?"

Louise excused herself and veered off to visit the ladies' lounge. By the time she came out again, the crowd had dispersed. As she continued on alone across the lobby toward the bar, a little party of people abruptly stepped from behind a huge Japanese screen set in a corner of the lobby.

She almost laughed, as if suddenly she'd been thrust onto the stage in the midst of a Restoration comedy. This feeling was only enhanced by the theatrical remark made by one of the group: "It's best done quickly, if done at all." There were three familiar faces—Fenimore and Lily Smith, and Joanna Heath. The others were nursery owners from the Midwest and West Coast. Still deep in conversation, they looked suspiciously at her as she passed, as if she might be trying to eavesdrop.

"Hi," she said innocently, and breezed on by. All of a sudden it occurred to her. "Of *course*—why *not?*" she muttered to herself. Bunny's murder could have been a conspiracy of nursery owners.

"You're talking to yourself," observed Shelby Newcross, who had silently come up and fallen into stride alongside her.

She started. "Oh, Dr. Newcross, I didn't know you were here."

"I'm curious. What is it that you were saying to yourself?"

"Just a silly thought about those nursery owners. They were being ruined by Bunny and her millions of reasonably priced, tissue-culture–produced plants. Mail-order businesses have been diminished and some of them ruined by the presence of Bunny's plants in every chain store and neighborhood plant store in the country."

The botanist smiled down at her. "So it follows that they might have formed a cabal and got rid of her. A *joint* venture, so to speak."

She sighed. "It's a crazy idea."

"Not that crazy. They're the people who suffered the most from Bunny, I suppose, except for the others she may have hurt that we don't know about. The thing is, Mrs. Eldridge, you will just never know if it was a conspiracy. The garden community is very close, in the end. Nursery owners, in particular, hang together. They are very tidy, sanitary people, and I doubt they'd leave clues around if they *had* conspired to murder our inestimable Bunny Bainfield."

"Just as we all suspected, this murder may never be solved."

"That's true. But surely that doesn't surprise you? You must know that many murders are never solved. Ah, here we are at the bar. Are you coming in?"

They found that Nathaniel Poe had claimed a booth in a corner, and joined him. With the great botanist sitting beside her, and the great landscape ecologist across from her, Louise reckoned she was about as happy as she could get. Then the gruff-looking Clendenin arrived.

"Come join us, Gene," Poe called out. Since the burnished chrome fixtures had been dimmed into ghost shadows, the disheveled, balding bureaucrat peered blindly into the gloom.

"You've got to come in on a candles-only landing," joked the professor, and waved a hand in the air as a guide. Clendenin shoved into the seat beside Poe. Now Louise had the cream of the conference sitting right at her table.

This, she realized, was the moment to persuade the publicity-shy Newcross to relinquish his privacy and appear on her Saturday morning garden show. She smiled when she thought of what it would do for her ratings.

The day was almost over, but there was suspicion in the air, floating like pollen over the fields on a summer day. It was time to plan the next move. There were so few who could have guessed the plan and how it was done, yet one had, at least. That person must be silenced, but it would not be easy with so many police around. A very natural-appearing and quick maneuver must be made—and then, an innocent-looking exit from the hotel. But how to accomplish that, with a cop at every door?

25

Louise sat comfortably in the booth in the bar, sipping Perrier water with a slice of lime and nibbling on some tasty morsels the waiter had produced. The day wasn't a waste after all: she'd now corralled a total of six people for guest appearances on her TV program.

Of the six, her biggest catch was Shelby Newcross. The minute they'd settled in the booth, he'd surprised her by turning to her and saying, "I've thought it over and decided I'll appear on your show. But first you must tell me what you want."

"I'd like to get together with you soon to plan it. We'd tape the program in April, just as the cherry trees open in Washington. We'll take a walk through your garden and talk about some of the plants you've discovered, how you visualize gardens, how you dream of them—"

"Oh *my,*" said Newcross, "how romantic you are, Mrs. Eldridge."

Nathaniel Poe pointed at his friend Newcross. "The romantic one is you, Shelby. Why, you even distill perfume, I hear, in your little lab, and surely what more romantic occupation for a bachelor?" He began to talk about how the two of them had taken field trips to Africa and South America to scout out new plants, and how Newcross's keen eye and instinctive vision had led them to new discoveries to be brought into cultivation, including the unique Newcross maple-leaf hydrangea that now graced gardens all over the world.

"Armed with his plant-collecting tools and a small pistol to handle dire emergencies, he'd trek over the most astounding rough country seeking out plants. Why, I'm his junior by, what? Twenty years? I could hardly keep up the pace."

Newcross looked sad. "That was years ago, Nate. I doubt I could even make a field trip through Rock Creek Park these days."

As they talked, Louise could see the familiar grouchy concern spread over the face of Gene Clendenin. "You plant explorers are okay as long as you're careful about what you drag into this country. Some exaggerate this problem, I know, but don't think it isn't real. Invasive plants are a worldwide problem. Foreign plants like Russian knapweed and Canada thistle are winning the American West."

Poe said, "But you've erred, too, Gene. In the name of saving native species, government agencies like yours have brought beneficial insects into the country that have turned into rampant killers of just the native plants you wanted to *save*."

Clendenin gave a brief laugh. "You're right, Nate. In government, I'm afraid that we operate on Murphy's law, or what the British call Sod's Law—"

Shelby Newcross nodded. "That anything that *can* go wrong *will* go wrong."

"Mistakes have been made," said Clendenin, "no doubt about it. Our agency has made them, and well-meaning saviors of the earth also have made them. Now, I'm a strong believer in applying Occam's Razor—"

Newcross chimed in again. "William of Occam was a genius: 'The simplest explanation is usually correct.' That means we must strip ourselves of those things that complicate our lives, whether we're talking about the environment, or whether we're talking about our personal affairs."

Louise was feeling slightly adrift in this conversation, but Clendenin brought it down to earth: "When we're dealing with our environment," he said, "this means that we must do things slowly but deliberately, then be patient and wait and see what nature tells us of our efforts."

The talk moved on to more concrete things, stories of people like John and William Bartram, who trekked by horseback through the wilds of the Eastern Seaboard in the 1700s, searching out beautiful trees and plants and finding thousands, and of the plant prospectors from earliest times bent on bringing new horticultural discoveries to the attention of people who loved gardens.

She was sitting forward, mesmerized, wishing she could take notes. Others came up and leaned against the booth, joining the conversation for awhile with these botanical giants, then drifting off. Gail approached the group and looked unsmilingly at Louise with her catlike eyes. The woman's troubled expression reminded Louise of the biblical story of Martha's jealousy of her sister,

Mary, and how she was told by Jesus that Mary had chosen the "better part."

Truly, Louise had chosen the better part by sitting in this booth.

Out of the corner of her eye she could see Fenimore and Lily come into the bar with Joanna and sit down. Joanna, still looking distracted, hopped up from the table and wandered about, chatting with first one, then another gardening colleague, while the Smiths simply sat looking truculent.

A remark someone made had faintly troubled Louise. Shelby Newcross made perfumes from plants. Did he also know how to make poisons from plants? As quickly as the question formed, she dismissed it, for she'd mistrusted her new acquaintances enough. She didn't want to add to the injury by thinking badly of this dignified old botanist.

Anyway, she had another concern as she glanced at Newcross. What she saw caused her to sit forward in alarm, for his eyes had suddenly brightened as if with fever, and his face had turned yellow-gray.

"Good heavens," cried Louise, turning to the old man, "are you all right?" For a moment she wondered if he had been poisoned like Bunny.

Nathaniel Poe, noticing what she had, said, "He's having one of his spells of pain. Quick, Gene." Clendenin and Poe slid out of the booth and rushed around the table to their friend.

"Shelby," said Poe, "let's get you out of here. Do you have some medicine in your pocket that you can take?"

Newcross shook his head. "It's in my room. I'd better go and lie down there for a bit." His friends supported him on either side as he walked slowly through the dimness of the bar. Louise watched him with deep regret. It was clear now that Newcross was gravely ill; his close colleagues all knew it.

It was a heartless response on her part, but she realized that she needed to get him on her television program quickly, for he soon would fade into the annals of horticultural history.

26

Word got around the bar that Ron Goheen would talk to the crowd at four and then let them go home. Louise left her companions behind and went out to the lobby to see if Bill had arrived back at the hotel. He wasn't there, but Mike Geraghty was, lounging against a wall near the registration desk and looking flushed and angry.

When he saw her, he nodded curtly, then cocked his head toward the side door. Her heart began to race. The detective must have learned of her unauthorized prying into the murder.

To reach the door, she had to pass a dimly lit alcove. As she did, she heard a quiet, bitter argument going on and recognized the voices of Fenimore Smith and Joanna Heath. *For some,* she thought, *this day can't end too soon.* She turned quickly on her heel again and chose a longer, more circuitous route to the exit. The policeman still stood guard, and he appeared to have no memory of her exodus this morning with Geraghty. He obviously had no intention of letting her through this time, so she just stood and waited for the Fairfax detective to come.

To her dismay, Mike Geraghty and Ron Goheen both appeared, and quietly scooted her through the door and out into the far corner of the tidy boxwood garden. They stood and looked at her in silence for a moment. Geraghty's arms were crossed and his brow furrowed. Goheen had his hands casually thrust in his pants pockets, but his face was blank and dangerous.

"What's the matter, Mike?" She had never seen two more vexed-looking men.

"You *know* what's the matter, Louise," barked the detective. "What's the matter is this crazy *reenactment* I heard about. What the hell were you doing, and who gave you leave to do it?"

Captain Goheen merely looked on in quiet disgust. He must have felt that it was only fair that since she was a county resident, she be chastised by the Fairfax County detective on board.

"I—I thought it was a good idea."

Mike Geraghty threw his hands out in exasperation. "Good *idea*? I hear you told people it was *my* idea—and if they cooperated, they'd be off the hook as suspects."

"I just hinted at that, Mike, I didn't exactly say it outright. You said something like that at breakfast—"

Geraghty glanced quickly at his detective colleague. Louise realized she shouldn't have mentioned their breakfasting together. "What were you trying to accomplish, if you don't mind my askin'?" said the Fairfax detective. "I told you at breakfast to stay out of this."

Caught once more in a misunderstanding with

the authorities, thought Louise. It always happened when her natural instincts led her to probe, as she had today, into criminal affairs that the cops preferred to handle by themselves.

Louise suddenly felt so weary that she couldn't think. She looked up at the leaden sky, as if for inspiration. A few snowflakes were falling, which made it seem more like the Christmas season. . . .

Goheen took her by the elbow. "Now wait, you're not spacing out on us, are you, Mrs. Eldridge?"

She refocused on the two formidable detectives. "No, I'm not."

"We've heard from a couple of different sources that you've conducted this little reenactment," said the detective chief. "Now, let's set aside whether or not this was a good idea, for what's done is done. What I'd like to know is whether you learned anything. Did you?"

"Yes, I did. But it wasn't only the reenactment—I talked with a lot of people today, just in passing. I wasn't *trying* to meddle, but every time, I learned something new. Gail Rohrig, for instance, had a terrible grudge against Bunny. I have no idea if it was strong enough to persuade her to kill the woman. The thing that bothered me most was that she lied about being sick last night."

Goheen's eyes widened. "Really? What else've you learned?"

She sent an uncertain glance Geraghty's way, and said, "Just as you've heard, I sat down with the people at Bunny's table, and some others, too, Ken Lurie, Richard Ralston, and Bob Touhy, and we reconstructed the evening. Since you were doing all those individual interviews, a group interview seemed like a good idea." She pulled in a breath. "Um, do you want to know what I found out?"

"Of course."

Pulling out her notebook, she said, "Here's my graph of people's movements."

The Alexandria captain of detectives studied it for a moment and said, "What does this tell us?"

"That there were a dozen people in that crowd who approached Bunny's place at the table, stumbled over it, brushed against it, or sat near it." She read him her list: Nathaniel Poe, Ken Lurie, Richard Ralston, Joanna Heath, Fenimore Smith, Lily Smith, Shelby Newcross, Gene Clendenin, Peg Roggenstach, Bob Touhy, Gail Rohrig, and Mardi Lischer.

"I'm not counting Bill and me," she said, sending Goheen a chilly look, "because I gather that you don't suspect us; but if you do, make that fourteen people. The Sandovelds at our table, and the Van Sickles at the neighboring table, are also off the hook, because they didn't leave their chairs. Two Agricultural Research Service people at the next table also didn't mingle; they must have realized it pays to mind your own business and not gape. I don't know their names."

Goheen said, "Can I take this?"

She tore the pages out of her notebook and handed them to him. Goheen turned to Geraghty with a brooding look on his face. "I thought she might have eliminated somebody. But no, she's added possibilities."

"You already know that almost everyone had some kind of motive, everyone except the ones I mentioned to Mike this morning, the Van Sickles and Dr. Newcross. Though Newcross did seem to hold her in very low esteem, if you want to call that a motive. Oh, and you can add Mardi Lischer to that list of non-suspects, too, because she didn't have a problem with Bunny. In fact, she seemed to accept her for just what she was." Privately, Louise had decided Mardi was as flamboyant as Bunny had been, and that this had helped them understand each other. It probably was some associate editor of Mardi Lischer's who kept *Horticulture Today* from going over the top.

Louise gazed out into the wintry little garden patch and shivered. "Maybe you have to approach this another way and look for the weapon. After all, dropping poison into a glass cup leaves no fingerprints."

Goheen gave her a long-suffering look that told her that he'd thought of this light-years ago.

"Um, I have a few more tidbits. Would you want them?"

"Of *course*," said the chief of detectives.

She recounted the gossip she'd heard about Bob Touhy's contest with Bunny for influence with the First Lady. Goheen nodded, as if he'd heard it, too. Her conversations with Fenimore Smith and Joanna Heath in the pool, the unexplained nervousness of the usually ebullient Joanna Heath, and even her far-out fantasy of a murder conspiracy by nursery owners were things he didn't know. "From the way those nursery people looked, I thought for a minute that they'd planned the murder together. I guess that's pretty far-fetched."

"Any other far-out theories?" asked Goheen in his dry, emotionless voice.

She pursed her lips thoughtfully. "I suppose it could have been a political murder, someone trying to ruin Maud Anderson's project."

"That's why we were interested in Gene Clendenin."

"Gene isn't the only one with a political agenda at this conference," she said. "How about a botanical garden director? They're frustrated with the thought of native plant crazes, because they don't want to limit the use of exotic plants."

"But there's no botanical garden director on your list," said Goheen matter-of-factly, "while Clendenin *is* there."

"But Gene's such an honest man, and so interesting. He's going to appear on my show."

The Alexandria detective looked at her with open disapproval. "So it's 'Gene' now, is it? I can't believe you're hitting these people up to appear on your program."

"Six of them."

"Don't you realize," said Goheen, acid dripping from his voice, "that one of your group is a pitiless killer?"

"Yes, Captain Goheen, I've not forgotten that fact. But I was sure you'd have this murder solved before the associate producer puts them on the schedule."

He exhaled a large breath of air and turned to Mike Geraghty. "She's in this thing now. You might as well tell her a couple of things."

Geraghty said, "The musician has admitted that an unknown person, with a voice that could have been either a man or a woman's, phoned him and promised him $300 if he would play that little 'joke' the night of the party. It was supposed to be a kind of musical surprise for our new president-elect and his wife. The fellow naturally took up the offer without thinkin' that someone was up to mischief."

Goheen took up the story from there. "We're trying to trace down the caller. After the phone call, he sent the money in an envelope postmarked from New York City."

"Too simple to think it was a New Yorker, I suppose."

Goheen's mouth got thinner. "Yes, Mrs. Eldridge, way too simple to conclude that."

The Fairfax County detective said, "On the other hand, Ron, that could be what the person wants us to think."

Just as Louise realized she was now half-frozen, Goheen decided he'd heard enough. "Let's get Mrs. Eldridge indoors again before she gets a chill. Then we'll meet the gardeners in that conference room, give them a few words about staying in touch, and send them on their way."

As they moved toward the entrance, the shadows of several people appeared on the inside doors, like fluid reflections in a pool of water. The sight of them sent a tremor through her body. She turned to Mike Geraghty and said quietly, "I hope those people inside didn't notice me. They might think I'm a police stoolie."

Goheen snapped, "And not a meddler who may have impeded a police investigation?"

"I didn't mean to meddle—"

"Yeah, I know your reputation. I also know Mike thinks a lot of you. It's the only reason you aren't in deep trouble with me, Mrs. Eldridge. From now on, I want you to stay on the sidelines and let us catch the murderer, okay?"

She exhaled gratefully. "Okay."

27

Louise, sitting in the back row of the meeting room because she'd arrived late, was impressed. Somewhere in his years in police work, Captain Ron Goheen had learned the mixed skills necessary to manipulate a crowd of forty-six people, one of whom was a killer.

He looked out at the crowd of garden aficionados and a bland smile broke over his rough-and-ready face. "Thanks for being patient today and cooperating so fully with the Alexandria police." Next he issued a brief weather report. "There's a high-pressure system covering the country at the moment, so the weather's predicted to be good all across to the West Coast. That will be welcome news for those of you who plan to fly home tonight or tomorrow morning."

Then came his first demand, a simple one. Waving a yellow lined pad in the air, he said, "We must be able to contact you, so don't leave until you've noted down your phone numbers and addresses. We need to know *everywhere* you can be reached— in case you aren't going to be at your home or office numbers." He bent his head and peered out at them, as if looking at a class full of naughty students. "If anyone's planning on leaving the country in the near future, please raise your hand."

No one raised a hand.

He set the pad on a table near the speaker's podium and turned back to his audience. Perhaps to give them a little feeling of ownership in the investigation, the head of detectives shared a few of the facts he'd dug up: "We've questioned not only you people here, but everyone who had anything to do with that Christmas party last night, from the janitors on. And we will continue our investigation until we find the killer. We know that horn-playing was a diversion, and was part of the murderer's plan. The confusion allowed the perpetrator to drop poison in Ms. Bainfield's glass."

Then came an actual threat. "As I've indicated, this was a cold-blooded crime. The wine was doctored with a potent poison for which there was no available antidote. Her death was inevitable. We don't intend to let this murderer get away."

His face was so intense and threatening that it was hard for Louise to tear her eyes away. If she'd been the criminal, she would have stood up and confessed on the spot, lest the man's face haunt her dreams. Glancing along the back row, she saw her colleagues were similarly transfixed. Maybe this was the moment when they began to appreciate the horror of Bunny's murder.

Her gaze was caught by a movement of someone standing near the back of the room. It was Mike Geraghty, his large frame shifting a bit as he leaned against the mauve wall of the conference room, his eyes also fixed on the Alexandria chief of detectives.

Mike looked grumpy. Maybe he was still angry with her, or was he just distracted, thinking about that wider list of suspects she'd given to police?

Goheen now was digging in a little. "What I'm proposing next is that you people might know something that you haven't told us. In the intense trauma that you've all suffered, we think one of you might have forgotten something, some small thing, that could lead us to the criminal. It seems unusual that with so many people around, a person could drop poison into a wineglass without *someone* noticing. But so far, that's the case. We *need* your help. Try to think of any seemingly unimportant detail. Don't be afraid that we'll think you're a pest. You could be a hero or heroine in this case. I've given each of you my card so that you can reach me directly."

Now he came in for the kill, leaning his palms against the podium and fixing them with a hard stare. "If any of you should be withholding evidence for any reason, I hope that you realize you could be prosecuted. Withholding evidence in a murder investigation is a felony."

He let that sink in for a moment, then said, "You can leave the hotel now. It's been a pleasure to meet you, and I appreciate your continued cooperation."

Mission accomplished. Ron Goheen may not have "got his man," but had probably scared the wits out of the forty-six people in the room. He picked up his notes in a gesture of dismissal. As if unlocked from a spell, the sober crowd began to murmur in low voices.

The doors of the conference room opened, and Bill walked in, searched the room for a minute, and came over to where she stood.

"It's good to see you," she told her husband, with quiet gratitude.

He gave her a light kiss on the lips. "Can we go home now? Then maybe I'll tell you what I've learned about your gardener friends."

Louise realized Bill had access to the best records on people through his connection with the CIA, especially when it involved a person from overseas, like Bunny.

"Before we leave, we have to sign out with the police and say where we can be reached."

"You look tired, Louise."

"It's no wonder. What a day it's been, though I'll admit that some good things happened. I enjoyed listening to great gardeners discussing gardening. And I signed up six of them for guest appearances on my show."

"Louise, you didn't. What the hell are you doing inviting them to appear on your show? Any of these people could have committed that murder."

"Not to worry, honey. As I told Mike Geraghty, the murderer will be tracked down by the time my associate producer does his research and gets these people onto the schedule." Like a delighted child who's just received a bonanza of gifts, she said, "I'm going to have Ken and Richard. You know them and how upbeat they are; they'll be a hit. And then three giants in the garden industry—"

"You must have signed up Poe."

She smiled. "And Newcross and Gene Clendenin. I don't think you met Gene, but he's going to be great. He is *so* smart, Bill. I talked Joanna Heath into letting us come down to her nursery for a spring program, mostly because she got pretty upset with me this afternoon during the reenactment."

"You staged a reenactment?"

"Yes. The police didn't like it much. But they took all the information I learned."

She paused to wave at Ken and Richard, who were just about to leave the room. Maybe they didn't see her, for they ignored her and strode out the door. It was then that she noticed she was getting the cold shoulder from other people.

Just an aisle away, Gail Rohrig gave a sniff and turned away—though that could have been because she realized Louise's patience with her had dried up. True, Nathaniel Poe and Gene Clendenin gave her friendly waves as they left the room, Poe holding a hand up to the ear as if holding a phone, and mouthing, "I'll call you," Clendenin nodding as if tersely agreeing they'd be in touch. The trouble was that others seemed to be moving away to avoid talking to her.

The explanation became clear when she saw Joanna and the Smiths staring her way. After their heated argument, they must have turned down the seldom used hall leading to that exit. They would have seen Louise as she reentered the hotel with Goheen and Geraghty.

That would have been all right if she had been in the company of only Mike Geraghty. Ron Goheen's presence must have made them believe that she wasn't just an innocent fact-gatherer but had burrowed right in there—like a worm in an apple—with the honcho heading the investigation.

She realized that they had passed the word to everyone else, for they all were giving her knowing looks, thinking she was a stool pigeon. As far as they were concerned, she'd broken the code of trust among colleagues, something that was very precious to the hardworking people in the gardening industry.

"Let's hang back a little, Bill, and then we'll go." But as they skulked at the back of the departing crowd, a small figure cut back through the big hallway tunnel and headed straight for Louise.

"Oh, oh," said Louise, "here comes trouble."

Gail Rohrig looked a little the worse for wear, her eyes bloodshot and her streaked gold hair lying lifeless on her shoulders, though her western outfit with its beaded jacket and heavy denim skirt had held up well over this difficult day. "Just the person I've most wanted to say good-bye to," announced the seed expert. Then without missing a beat, she continued, "Hi, Bill," and smiled up at Louise's husband. "Consider yourself out of this." And she dragged Louise to the side of the hallway and proceeded to give it to her.

"For God's sake, why did I make the terrible mistake of thinking we were friends? I spilled all my little confidences to you, and what do you do? You blat it all to the Alexandria cops and that big white-haired dick from your neighborhood."

"Look, Gail, I didn't say anything about you to the police." That wasn't one hundred percent true; she just hadn't said anything to Geraghty and Goheen that they didn't already know.

The woman had her hands on her hips, the classic pose before a guy or gal pulls a gun, or maybe a fist, and Louise could see from the corner of her eye that Bill was looking on with concern.

"Do you know," rasped Gail, "that those creeps ushered me into their interrogation room again right before this *meeting*?" Sparks were flying from her eyes. "That's the third time, and there'll be a fourth, because they want me to hang around and talk to them yet again before I hop a plane tonight. *Now* I find out from Joanna that you're a common snitch, and the reason I'm bein' given a hard time is because you're feeding those two dicks a lot of lies."

"Gail, I'm not a police snitch; I was investigating on my own." She pulled in a deep breath, because in the excitement she'd neglected to breathe regularly. "My question for you is, where did you disappear to Sunday night, immediately after Bunny was stricken?"

"I'll be *damned!*" yelped Gail, her hands down at her sides now, fingers flexing. "You're accusing me of *murder?*"

No one was left in the far corridor where they stood, though the last people boarding the escalator looked back at the threesome in some alarm.

At any moment, Louise thought, she was going to get a shot in the jaw from her erstwhile friend. "Gail, I'm not. I'm only saying that you ought to tell the police the truth about being sick Sunday night."

"You're going to tell me I wasn't sick? How dare you, Louise Eldridge—"

Gail took a step closer to her.

Bill, she noticed with relief, was coming up in back of Gail, and now he reached out and gently touched her arms with either of his hands, like a trainer trying to steady a frisky colt. "Excuse me, ladies, I think this is going over the top. How can we resolve this amicably?" He slid in beside Gail, and they now made an uncomfortable little clique in the hall.

"You can damned well apologize, Louise, and take back what you damned well said."

A huge wave of fatigue overcame Louise, and this was always bad, because when tired she tended to abandon her normal tactful manner. But this Girl from the Golden West wouldn't respond to tact, anyway.

It wasn't the first time Louise had been bullied by a short person. Maybe it was something short people liked to do. But two could play this tough-broad game, she thought to herself. She had the woman by at least six inches and ten pounds. She planted both feet firmly apart, moved her shoulder purse back, looked down on Gail, and said, "I'm not sorry for pointing out the truth. And don't try to intimidate me, because it won't work. Nor will I apologize for wanting to find a killer who got rid of an enemy in a sneaky, criminal way rather than fighting her on fair grounds. So if the shoe fits, put it on."

Then she grabbed her husband by the arm and strode down the corridor toward the escalator.

"Wow," muttered Bill, "you women are tough." He gave Louise a sideways glance and then shot a suspicious look back to where Gail still stood. "All I can say is, no wonder the police questioned her three times."

Louise desperately wanted to get out of the stultifying atmosphere of this luxury hotel and return to her home in Sylvan Valley. When they reached the lobby, she saw that The Federalist was returning to normal, with normal guests, and not garden experts, populating the lobby and probably not even realizing what had gone on here in the past day. Several of the gardening group were still waiting in a line to sign out with the policeman at the front door.

She touched Bill's arm. "Let's just wait to sign out until those others leave," she said.

"That argument with Gail must have been up-setting," said her husband. "But there's something else. What's wrong?"

"It's much worse than that. These people have got me all wrong, and I've just lost something that I cherished—their friendship. I don't know if I'll ever get it back again."

28

Bill had suggested that before they went home they leave the car in the underground hotel parking lot and have dinner in Old Town. They were no more than a block from The Federalist when they were intercepted by Charlie Hurd and Peg Roggenstach.

Louise grabbed Bill's arm when she saw the two of them approaching. "What a combination that is," she murmured. "I bet Peg will spill everything she knows to Charlie."

Bill slowed his step, and she saw a look of concern cross his face. "Louise, don't confide a thing to that woman, do you hear? On the other hand, she could have information, so follow my lead, okay?"

She looked at him curiously. "You'll have to tell me why later."

Charlie strode up to them. "Bill, Louise—glad to see you. We're out here in the fresh air, and I'm no longer muzzled." He turned to the tall woman standing beside him, who was muffled up in a mohair coat and scarf and looking dramatic, like the female lead in a foreign thriller. "In fact, I've met Peg, here, and she's promised to tell me all she knows. What about you two? How about us all getting a cup of coffee at the little place down the block?"

Bill said, "Sure, we have a minute, don't we, Louise? We'd enjoy coffee." He took Louise's arm and gave it a meaningful squeeze, and she knew her husband was up to something.

Peg put a hand on Louise's sleeve. "Anyway, I need to ask a favor of you." They walked into the same coffee shop in which Louise had eaten breakfast. When they'd seated themselves and ordered, Charlie said, "I'd love to know what happened today in that hotel."

"Not much happened, Charlie," said Louise. "And anyway, I don't think the police want us to share everything we know with you."

The reporter sat back in his chair, a petulant expression on his face.

The German woman turned to him and settled the matter. "I agree with Louise. Nothing happened, except that we were questioned by police. They took our fingerprints, just as if we were in a police station. Then, Louise conducted a sort of 'play' and we all tried to remember what happened the moment my—Bunny was poisoned."

Charlie sat forward eagerly. "So, did you? What did you decide?"

Louise looked at him disapprovingly. "Nothing."

Peg shrugged in a continental way. "Everything. Almost anyone could have poisoned her."

"Aah, I love that!" said Charlie, finally deciding it was worthwhile to pull out his Palm Pilot and take notes. "Just as I thought: this is a replay of *Murder on the Orient Express!*" Busily writing with his stylus, he cried, *"Man,* I hesitated going that way with the story, but since the cops don't have a perp, and people like you agree with me, Peg, I'm going with it. What else do you know?"

She turned her brooding eyes on him, and Louise realized the guy was about to experience the big deep freeze from Peg Roggenstach. "Mr. Hurd—"

"Aw, call me Charlie—"

"Mr. Hurd, why don't you just let Louise and me talk?"

He scrunched his shoulders, as if in so doing, it would harness all his creative energy for a moment. "Sure, sure. Go ahead."

Peg leaned toward Louise, and again Louise could feel her sympathy for the woman growing. This was the single person who was grieving for Bunny Bainfield, and it gave her an appealing quality.

Louise was burned out on hearing what a terrible person Bunny was, and appreciated someone who could view her as more than one-dimensional. Just like other unsavory people—Hitler, Mussolini, Stalin, Capone—Bunny must have had a little vein of goodness inside her.

"I want you to keep looking into this, Louise," said Peg. "You may be able to do more than the police."

Bill shoved his shoulders forward. "Sorry, Peg. She can't do it. I absolutely forbid it." He put up a hand when he saw Charlie scratching on his hand computer. "And don't write this down, Charlie, or I'll damned well have you thrown off the staff of that paper. This is a private, privileged conversation."

Peg opened her hands pathetically. "But why can't she—"

"Because the police have it well in hand," said Bill. "There's no need for Louise to put herself into danger by probing into this crime."

Peg looked at Charlie suspiciously, and decided to go ahead. "I have another theory now. I wonder if it wasn't to do with the fact that we're genetically altering native plants in our nursery."

Bill frowned.

Louise said, "Give us some details." And Peg proceeded to talk about the scope of the genetic engineering attempts on common native plants, and how both she and Bunny and key employees had a feeling that someone was trying to find out exactly what was going on in the nursery. "You know how it is: the plant industry is like the garment industry—"

"I heard Bunny say that, too," said Bill. "You mean, you're making a lot of hot designer models inside your plant laboratories there in Frederick."

"And from native plants, too. That's the big breakthrough." Peg's eyes grew larger. "It's very competitive, so our work is top secret. I wonder if someone from the USDA would hate that so much that they'd think the only way to stop it was to kill Bunny."

"You're *kidding!*" cried Charlie. "I love it; I can see the headline now: '*Scheme to Genetically Alter Native Plants Leads to Poison Death.*' Subhead would read, '*Federal Official Implicated.*' So which federal official do you think might have done it?"

Ignoring Charlie, Louise said to Peg, "It's too ridiculously far-fetched to think a solid career bureaucrat would risk everything and *kill* somebody to stop this research."

"I agree," said Bill. "Now, why don't we talk

about other things? Peg, you must have had a fascinating life in East Germany."

Louise realized that this was Bill's purpose in stopping off for a cup of coffee. He wanted to pump Peg on her experiences in the Eastern Sector.

The German woman calmly recalled stories of her upbringing on a farm, then repeated the story of how she had gained a small fortune by selling bat guano. Before anyone could express doubts, she quickly moved the story to Britain. She told them, "I hit my—what do you call it?—stride when I found such a wonderful partner in Bunny."

Bill listened, keeping all his skepticism to himself. Soon, Louise suggested that they should be on their way.

Peg handed Louise her card. "If you accidentally learn anything, remember, I'm only an hour away."

She gave the woman a sympathetic hug as they departed on the street.

They'd given up the idea of eating in Alexandria, and decided instead to go home. As they walked back toward the hotel, Bill said, "Peg acts as if she's lost her soul mate. I hope she doesn't think she can pick up a new one in you."

"I think she's stricken with grief, as anyone would be in that situation. So don't be mean."

"But you don't really want to have anything to do with her, do you?"

"I don't see us having much in common, no."

Her husband's lips set into a grim line. "You give everyone the benefit of the doubt, and I like you for that, honey. But in this case, I don't want you to. Let's go home, and when I tell you about Peg Roggenstach, you might not feel so warm and fuzzy about her."

29

Since their route home took them by their favorite local eatery, Ernie's Crabhouse, Louise and Bill stopped for dinner. The sloppy, physical job of eating the crabs—cracking the legs, extracting the meat, and dipping it in melted butter—was just what Louise needed. It gave her a sense of respite after almost twenty-four hours of unabated tension. She'd witnessed a sickening murder and fallen into her usual compulsion to try to solve the case. No wonder she'd been tagged at the end of the day as a police snitch.

Bill again delayed telling her what he'd learned today. "I won't ruin your meal. Eat, and then we'll go home and talk about it. As for your friends being mad at you, you'll just have to set them right someday."

At the moment she didn't care what anyone thought of her. She was occupied with the sensory pleasure of eating, and a half dozen crabs and a couple of mugs of beer later, Louise felt almost normal.

When they arrived home, they found an indignant cat yowling for food, and three messages on the answering machine. One message was from the tiresome Charlie Hurd. "Hi, Louise—I thought you'd be home by now. Peg was pretty helpful, but I'd still like a private conversation with you. Call me, will you?"

"Flattery won't get him anywhere, doesn't he know that?" said Louise, opening a can of cat food.

The second message was a hang up, the call made from an unrecognized number in Washington, D.C. She jotted it down on a pad. The third call was from Mike Geraghty, still in the makeshift investigative headquarters at The Federalist Hotel. He told Louise to call him back "quick as you can."

The call was puzzling, for Geraghty's voice was full of strain. He'd phoned only half an hour ago. Did that mean there was a break in the case shortly after she and Bill left the hotel in Old Town?

Louise got hold of the detective on the first ring, as if he'd been hunched over the phone, waiting. "Coupla things," said Geraghty in a cautious voice. "I'm keeping you informed for your own protection."

Why did the detective sound as if he were walking on eggs? "Let's take this person by person. First, we'll get the subject of Gail Rohrig out of the way. Gail finally leveled with us before she took off for Santa Fe. Turns out she was in a major battle with Bunny Bainfield that was just short of landin' in court."

Louise held the portable phone against her ear and paced the living room as she talked. "You mean Bunny was threatening to sue her?"

"Yeah. Gail hired a private detective to tail Bunny, and he found out some things."

"That's turning the tables. Bunny was the one who hired investigators to dig up dirt on other people."

"That's what Gail said, and that's why she went after the woman in the same hard-boiled way. It's how she found out that Bunny and Peg were lovers. The whole thing was about to be blown wide open, with Bunny threatening to file a multimillion-dollar slander lawsuit. Now that just might be a good enough motive for murder."

"And that's why she took off after the murder?"

"Yep," said Geraghty. "The minute she understood something terrible was happenin' to Bunny, she slipped out to the women's lounge and pretended she was sick. She figured if the police discovered her motive, she would become a suspect. As far as *Goheen's* concerned, she *is* a suspect. He has people in Santa Fe checkin' out her and her business establishment."

Louise was glad of that. This woman who broke horses and fought like a tiger was plenty tough enough to commit murder. She shared a few details of her tiff with Gail, and Geraghty agreed that the spat had something to do with the woman's decision to level with authorities.

"Um, but Gail Rohrig's not the only reason I called. There's also the Smiths; they've disappeared."

"How'd they manage that?" The scene at The Federalist Hotel had reminded her of that desolate novel, *No Exit.*

"We were checkin' off people as they departed at the front door. But they scooted out the back way. They had a bellboy bring their luggage to a back door, arguing that their car was back there and not in the underground lot. He assumed, with all the rigmarole going on in the lobby— people signing out and the like—that they'd already checked out." The detective chuckled. "The kid said, 'They were so dignified that I couldn't believe they'd lie.' "

"Class will get you everything," murmured Louise.

"We thought Joanna had done the same thing for a while."

"What do you mean?"

Louise could hear a big exhalation of breath on the other end of the phone. "I hate to tell you this, but I have to. I know you're all worn out."

"And my gardening colleagues are convinced I'm an eavesdropping stool pigeon."

"Yeah, I could see you were gettin' the cold treatment this afternoon. All I can say, Louise, is that this time you brought it on yourself."

"Why are you beating around the bush with me, Mike? What's up with Joanna? Is Goheen going to lay Bunny's murder on Joanna?"

"He just might, he just might. It's up in the air at the moment."

The man sounded spacy, which was incredible, because Mike Geraghty was the most down-to-earth man she'd ever met. She patiently repeated, "What has happened to Joanna?" By the time the words were out she knew it was something she wouldn't want to hear.

"Joanna's dead. She's taken poison. We found her in her locked suite at The Federalist."

"Oh, my *God.*"

She touched Bill's arm and he headed for the phone extension. He said, "Mike, I'm on the line now, too."

The detective repeated the news.

"How could that have happened?" Louise asked in a quiet voice.

"She wasn't checked out, so we asked a hotel employee to go up to her room. It was locked and had to be forced open. It appears that she killed herself, Louise. Goheen speculates that she killed Bunny, too, and then suffered remorse over it."

"Joanna, killing herself?" Louise felt drained. She remembered her as a person with a tough but optimistic point of view, who worked hard and went charging around the country conducting garden seminars to educate the public on how to grow flowers. Why would such a woman kill herself?

And yet Joanna had been an emotional wreck during that playacting exercise, talking mysteriously of heavy things that were on her mind. "I don't want to believe it, Mike."

She could hear him breathing heavily. "Look, there's somethin' behind this suicide theory besides a dead woman behind a locked door, something that practically clinches it. We found a supply of poison in Joanna's purse."

"Are you sure it was suicide? Is Goheen sure?" She couldn't get rid of that image of the spirited Joanna Heath.

"Not a hundred percent, and I'll tell you and Bill why, if you want to hear it."

"Go ahead," she told the detective, as her husband viewed her from across the room with concern in his eyes.

"She's lyin' on the floor in this white and gold and tan-looking bedroom—"

"We know those bedrooms," said Bill.

"She was a very, oh, how can I describe it? A very *regretful*-looking corpse. Rictus mouth, contorted body, fluids flowing from every aperture—"

Louise shuddered. "Just like Bunny."

"Except Joanna Heath had this disconnected

phone cord wrapped around her wrist, as if she were lookin' for the end of it."

"*Wait,*" said Louise. "That doesn't make sense."

Bill, always a man to analyze the facts, said, "The locked room, plus the extra poison in her purse, indicate that Joanna killed Bunny and then herself. But the disconnected phone cord might point to another theory."

"Couldn't a' put it better," said Geraghty. "Goheen thinks there's another way to look at this, that Fenimore Smith was in cahoots with Joanna to poison Bunny, and then Joanna suffered remorse and took a dose of poison herself. This is somewhat supported by the fact that we found Fenimore's fingerprints all over Joanna's room."

"It *could* mean that Fenimore killed her."

"Then how did he get out of that room?" asked the detective, a shade of impatience now entering his voice. "It's true, the disappearance of the Smiths makes us uncomfortable, though it could be perfectly innocent. They did just what we told them *not* to do, which was to go off without leavin' a number where they could be reached."

Bill said, "It's important for you to know that we received a hang-up message when we got home tonight."

"Damn," said Geraghty. "See, that was my main reason for tracking you down so quickly, Louise. You've gotta be very careful, because we may or may not have found our killer. If we're wrong about the Joanna Heath theory, then you have to worry about the enemies you made this afternoon; one of *them* could be the killer."

Her husband was grim. "Mike, I don't like this. Has Ron Goheen read my memo yet? When he does, I bet he'll put Peg Roggenstach high on his list. I'd like to know what he's doing about all this. How are you handling the news about Joanna?"

"For one thing, we're tryin' to locate the Smiths. And Goheen's keepin' a lid on the news about Joanna Heath for a while at least. That's not an easy job with Charlie Hurd sniffin' around. If it should turn out that she didn't poison Bunny, then the less that comes out about her death, the better. For instance, say Fenimore Smith killed Bunny, or plotted with Joanna to kill Bunny. It would only be an advantage to him to know that the woman committed suicide."

"If she did kill herself," added Louise.

Acting as if he hadn't heard that, Geraghty said, "Bill, you take care that Louise is not alone, and I'll have a patrol car circulate in the neighborhood a coupla times tomorrow. And by the way, thanks for sending those faxes on what you learned today. Goheen is just gettin' around to them. Louise, just a parting bit of advice: as for further investigatin' anything, well, just don't do it."

"That goes without saying," said her husband.

As he said good-bye, Geraghty promised to stay in touch. Bill came into the living room and sat down beside Louise on the couch, looking worried. "Do you understand what Geraghty's trying to tell us? Fenimore Smith, for one, is out there somewhere in the Washington area, and he could be the killer. After this afternoon, he might think you have something on him. What's to stop him from finding his way to Sylvan Valley? And Peg Roggenstach: she's even more of a concern. I sent the information on her to Goheen hours ago. He hasn't bothered to read it, even though when I left the hotel this morning he pressed me to use my resources to check these people."

"What did you find out about Peg?"

He slumped back on the sofa. "She's actually Peg Reuter; she changed her name. In East Germany she was a lower-echelon member of the *Stasi*. She wasn't prosecuted after Germany was reunited because there were so many higher-ups they were more intent on pursuing. The statute of limitations has run out on those cases now. But recently it's come to light that Peg Reuter was part of a gang of anonymous, paid assassins sponsored by the Secret Police. They committed a great many crimes in the name of patriotism. There's no statute of limitations on murder, and provided they can get more evidence, I hear that the long arm of German law may reach out and bring her back to stand trial."

"Good grief."

"What she said about earning a little fortune was true, but it was by killing people. Then she slipped out of the Eastern Sector, changed her name, and went over to Britain with no trouble."

"I have to admit that sometimes, when Peg looked my way, she scared the living daylights out of me."

He looked at her soberly. "I hope you don't forget that; I don't want you to have anything to do with her. There were even more European connections."

Louise laughed. "I always suspected that Europe had something to do with this: European gardening snobs versus American environmental purists."

"There was something on your favorite gardener, Shelby Newcross. Seems he had problems years ago when he worked with the British Secret Service unit. Sounds as though he had a bad rap hung on him, something that temporarily tarnished his reputation. There was lots of activity in eastern Europe in the early fifties, with all the tension between the Allies and the Soviets. Newcross was in charge of a British team trying to set up a double agent in the East. The Brits' cover was blown, and two of the three British agents were killed. All except Newcross, that is. He was blamed at first, then later completely exonerated. But it left him so bent out of shape by the agency's lack of confidence in him that he left government service and went into a whole new field: botany."

"Good thing he left the spy business; he's one of the world's great gardeners." She wondered if Peg Roggenstach, in her wide-ranging investigations, had ever dredged up this old affair involving the botanist. It could make a motive for murder, given his cherished reputation as a botanist.

"I also got a reading from the British on Bunny Bainfield," Bill continued. "The general consensus is that she's a racy woman with a bent for gardening who used her sex appeal to get ahead on British television, and then emigrated to the United States and became an American success story."

"That's no surprise, Bill. We all knew that."

"Also, she's a good daughter to her mommy and daddy, who live in London's East End, and generous with her many siblings."

"That was in the *Washington Post.*"

Bill grinned. "I always told you Charlie Hurd was better than we give him credit for. So, what I conclude is that Peg Roggenstach's the one you have to be careful of."

"A woman who's quite familiar with killing people, and certainly knows how to lie with a straight face."

"The *merde* story, you mean," said her husband. "That gave me my only good laugh of the day, and I had to keep it strictly to myself."

* * *

At ten o'clock, Janie, who'd been at a friend's house for dinner, arrived home. She was hardly in the front door when she started grilling her parents on details of the murder. They didn't mention there had been a second death connected with what the girl jokingly called her mother's "garden gang."

Bill said, "It's been a hard day for your mother. Can we talk about this later? And by the way, is there any chance of you staying home tomorrow from school?"

Louise felt like someone who'd lost all ability to contribute to family life. Now, she even needed a sitter.

Janie gave her mother a disapproving look. "Don't tell me you're in trouble again. . . . Have you gotten involved in this thing? Haven't you learned when enough is enough?"

"Janie, get off that tack," said Bill sharply. "What about tomorrow? Can you or can't you?"

Their daughter shook her long blond hair in a careless gesture. "Sure. I can't do it in the morning, unless you don't mind me missing my test in trig. But I can be home by one-thirty or two. How's that?"

"Fine," said her father. "Be here, please. It's important. We'll fill you in tomorrow."

Janie came over and put her slim arms around Louise and kissed her. Softly, she said, "Sorry to scold you, Ma, but *really*, you get in more trouble. You know I'll help protect you, though, anytime."

The girl went to her room, and Louise and Bill plodded their way down the hall to their bedroom and got ready for bed. After they'd both read for a while, they turned out the lights. Bill gave her a kiss, then turned away from her, and she curled up against him and lay silently for a long time. Still, sleep wouldn't come, so she loosened her hold on his waist, got up and roamed the silent house. Janie, too, was fast asleep.

Louise peered through the floor-to-ceiling living room windows into the vast woods at the back of their house and, not liking the feeling that someone could be looking in, drew the curtains shut. Wandering into the guest bedroom, she stared out the window into the woods of the front yard. A car was slowly circling the Dogwood Court cul-de-sac.

Her heart skipped a beat. She tried to remember whether or not Bill's Beretta was still in the safe in their bedroom.

A couple of moments later the car stopped at the next-door neighbors', a car door slammed, and a young man escorted the girl who lived there to her front door. Louise relaxed and exhaled the breath. The neighborhood was quiet and safe-appearing again.

Suddenly realizing she was dizzy with fatigue, she grabbed the windowsill for support. Surely, after the upsetting events of the last day and a half, the murderer—if there was a murderer on the loose— was just as worn out as Louise was. She was going to count on that. She went back to bed, gently cuddling up to her husband. But there were sounds, the odd creak of the house settling, or the hum as the refrigerator motor turned on. And sounds in the woods, the odd animal cry. . . .

It was a long time before she drifted off to sleep.

30

December 17

Though Louise had slept fitfully, life appeared normal when she got up. While in the background National Public Radio calmly related the news of the day, her tousled husband finished dressing, and her frantic daughter darted about the house getting her possessions ready to take to school. Events of the previous two days seemed almost unreal.

Not in a hurry to go anywhere, Louise, accompanied by Hargrave, traveled through the house and opened the drapes to let in the brooding light of the December morning. Then she went to the kitchen to fix breakfast for the family.

Over their second cup of coffee, she told Bill she would spend the morning Christmas shopping in Alexandria. When she saw a frown forming, she said, "How can I not be safe Christmas shopping in Alexandria? And by the time I get home, Janie'll be home from school to keep me company."

"Don't worry, Dad," said Janie, with a slight smile. "I've done it before, I can do it again." She patted her mother's forearm, as if patting a child. "I'll save this woman from herself."

Bill's face turned solemn. "Jane," he said, "this isn't the least bit funny." He called her "Jane" only under the harshest circumstances. "You wouldn't make jokes if you'd seen that poor woman retching her life out, green poison spewing from her mouth, every nerve twitching—"

"Please!" cried Janie, shoving a hand out in front of her. "Stop; that's enough."

"Fine," said her father. "Then you stop acting as if this were some trifling thing. What we want to do is keep your mother safe."

"Sorry. I didn't mean—"

Louise watched the two of them as they first contended, then apologized to each other, and was grateful when they left her alone in the house and drove off in their respective cars. Janie had inherited Louise's nine-year-old Honda station wagon, which carried the aromas of garden mulch and fertilizer, while Louise had a new black PT Cruiser. She felt like a character out of a 1930s movie when she drove it.

She was restless, and had no desire to hang around the house and read the paper and drink coffee, her normal routine. After finishing up the dishes, she looked at the outside thermostat and saw that it was forty degrees, a typical "spring" Washington day in winter. So much for those promises of a snowstorm: it had been delayed again.

She put on a wool sweater, an old hound's-tooth wool jacket, wool slacks, and boots; that would be more than enough to withstand forty-degree weather. She swung happily into her new car and drove the four miles north to Old Town, her favorite place, after mail-order shopping, to buy Christmas gifts. As she pulled into the bustling little neighborhood with its twinkling Christmas lights and pure early-American architecture, it was easy for a moment to forget that just three blocks north was Gadsby's Tavern, the scene of Bunny's murder, and three blocks beyond that, The Federalist, scene of Joanna Heath's demise.

After a day and a half of close contact with her gardening colleagues in an atmosphere of appalling stress, she suddenly felt very much alone, like an untethered balloon floating in the ether and prone to crashing.

Even a simple thing like parking her car in the gloomy basement lot of the Torpedo Factory seemed perilous. She hurried quickly to the street, and soon found that shopping was a way to come back to solid ground. She spent a pleasant hour browsing in the small shops of artists and potters who occupied the huge space once used to produce World War II weapons, buying a few gifts.

As a present for her mother-in-law, Louise nearly bought something she herself would have treasured: a set of thick-cast Solveig Cox mugs. But after a moment's thought, she set them aside. A gift for Jean Eldridge was something that had to be thought over carefully.

There was something out there for Jean that was better than coffee mugs, and it would come to her eventually.

From the Torpedo Factory, she walked up King Street, visiting a few shops and the bookstore, then headed over to Cameron Street to Nuevo Mundo, with its funky clothes and jewelry. She found a wide, ropy Philippines bracelet made of brown resin for her other daughter, Martha, and a feather-bedecked

Incan purse for Janie on the theory that Christmas presents should be exciting, not supplies of needed goods such as underwear or socks.

With her purchases in hand, she prepared to leave, but stopped as she glanced out the front window of the shop. She hadn't realized she'd come so close: Gadsby's Tavern and the City Hotel were kitty-corner on the next block and plainly visible from where she stood.

It was time to get out of this neighborhood before nightmarish memories returned. The charming Christmas glitter of Old Town had lost its magic, and that approaching storm cast an ominous light on the old city's dignified colonial buildings. She hurried out the door, as if being pursued, but she was too late. Just as she feared, the grisly pictures returned to her mind. Bunny Bainbridge in death throes in the hotel ballroom. Joanna Heath, dying a horrible death on the taupe carpeting of a white and gilt hotel room.

As she walked the uneven sidewalk, the images flashed repeatedly through her head as if she were playing and replaying a movie in the back of her eyes. And there was some small detail that was wrong. . . .

She walked back to King Street, staring without seeing. She knew what still bothered her: why would a frantic Joanna clutch at a disconnected telephone cord if she'd chosen to poison herself? That was not the act of a person who wanted to die, but of someone who desperately wanted to be saved. The suicide theory didn't hold. Somehow, both Bunny *and* Joanna had been murdered, and the murderer was still out there.

She felt her heart thump wildly as her mind groped for an answer. Fenimore Smith had strong reasons to get rid of them both. Bunny had ruined him and Joanna had stiffed him by not allowing him to pull out of the sales agreement on Wild Flower Farm. First, he poisoned Bunny, expecting that would solve his problems. In the hotel pool the next day, when he was talking about the sales deal with Joanna, it had all been couched in past tense: "I almost lost Wild Flower Farm."

At that point, Fenimore Smith must have been convinced that Joanna would tear up the contract on Wild Flower Farm. Later, he must have demanded that his colleague void the agreement. Louise was convinced that was the crux of the argument she'd heard in the hotel alcove. When Joanna refused, Smith had to kill her, too.

But then Louise hit a blank wall. How did he do it and leave Joanna's body in a locked room? She shook her head, so frustrated that she almost went back to the more plausible theory of Joanna as murderer/suicide victim.

Still staring into space, she tripped over the cobblestones in the ancient sidewalk and would have fallen if two men had not reached out and steadied her.

"Oh, thank you," she said.

"Louise!" cried one of the men, his golden-brown eyes filled with concern. She focused in on him; it was Ken Lurie. Standing next to him was Richard Ralston. They wore down jackets and their arms were full of packages.

"Richard, Ken—what are *you* doing here?"

Richard gave her a guarded look.

Oh God, she thought, *he's still thinking I'm a Judas.*

"Evidently doing the same thing you are, chilling out after our two days of jail time in Alexandria's finest hotel." His eyes widened. "Have you heard the terrible news about Joanna?"

"Yes. It's just awful."

Ken shook his head in puzzlement. "Joanna was my good buddy, and I can't figure this out. If she committed suicide, what does it mean, that *she* killed Bunny? I'm staying at Richard's condo for a few days, hoping the police clear up this case before I go back to New York. When they called last night to tell us, that was the end of sleep."

"For me, too," she said. "I was up half the night, just thinking about it."

The three of them were a desultory group, hunched together on the old sidewalk like refugees from a disaster. She suddenly felt the weight of the packages she was carrying. "I've been Christmas shopping, and I'm about ready to drop."

"We could tell that, girl," said the garden writer. "Do you want to do lunch?" He looked up at a colonial sign hanging above them. "Il Porto—they look open."

They went in and found the restaurant empty of other customers and so dark that it was like a womb. Just what Louise needed, a dark, warm place where she could feel safe.

Richard briskly took charge. "Give us an out-of-the-way corner," he ordered the sanguine waiter, "in case you get a crowd."

"Oh, we will, sir," said the man, his dark eyes smiling merrily. "We barely opened the doors." He took them up two steps to a removed alcove, where the main illumination was a flickering candle set in a red glass chimney.

It was wonderful to be inside, away from the bustling streets of Alexandria, inside with people she liked. But she felt her guard go up; it wouldn't do to trust her two new friends too much, for neither one had been removed from the suspect list. On the other hand, it was clear they didn't trust her, either.

Richard ordered a bottle of wine. The waiter's eyes sent her a good-natured challenge; she decided to have a glass.

"So what do you hear, Louise?" asked the florist. "And don't hold back. We know you have a pipeline into police headquarters." His ready smile didn't quite reach his eyes.

How much could she share with them? "It seems the Smiths are AWOL, but it's probably just a failure in communication. Nothing much else—"

"Sure, okay, we get it," said Richard, a touch of bitterness in his voice. "You're still undercover, aren't you, Louise?"

"No, I swear—"

"Maybe Fenimore did it, maybe he didn't, huh? Whatever you know, you're keeping to yourself." He turned to Ken, who was hunched over the table, looking as exhausted as Louise felt. "She's not talking, Ken. She's withholding facts. So we won't tell her what *we* know, either."

With a deep sigh, she said, "I truly don't know anything more, Richard." She could see by his face that this plea of innocence annoyed the husky florist even more.

"Ken and I've been talking about this into the night, and it gets spookier the more we talk about it. Who did it, this one, or that one? Who's going to get it next, Ken, or me? I've decided that there's not one person in that whole bunch of guests who *couldn't* have done it. We're all gardeners, and many of us are well-schooled in the art of alchemy." He shrugged contemptuously. "It would be nothing for us to cook up a little special poison dose for a person like Bunny. We're no strangers to poisons."

Louise stared across at Richard. His face was usually so innocent-looking, but at the moment it was the picture of ambiguity. Moist red curls glistened in the semidark, giving him the look of a devil—or an angel. He stared back without smiling. "Or, to make it even easier, I could have brought in a little stash of prepared arsenic to do the job. And I'd have hidden it in one of those flower containers in the ballroom, maybe under the lip of a pot, where the cops wouldn't have found it."

What was going on with this man? Was a stain of guilt leaking out? With a hand that felt quite weak, she raised her glass and took a sip of wine.

Ken looked around, saw the waiter hovering, and poked his friend in the arm, not too gently. "Shut *up*, Richard. Two people are dead so far, and don't think the police aren't going to hear about everything you say."

Louise felt defensive. "Look, the police came to me, not the other way. I swear, my husband would leave me if I got involved anymore. And if it's any comfort, I told Geraghty from the start that you two definitely were not viable suspects."

Ken refilled her glass, then smiled down at her and bent his glass to hers in a little toast. "Here's to friends. I believe you, Louise. I'm tired of this thing straining friendships. I'm not going through life being suspicious of people."

"Nor am I," said Louise. "Why don't we talk about something other than the tragedy."

In a sad voice Ken said, "I knew Joanna for years. She just wasn't the suicide type."

"Not *that* old gal," said Richard.

"I agree," said Louise.

"So let's change the subject," said Ken, as their main courses arrived. "What're you doing for Christmas, Louise? How does a nice, nuclear family like yours spend the holiday?"

She picked at her scallopini alla'Angelica and

tried to describe the trauma of getting ready for Christmas. "The whole house still needs decorating. And this year we have a cat, so our Christmas tree is going to look funny. Most of the ornaments will have to go on top."

Ken nodded. "Kitties are hard on Christmas trees."

Louise laughed. "This is an old tabby that ought to know better. He loves to play, and when he sees those shiny baubles, I know he'll go wild, so best not to tempt him. But there's not only the decorating, there's the shopping. Today I got some of it done, but it's an enormous job, terrifying, really, because in six days my parents and Bill's parents arrive, as well as Martha and her boyfriend Jim, and Janie's boyfriend Chris—"

The wine was loosening her tongue, as it always did, and soon she was even telling them that the two sets of parents disagreed on politics.

Then the humiliating bottom line: "And my mother-in-law doesn't care for me much."

"That *can't* be true," said Ken.

Richard chuckled meanly. "Maybe she withholds *facts* from her mother-in-law."

Louise decided to ignore Richard. "Oh, it's true, all right. She disapproves of me more these days because occasionally I've helped the police with, um, criminal matters."

"We *know* that," said the florist, snippily.

Again, she decided to ignore the slight. Smiling confidently, she said, "But I've decided that I'll clean the kitchen and bathroom cupboards and put in new shelf paper before she comes."

"My, my, my," drawled Richard, with a total lack of sympathy, "is that a non sequitur, or *what*? What the devil has shelf paper got to do with your mother-in-law hating you?"

Louise realized she shouldn't have confided such a domestic detail to two professional men; they hardly knew what shelf paper was. "It's just a way to try and impress the woman," she admitted.

All sympathy, Ken reached over and put his hand over hers. "First thing you have to do, Louise, is to stop calling her 'the woman' when you talk about her. If you don't, you'll never get anywhere. What do you call her to her face, *Woman?*"

"No, of course not." She felt like bursting into tears. "You're right. Jean is her name, and that's what I've been calling her, because I call my own mother by her first name. But maybe I should go more traditional. She's never completely accepted me, neither my cooking nor my lifestyle, but I'm going to find some way to earn her approval if it kills me."

Richard Ralston began to laugh, whether with her or at her she couldn't tell. "More power to you, Louise. By God, *clean* those cupboards, *change* that shelf paper, *coopt* that mother-in-law." He sounded desperate and bitter.

Richard's forced smile vanished, and he leaned toward her with an intense expression on his round face. "And while you're at it, use those detecting skills of yours to figure out who in the hell killed Bunny Bainfield and Joanna Heath. Otherwise, we'll all spend the Christmas holiday looking over our shoulders wondering if we will be the next victim."

31

When she returned home, it was one o'clock, and Louise had five messages on the answering machine.

Mike Geraghty had called, which was no surprise. Though she doubted that either he or Ron Goheen would believe her, she needed to tell him that she had strong doubts that Joanna committed suicide.

She'd have to approach the subject carefully, to be the soul of tact and sweet reason, for the last thing they needed was to try to fathom a locked-room mystery. They hadn't even pinned down the grossly public murder of the nation's top garden entrepreneur.

There was another hang-up message, this time with the sound of breathing. As if echoing this scary sound, she pulled in her own breath and felt her heartbeat quicken. She jotted down the number from which the call originated. It was different from the one last night.

Next was another even more frantic message from the *Washington Post* scribe. Charlie Hurd rasped into the phone, "Louise, please call me—I've just learned another one of your gardening buddies got offed. This is a veritable botanical *bloodbath!* Why, *you* could be next! But the cops are really making this hard for me. I need your input on my story or I'm—" Before it finished, she erased the message.

The next was from Wilmette, Illinois. It touched her heart that her wonderful, laid-back mother had phoned her. "Louise, this is your mother. Dad and I are looking forward to seeing you in less than a week! Tell me if I can bring anything. For instance, do you want copies of recipes I've given you that you might have lost in moving—things like that, that might help you out—"

Did her mother, the wise Elizabeth Sharpe, sense that Louise was getting nervous about Christmas dinner?

The last message was from Janie, who said she'd been delayed at school. "But since you're not going to be home until two anyway, it will be fine. I'll be home by then, or a little after."

The calls made her think for a moment that she should get a cell phone, like Bill and millions of other world citizens. And yet if she'd had one with her, she would have been trotting around in Old Town with a phone hooked into her ear, getting freaked out. Talking with the police about a murder investigation, gossiping about details of the family Christmas party, or scared out of her wits by the mystery caller. . . .

Did that caller merely want to check on whether

or not she was home? She searched her mind for someone local who would have phoned and couldn't think of anyone except possibly Gene Clendenin. Maybe it was the terse Department of Natural Resources executive wanting details on his guest appearance on her show.

Suddenly she felt quite unsafe. At times like this she regretted living in what was essentially a glass house in the woods. She went around the house again, just as she had done at midnight last night, and pulled the big drapes closed. Too bad her temporary dog, Fella, had had to be returned to her world-traveler neighbors. She'd taken care of the little Westie for six months, and though small, he'd been good at announcing arrivals.

Grabbing the portable phone, she sat down at the dining room table and pressed in the number from which the call was made, but got no answer.

Next she called Geraghty back, promptly telling him about the new hang-up call.

"Oh, shit," he said, his voice heavy with fatigue. She doubted the man had slept for the past two nights. "We'll check the number out right away, but I suspect it'll be another call from a pay phone. The one from last night came from a phone booth in Georgetown—corner of M and Pennsylvania."

"Oh. I wish it had been someone I know."

"Like I told you, Louise, I have a patrol car out there makin' rounds in your neighborhood. I'm glad to hear Janie's comin' home soon. Meantime, I'm sorry to say that we haven't located the Smiths."

"You haven't gotten any closer to solving the case, have you?"

"Sure we have," he said in a voice that sounded to Louise like false bravado. "At least Goheen has found out a lot about people, and Bill's been a big help with his overseas sources. We've learned that gardening folks aren't quite as goody-two-shoes as we thought they were."

She smiled. "You mean they didn't escape being human just because they dig in the soil?"

"They sure didn't. We got some pretty sensational stuff."

"Do I get to hear about it?"

"Take Gene Clendenin, for instance. He's on that list of twelve. Years ago, he was charged with assault and battery; he nearly killed a man, all for the honor of his wife, allegedly, so *he* got off, too."

"I knew he was a tough cookie."

"Then there's Peg Roggenstach, who is actually Peg Reuter. Bill tell you about her?"

"Yes, just as he told me that Shelby Newcross was once with British Secret Service."

"Yeah, Peg tipped us on that, too, but she didn't know the details. Plus she dished some other dirt on Ken Lurie and Bob Touhy, namely, about Lurie's numerous affairs, and being named corespondent in a New York divorce case. But no surprise there. And I learned about Bob Touhy's clumsy plan to put Bunny in a bad light with Maud Anderson."

"Really?"

"Yeah, a little 'She's a lesbian!' smear campaign he was tryin' to orchestrate so he could become Maud's main man on this plant project. But people like Lurie and Touhy and even that cocky little Richard Ralston are not Goheen's top concerns at the moment."

She was happy to hear that about Ken and Richard. "Why is that?"

"Their motives aren't strong enough."

"That's comforting. I just ran into Ken and

Richard in Alexandria. Ken's pretty despondent, so it would be a great thing for him to know you don't suspect him anymore."

"I didn't exactly say that, Louise. Things can change in a minute. You saw 'em, huh? And what didya think? I personally disagreed with Ron on Ken Lurie. I liked Lurie for Bunny's murder 'cause she'd humiliated him in public. Or it could have been Lurie and Ralston together. D'ya like *that* scenario?"

Louise felt a sense of exasperation as she listened to Geraghty wobbling back and forth with his theories. The authorities didn't have any more of a clue than she did as to who was behind this crime, or crimes. She put her free hand to her brow and felt the beginning of a headache. "I've already told you, I don't think Ken could kill anyone. Richard just talks irresponsibly, that's all."

"He does? What does he say?"

"What does he say—" She wished she'd included him in her disclaimer. "Oh, he jokes around about things, you know how he is."

"Not really," said the detective. "You tell me."

She remained silent, reluctant to squeal on friends with whom she'd just barely reestablished good relations.

"Look," said the impatient detective, "you may think I'm waffling or something, but I'm not. Each new contact with a person can reveal something new and valuable. So let's not hold back, okay. What about Richard?"

As best she could, she repeated his casual remarks about how he could have sneaked arsenic into the Christmas party and concealed it in a plant pot. "You see, that was just silly talk, because Richard *didn't* do that. The Secret Service spent hours going through those plant containers before they ever reached the ballroom."

All the while that she scrambled to recover Richard's reputation, she wondered if she might be wrong. The fact was that Richard had unnerved her by the time they'd finished lunch in Il Porto. She didn't know whether it was his caustic personality or something more dangerous. To Geraghty she said, "Let's talk about other people who used to be on your suspect list. How about Gene Clendenin?"

"Aw, Goheen gave up on that theory last night. The guy has impeccable credentials in Washington. Outstanding research chemist until he went with the Feds. Recently widowed after taking care of his Alzheimer's-afflicted wife for years. Strong, successful family of sons to support him. Good record of achievement at Natural Resources. So who does that leave us with? We still have Gail. We still have Fenimore Smith. We still have Peg Roggenstach. That makes three live ones—to which, I stress, we could always later add your friends, Ken Lurie and Richard Ralston, and your *non*-friend, Bob Touhy. In fact, I'm gonna call Goheen regarding Richard. The results on the poison used should be comin' in any time from the FBI, and we can search his florist shops and see if we find any matches."

"You make me so sorry I told you anything," she said in a glum voice. She felt like crying. How could she know whether this new friend was being unjustly treated or not?

"Don't let this get to you, Louise," advised Geraghty. "You've gotta be tough. You can't get too close to people who may be suspects. By this time I thought you could stay a little more—professional."

This rebuke, and the two glasses of wine she'd

had at lunch, were all she needed to launch into a deep depression. She felt like going to bed and pulling the covers over her head. "I'm afraid I'm just an amateur, Mike."

"Well, don't let it get you down. I need to fill you in about Peg Roggenstach, too. Again, it's for your own protection. Bunny's housekeeper has verified that although Peg and Bunny had a long-standing romantic relationship, Bunny wanted to break it off. She was two-timin' Peg all over the lot, and even threatenin' to fire her."

As an afterthought, he added, "Thinkin' on those hang-up phone messages, we have to remember Peg's local, too. She's about forty miles from you in Frederick. Easy to jump on two-seventy and drive down to D.C.—"

Louise groaned. "I know. So it could be Fenimore Smith *or* Peg Roggenstach who's making the phone calls." She stared at her drawn dining room curtains and felt claustrophobic, just as she had at The Federalist. It was as if she were in a prison.

"Have you told us everything that these people spilled to you? That's what I'm wonderin'."

"I told you everything, but not in the proper tense."

"Huh?" said the detective.

She repeated word for word the conversation she'd had with Fenimore and Lily Smith in the hot tub, and in retrospect how it sounded as if they were convinced Joanna would tear up the sales agreement on Wild Flower Farm. "Is it so wild to think that Fenimore poisoned Bunny, thinking that would save his nursery from being sold, and then Joanna wouldn't go along, so he had to kill her, too?"

"Not too crazy, 'cept for that lock on Joanna's hotel room door."

"Let's talk about that for a minute." She kept her voice calm and unexcited. "I could never believe an ebullient person like that would commit suicide."

"Ebullient? Gimme that one more time."

"Ebullient: exuberant, lively. And why did she clutch the phone like that if she were trying to kill herself?"

"Simple. People change their mind in mid-suicide, that's why. But I agree with you that we have to explore all theories. The forensics lab has found it difficult to analyze the poisons used in the two cases but ought to have the answers soon. The police in North Carolina are still combing Joanna Heath's home and office and nursery for evidence of poison."

Louise persisted. "I don't believe Joanna murdered Bunny. And I'm sorry if that means that you have to go to all the trouble of finding out just how Fenimore Smith, or somebody else, poisoned her and then got out of that room. Neither Ken nor Richard believes she killed herself, either."

She heard Geraghty's big sigh at the other end of the phone. "Swell. You got a couple of people who *could* be suspects givin' you theories on who did it, and how. Okay, so you don't think Joanna killed herself. We'll try to see where we can get with that."

"At least consider it, okay?"

"Now, another bit of news. Maybe you saw it in the *Washington Post* this morning. Your Dr. Newcross was slated to be knighted by the queen for his life-long achievements in gardening, but the old guy apparently won't go to accept the honor because of, quote, 'health reasons.' "

She realized the import of it all. Newcross was sicker than she thought. She had to get an immediate interview with him or she would lose her chance.

"Mike," she said, "I'd like to call Dr. Newcross and go to see him." She told him about the interview and of the need to schedule it as soon as possible. And while she was there, she could lay to rest those nagging suspicions she had of the famous botanist. "Is that all right with you? He lives in a mansion down on the Potomac, so he'll surely have servants of some kind on hand. I think I'll be safer visiting him than if I stay here alone waiting for Janie."

"No reason not to go," said the detective casually. "But be cautious; keep your eye open for Fenimore Smith and Peg Roggenstach. When you're done talking to the guy, go home and hunker down with your family for awhile."

The situation was still precarious, but that was not surprising. The FBI lab soon would know what poison was used, but it still wouldn't be possible to trace it. Hidden was hidden. Police were confused when they found Joanna in the locked room, and with luck would stay that way. The wild card was Louise Eldridge. Those wide, hazel eyes of hers were the eyes of an eternally prying person, like those biddies in British mystery stories. Her weakness, though, was that she was gullible, and trusting—but not to be trusted herself. Were their paths to cross—and they could soon—it would be necessary to try to deflect any suspicions she might have as of today. If it turned out that she was a threat to the continued enjoyment of life, she would have to be removed like the others.

32

Louise made a phone call to Marty Corbin at
WTBA-TV to see if she could get approval for
the Newcross interview. Her free-wheeling producer was taking the day off, watching old movies,
and when she caught up with him at home, he didn't
particularly welcome her call.

"So this is another of your last-minute ideas," he
grumbled. He could have been more good-natured;
after all, until the recent inroads of Bunny's rival
show, Louise's program had steadily improved ratings that were enhancing the reputation of both
the station and Marty himself. Yet she knew these
last-minute requests drove him wild, and strained
their relationship. Now he'd have to go to the program director practically on bended knee and beg
him to shift the schedule.

"Marty, this one's hot, very hot. We've tried for
three years to get Shelby Newcross to come on our
program, and yesterday he finally said yes. Normally,

we'd schedule him in the spring, but I just found out we have to do it now or never. The man's very ill. He's too sick even to travel to England to be knighted by the queen."

"That's pretty damned sick," said her robust producer. "Is he strong enough to walk around his own *garden?*"

Her tone rebuked him. "I'm sure he is. And he's just one of the world's greatest gardeners. You'll understand that when you see the tapes."

"How much time would you need?"

"I thought we could run it as a two-part special, a half hour on the Saturday before Christmas, and a second half hour on the Saturday before New Year's. We could call it 'Strolls Through the Christmas Garden.' "

Marty said, "Lou, this is crazy. The Saturday before Christmas is four days from now."

"I know," she agreed, sighing audibly. "Short lead time, isn't it? I guess it's impossible and we ought to just forget it." Her feisty producer hated the sound of the word, "impossible"; maybe he'd rise to the bait.

"Wel-l, I suppose we could get a camera crew down to this guy's estate. But it's gonna have to be tomorrow or Thursday, because we'll need Friday to edit. And I'm warnin' you, Lou, we're running over budget already with some of these ideas you've thrown at us."

"This is a once-in-a-lifetime opportunity; you'll see."

"So you wanna call this, 'Strolls Through the Christmas Garden.' What in hell is that supposed to mean? Is this gonna be an end-of-life interview, or what?"

"It'll be mainly about his career in gardening,

though I suppose we might get around to the subject of his health—"

"I know you could handle it if that happens, but you'd better know goin' in what not to ask the man. Some people are sensitive."

"I'd guess that what he'll like best is reminiscing about his plant explorations. And this will be as we're walking in his gardens, which I hear are wonderful. It's supposed to snow tomorrow, so all the plants will be kind of freeze-dried, like beautiful white ghosts."

"Hold that lyrical stuff. I just ate my lunch."

She pulled in a breath, exasperated at this man who produced her successful TV gardening show but at the same time mocked her whenever she waxed poetic over gardens. But she had to keep her temper and take some of his flippant remarks if she wanted to get her way on this issue.

"Now don't get mad, Lou," soothed Marty. "I can practically hear you gettin' pissed off at me over the phone lines. I was mostly kidding, but not a hundred percent. I'd prefer you didn't do things this way, at the very last minute. I think I can talk our program director into this; I'll phone you later and let you know for sure. And meanwhile, save that creative stuff until later. In other words, you're gonna have to give us lots of input if we go through with this harebrained scheme."

"I'm willing to work overtime if that's what it takes to get these interviews on the air during Christmas. I thought I'd drop in on Newcross this afternoon to look the place over."

"Thatta girl. The more we know of the lay of the land, the better. Well, I gotta admit you're a bit of an opportunist, talkin' me into this. I mean that in some ways as complimentary, because you do have a lotta get-up-and-go. But what you need more of is *discipline*. You have to think ahead better and try to stay within budget and within the limitations of our shooting schedule."

"Otherwise, you love me, right?" she said drily.

His tone turned affectionate. "Aw, of course I love you. But you've caught me right in the middle of something."

"I know. A good movie."

"Yeah, *Purple Noon* again." Then his voice became serious. "Say, I heard about that poisoning at the First Lady's Christmas party. Are you all right? I see by the papers that the cops don't think you did it, even though I personally couldn't restrain a little happiness over the fact that someone got rid of your biggest garden show rival."

"Really, Marty, that's a terrible thing to say."

"Aw, c'mon, I was just kiddin'. It was terrible the way that the woman died. It reminded me something awful of Madeleine."

"Me, too."

"Well, saccharine words aside, now, I hope *you* aren't involved in the investigation."

She didn't say anything.

"Damn, you *are* involved."

"Marty," she said wearily, not wanting to confess how deeply involved she was in the affair, "don't ask and I won't tell."

What would he think when he found out on tonight's news that another garden expert had met her death? She didn't intend to tell him in advance.

There was silence on the other end of the phone. "Hell, Lou, keep out of trouble, will ya? Don't go to jail, and don't get poisoned. We have a lotta work to do for the next season's programs.

I'd hate to lose you. And anyway, I love ya, sweetheart."

When Louise phoned Shelby Newcross, she was of two minds. If she told him of the death of Joanna Heath, he might suffer shock, since he and Joanna were old friends. But if she withheld the news, he might hold it against her later.

The matter was solved when the botanist quietly said, "The police called this morning, Louise, and told me that Joanna has apparently committed suicide."

"I'm so sorry," said Louise. "I was contacted, too. Maybe this isn't a good day to invite myself to your house."

"No, actually, it's good to talk to someone who knows about all these dreadful things that have happened." The man sounded lonely.

"I won't stay long, Dr. Newcross. Since you've agreed we can tape the show later this week, I need a quick look at your place; it will help my associate producer enormously in planning the shoot."

They agreed that she'd come immediately. Louise tore a sheet of yellow, lined paper off her pad and wrote Janie a big note:

Janie, dear—
A small emergency—had to go to see Shelby Newcross, a guest for the show. Will be only 4 miles away, near Mount Vernon. Will be back at least by three.
Love, Ma

Louise smiled at the "Love, Ma." She had never been able to figure out why her two fairly sophisticated children called their fairly sophisticated mother "Ma." But she liked it. It was like a time warp: in some way she must be viewed by her daughters as a comfy, old-fashioned mother, not only as a newfangled career woman who mismanaged household and family on a regular basis.

Coat and purse in hand, she was nearly out of the house when the phone rang. She picked up the kitchen extension.

"Louise, my dear, at last," said the urbane voice. She experienced a thump of excitement in her chest. It was the salt-and-pepper-haired faux lothario from Connecticut and New York City.

"Fenimore Smith. I recognize your voice."

"Good," he said smoothly. "I'm glad I reached you."

"Why didn't you leave a message? Was that you, earlier today, and you last night?"

"That was me. Louise, the police left a message about Joanna. I have few details, and searched the paper for a story, but have found none, so I gather Captain Goheen is quashing the news for the sake of his many-faceted investigation. I'm guessing, however, from the wary tone of the officer who left the message, that there's some evidence against me. Now, you may not believe this"—his cultured voice was totally without emotion—"but I had nothing to do with her death."

"But what about Bunny's?" said Louise, then regretted she'd spoken up.

"Bunny's death? Nonsense, Louise. It was quite apparent that the police had nothing to tie me to that poisoning, and *really*, do I appear to you to be a man who would poison people? That's a woman's game. If I had to do it, I would have used a pistol."

"That's so reassuring, Fenimore."

"I didn't call to spar with you, Louise. I called because I know you have an in with that local police fellow, and I think with the Alexandria police as well. That was apparent from the way you were sneaking around, getting information, and then dishing it to Goheen out there among the boxwoods."

The shame of being falsely labeled a stool pigeon had worn off, and Louise found she could be a little righteous about it. "I was only doing a little private investigating on my own, believe it or not."

He laughed, the remorseless laugh of a New York businessman who'd garnered record profits for his company last year but who couldn't let loose of a failing nursery business, because it represented part of his overblown ego. "That's why I'm calling *you*, Louise. Of course, Lily thinks I'm way off base on this. Thinks you're going to be useless. But you're in the loop, and I believe you could persuade the authorities that I didn't, that I couldn't, do this—that is, murder either of these women. Friend to friend, shall we say, or maybe just colleague to colleague."

"Fenimore, I would have no possible way of telling if that's true. So how could I smooth the way with the police?"

"Oh, just by the force of your personality. I'm not too far away from your house at the moment. At least I'm in the labyrinth that you call Sylvan Valley. I wondered if I could just drop in and talk this over. . . ."

Horrified, she realized he probably was talking from a cell phone this time; he could be outside the door for all she knew. Yet she probably was safe for the moment. Her address was not listed in the phone book.

"I—I have an appointment, an important doctor's appointment. What if we meet in a couple of hours?"

By that time, she could alert Geraghty, and he could advise whether she should meet Fenimore somewhere and try to pump him for information, or whether they would send in the police with flashing lights to throw the man in handcuffs into the back of a squad car.

"All right, where? I suppose it's too intimidating if I should come to your house."

A tricky man like Fenimore could soon pry her unlisted address out of some local source, if he hadn't already. Desperately, she resisted the urge to hang up on the man and flee.

"Why don't we meet in a restaurant I know on Route One," she said, trying to keep a tremor out of her voice. "It's the Dixie Pig, at the corner of Fort Hunt Road and U.S. One. You can't miss it; there's a little dancing pig on the sign above the restaurant."

His voice was larded with sarcasm. "It sounds like a gourmet experience. I'm sure you're dragging me there just to see me suffer. Since it's so public, do you think you could refrain from calling the police?"

"I think so."

"Then I'll see you there at what? Four? I won't come in if I see signs of the police."

"Make it five. My appointment might run on a bit."

"Five it is. You're a good sport, Louise. You won't be sorry."

That was enough; without bothering to say good-bye, she hung up, then quickly tapped in the speed-dial number for the Mount Vernon District Station, where she hoped she'd find Detective

Geraghty. He wasn't there, and she left a message for him to call her. Breathing fast, as if she'd just run a mile, she knew she had to take action. She hurried to the bedroom, opened the lockbox in the closet that held Bill's Beretta, and plucked out the gun.

In a world where Fenimore Smith was loose, she wasn't stepping a foot out her front door without a pistol in her purse.

33

Louise had stopped trembling by the time she'd traveled the four miles south to Shelby New-cross's house. But she hadn't stopped looking in her rearview mirror, especially at a Lincoln Town Car that had followed her for a couple of miles. It was the kind of vehicle that Fenimore Smith might own. The car continued on when she turned off the parkway.

Had Fenimore Smith truly wanted to talk to her just so she could intervene with the police on his behalf? If not, what was his motive? Would he dare try to murder her in a public restaurant?

Realizing she was nearing her destination, Louise turned her attention back to the road and to Shelby Newcross. He had given her very precise directions: *You will come upon a grove of pines bound by a split-rail fence, and a discreet green sign with the house number.* She found the heavily wooded driveway and followed it as it wended downhill toward the Potomac river.

It was all well and good to worry about Fenimore Smith, but she had to remember that Dr. Newcross was also on that list of twelve who had access to Bunny's wine goblet. And yet she agreed with the police that the frail botanist was an unlikely suspect.

Soon the woods thinned, and to her right she saw his two-story fieldstone house. It had been built in the early eighteenth century and added onto since. As she approached it, she caught an enticing glimpse of terraced gardens spilling down to the water. She pulled up the curving drive beside the front door and surmised that the sound of her tires on the gravel driveway had alerted Newcross, for by the time she'd turned off the engine he stood in the driveway of his classically styled front door.

Without his suit coat, Newcross looked as thin as a man made out of cardboard. Wearing a soft, old sweater over his formal shirt and tie, he strolled out on the porch to meet her, then ushered her through the door and into another world. He carefully turned the key in the deadbolt as if to assure there'd be no interruptions to its sanctity.

Fine eighteenth-century antiques and rugs and delicate porcelain pieces on tables mirrored the upper-class life of colonial America. She could well imagine the first owner of this place socializing with George and Martha Washington, who had lived a mile down the road; having them over for dinner in this long, beautiful dining room; showing Washington the terraced riverfront gardens he'd developed so lovingly. And hoping, of course, for a return invitation to Washington's home, Mount Vernon.

Newcross also lived only a few miles away from
Potomac Farm, where Theodore Van Sickle, his
good friend, who was head of the National Horticultural Society, presided. It must be a serene existence, she thought, out here just beyond the hubbub
of Washington, a place to contemplate, read, do
plant research, and enjoy the legacy of history.

Studying him now, she was worried by the elderly botanist's appearance. Was this man up for
the interview? They would need to shoot a lot of
footage in contrast to what would make air, because of the man's obvious infirmities. Then they'd
have to do a delicate bit of editing.

As if reading her mind, he said, "Don't worry,
Louise, I said I'd give you an interview, and I will
prevail in that. Let's take a quick tour of the gardens, so you can inform your cameraman, or whom-
ever, as to what eventualities lie ahead for him later
this week."

Newcross led Louise down the gravel paths, past
garden beds graced with those freeze-dried ornamental grasses and evergreens she'd tried to describe to her producer that were so picturesque
even in the off-season. Inexorably they headed toward the river.

When they stood on the high bank overlooking
the swift brown water, her nervousness returned.
In only seconds, that powerful Lincoln Town Car
could charge down Newcross's long driveway and
intrude upon their peace. Standing here, she
made a perfect target in case Fenimore Smith had
a weapon, and he could easily have stashed a gun
in his car. Had he purposely driven by and then
made a U-turn and come back? She kept darting
glances to either side to be sure no one was lurking behind the bushes or trees.

As they walked back up the hill toward the

house, the mastery of the gardens swept her away, and she forgot that a murderer might be tailing her. She looked up at the gray sky and prayed for snow, a scarce thing in the Washington, D.C., area. White powder would outline every curve of the bushes, every bold stand of the grasses, each beautifully desiccated and seed-podded perennial, the silhouette of every soaring cedar and cypress.

It was painful progress, for the botanist was walking very slowly. Louise was tempted but did not dare to invite the elderly man to take her arm for support.

In spite of long silences, a certain intimacy developed between them. At one point he looked down at her and said, "You must tell me about your family."

She described the busy life that she, Bill and Janie led, even mentioning the disparate family group she was expecting for the holiday.

"Ah, parents with differing political philosophies; good thing you and Bill agree on such important things."

Encouraged by his questions, she admitted, "I'm a nervous Nellie, especially in the face of the arrival of my mother-in-law, who's a marvelous housekeeper."

He smiled. "You mean you're a much better garden show host than you are a homemaker? To me, that reflects the proper values."

A man with dual citizenship in Britain and the U.S. because of his American mother, he told Louise that he had no family of his own. He had outlived his siblings in England, and had never married. "I must confess that gardening has been my whole life."

As they made the circuit and returned to the house, Newcross brought her into a fieldstone out-

building that was his greenhouse and plant laboratory. To her delight, she saw tissue-cultured orchids growing in test tubes, potted baby orchids,
and lavishly blooming mature plants, sitting on
benches or hanging in slatted baskets. "It's heavenly
here," she cried, almost spellbound by the beauty
of the flowers and the profusion of fragrances.

Newcross went down the greenhouse row and
took a hanging plant from its hook. Louise caught
her breath. It had large, purple-red, triangular-
shaped flowers that hung below the plant itself.
"This orchid is for you. It has a rather formidable
name—*Dracula bella*. It's a fussy fellow. I've raised
it from a corm. I need someone who knows plants
to take care of it."

Louise felt a pang of sorrow; the man was giving
away a favorite plant, knowing he didn't have long
to live.

He began detailing just how the orchid, native
to the high mountains of Ecuador, needed to be
kept: in a moist, semi-shady environment, and in
no temperature that exceeded seventy-five degrees.
"Take it home," he admonished, "and cherish it."
He handed it to her as if he were transferring a
baby into her care.

The sad expression on his face brought tears to
her eyes. "How can I thank you?" she said. She was
so moved that she decided she'd throw caution to
the winds and invite the old man to join her family
for Christmas dinner. He probably was planning to
dine with the Van Sickles or any number of other
friends, but she wanted to be sure he didn't spend
the holiday alone.

Newcross leaned for an instant against the sill of
the door to the lab. His plant experiments obviously took place here; she recognized some of the
equipment, for she had briefly worked in a plant

laboratory. There was a gas chromatograph, a scales, and a Rube Goldberg–type contraption of connected tubes and bottles. The corked beakers in a partial rainbow of roses and purples standing on a shelf must be his perfumes.

Noting her interest in the equipment, Newcross said, "Do you like my little distillery? I use a very ancient water process to make my perfumes."

The movement of white mice inside a cage caught her eye. "And the mice—what are they for?"

"That explanation, too, in a moment, my dear," he said, in a strained voice. When she turned to look at him, she was shocked to see his increased pallor; the brief outing had exhausted him. Sadly, he shook his head, as if he had somehow failed in his task. "It must be obvious to you, Louise. I'm sick."

"Oh, Dr. Newcross, do let's go back to the house. I've seen enough."

"I hope so, Louise. I'll give you more details on the laboratory when we reach the comfort of the living room." He gave her a large sheet of delicate tissue to wrap about the orchid, and they left the outbuilding, Newcross carefully double-locking it behind them. As they made their way on a short, open path, she saw a longer path that branched off and led to the living room. It was lined elegantly with twenty-foot-tall shrubs with long, narrow leaves that she didn't quite recognize. They'd probably taken this shortcut to keep the orchid from becoming chilled.

They entered the kitchen annex of the house. Again, Newcross meticulously double-locked the back door, as if he were as worried as she was over a possible encounter with an enemy. Her enemy, she was pretty sure, was Fenimore Smith, but she didn't know who Newcross's was.

Then he told her. "Can't be too careful these

days. There've been daylight burglaries in the neighborhood, virtually under the noses of our security patrol, and an atrocious incident of carjacking during which a woman was hurt badly." He patted his pocket and smiled. "I keep a little insurance here." She saw the outline of a small pistol. Then she remembered that she, too, had a little insurance in her purse, in the form of Bill's Beretta.

The kitchen was a picture of early-American charm, with natural-colored homespun curtains, a bit of calico wallpaper, the original brick walls, and antique cooking utensils hanging on hooks in the huge old fireplace. There was even the smell of a fresh-baked loaf of bread that a cook had left on the counter, but no sign of the cook; Newcross seemed quite alone this afternoon.

They continued up the stairs and through the elegant dining room to the sitting room, where the botanist directed her to the brocade couch, then sank down himself into a wing chair upholstered in crewel-embroidered linen. "Just give me a minute, Louise, and then we'll have a refreshment. You could hang your orchid from the crossbar of that floor lamp next to you."

"Of course." She carefully situated the *Dracula bella* orchid on the crossbar and set her purse down on the floor beside her. Then she occupied herself examining the long, featherlike red petals that sprang from the apex of each triangular-shaped orchid flower. The blossoms were as fine a work of art as the paintings on Newcross's living room walls.

After a brief moment, the scientist murmured quietly to himself, "Better now, much better." He got up shakily and went to a sideboard where there was a small array of liquor bottles. "Could I offer you a glass of sherry?"

With two glasses of wine at lunch, she'd already had more to drink than she usually drank in a month, and she thought of that righteous little lecture she'd given Bill about drinking not being the panacea people thought it was. She should say no, but, just as she had thought when lunching with Ken and Richard, to decline would spoil the moment. Besides, sherry came in small glasses and could do little harm.

"I'd love it."

He brought over a drink for each of them in a crystal glass, then raised a toast. "Here's to both of us, and a long life for you."

The words wrenched her heart. "And here's to—" she started, wanting to say something more, to elaborate and mention the fact that he deserved knighthood. But the words stuck in her throat. Newcross wouldn't toast to his long life, for that would be a lie; he didn't even have the strength to go to England to receive the Order of the British Empire. There was nothing safe that she could say to the man, except some silly detail about the interview.

She finally managed something neutral. "Here's to a successful garden tour shoot." For a moment, they sat as if in quiet communion. The sherry was tasty and warm as Louise rolled it around in her mouth and finally swallowed it. Newcross watched her alertly, looking like a large bird.

She took another sip, and then broached the subject of taping the interview. "I brought a recorder with me. It will help my associate producer if he has an idea of how we're going to handle this shoot. Do you mind?"

He looked at her for a moment, then said, "I have no objection, my dear. Tape away."

She pulled her small tape machine out of her

large purse, set the purse beside her on the floor, and positioned the recorder on the low table in front of her, halfway between her and her interviewee. "I thought we'd break the interview into two parts, and call the two of them, 'Strolls Through the Christmas Garden.' My producer said he will schedule them for the Saturdays before and after Christmas."

Newcross leaned his head against the high-backed chair. " 'Strolls Through the Christmas Garden.' It sounds quite wonderful."

She pressed the start button on the recorder and heard the soft whir that indicated it was functioning properly, then turned it off again. "I'm sorry. Can I ask another favor? Something a little upsetting happened just as I left home; would you mind terribly if I checked my messages, just to be sure things are all right?"

He nodded and pointed to a small Chippendale desk at the end of the living room. On the top rested a phone. She hurried over and tapped in her home number, at the same time checking her wristwatch and noting that it was quarter until two. She wanted to be sure that Fenimore Smith had not been up to any tricks while she was out.

As she waited to collect her messages, a horrible realization overcame her: she'd left home for safety's sake and hadn't considered that Janie would be coming home to an empty house. If Fenimore Smith were lying in ambush for Louise, he might harm her daughter instead.

She tapped her fingers nervously on the desk as she heard the playback of the single message, from Smith: "I'm calling again, Louise, to reassure you that I'll be at our rendezvous at five. I hope you don't let me down."

She exhaled a breath. He sounded on the level,

but how could she trust him when the police didn't? She should have tried to reach Detective Geraghty again before now.

"One quick call," she said, looking over her shoulder at Newcross. His eyes were closed, and he gave a faint nod of the head. An old man catnapping.

She tapped in the familiar number of Mount Vernon District Station. But Geraghty wasn't available, so she talked to his crabby sidekick, Detective George Morton, telling him about Smith's request to meet him, and her counterproposal that it be at the Dixie Pig at five o'clock.

"Why didn't you contact us sooner?" growled the detective. "You've let an hour go by when we might've been lookin' for the guy in the neighborhood."

"I left a message earlier. Detective Morton, please tell the officer in that patrol car to keep an eye on our house until I get there. My daughter Janie'll be home from high school at two; I want you to make sure she's safe."

"If you want that, then you shouldn't be negotiatin' with murder suspects on your own, Mrs. Eldridge. Now you contact us as soon as you're home, and we'll tell you whether or not we want you to be the one to meet this fellow at the Pig. The way I last heard it, this guy's a suspect."

Don't I know it, she thought to herself, but kept all sarcasm out of her voice; she needed the Fairfax County police to help her. "Thanks very much, Detective Morton. I just have a few minutes of business here, and then I'll be on the road home."

"And don't forget—"

"I know: be careful."

When she hung up the phone and returned to

the living room, she automatically turned the recorder back on, picked up her glass, and took another grateful drink of sherry. Newcross was sitting alertly in his chair now, not drinking, just watching her. "My, it sounds as if you have a lot of things going on."

"Unfortunately so. I hope life settles down quickly." She didn't want to mention that Fenimore Smith was a suspect on the loose. But she did think she should clear the air by talking of Joanna Heath's death.

"Though I didn't know either Joanna or Bunny well, I was upset by the terrible things that happened Sunday night and Monday," she said. "I'm sure you were, too. I want you to know how sorry I was, particularly about Joanna's death, since you were a close friend of hers." It was intended to be a graceful closure to this traumatic subject. But to her surprise, Newcross latched onto the topic like a fish grasping onto a piece of raw bait.

"Joanna was my friend of many years." The tremble in his voice became more pronounced. "And a finer woman, and a finer nurserywoman I've never met. Although not young anymore, she was quite . . . young in spirit, and strong, with a strength I only wish I had." His eyes misted over; Louise turned her head to look away, for fear of embarrassing him.

In the same quiet voice he went on: "Yet we both know the first one to die was like a barbarian at the gates, bringing the downfall of others, polluting the tastes of the American public, and dumping her products on gullible people whose simple desire is to have flowers in their lives."

He closed his eyes once more, as if fatigue had again overcome him. "She even spied on worthy people, trying to daub them with scandal, any old scandal, old or new, true or untrue, in order to bring them to heel—to drive them into some pharasaical business deal with her. She used sex and money to pervert the beauty and purity of gardening and nature. A truly execrable combination, Louise, sex and money. Again, the gullible bought from a person like this, actually *believed* a charlatan like this, and she grew stronger and richer, until the fantasy that she was invincible overcame the reality that the empress had no clothes."

As he talked on, a sense of uneasiness enveloped her. This indictment of Bunny Bainfield was brutal. Yet it was all true: there was no question Bunny had done great harm to people as she made her way to the top of the gardening industry.

He fell silent for a moment, then gave her a pensive look. "Forgive my diatribe. You don't want to hear that." Smoothly, he changed the subject. "Now, as for the details of our televised garden tour, I believe we should start at the top of the hill and slowly descend, garden by garden, the cameraman using as backdrops either the Potomac or the pine woods at the crown of the property."

He laid out a plan for the shoot that was worthy of her producer. The botanist obviously had taste, and knew his garden as a parent knew his child. She tried to concentrate as he talked, but her mind was elsewhere, and full of disturbing pictures.

Those tall shrubs lining the other path at the back of the house had caught her eye, and now she realized what they were: oleander. Why this should bother her, she didn't know, for oleander grew all around the Washington, D.C., area, including in her yard, and probably in thousands of places on the eastern seaboard. Undoubtedly, it was not the only poisonous plant growing on this magnificent estate. She was sure that Shelby New-cross, just like Louise, herself, had stands of other lethal varieties.

Richard Ralston had laid it out bluntly: to gar-deners, poison was just a basic supply. Not only did they have stores of poison chemicals, they also maintained apothecaries in their backyards in the form of beautiful plants. Oleander. Monkshood. Foxglove. No wonder one of them had chosen poi-son to kill the abrasive Bunny Bainfield.

Since the plant was so common, why hadn't her host taken her down that fabulous oleander-lined path? It led to the more acceptable living room en-trance to the house. Her heart skipped a beat. The last thing she wanted to do was to suspect the great gardener, Shelby Newcross.

Then new questions stole across her mind. Were those deep-tinted liquids in enclosed beakers really perfumes? And what of the experimental mice? No kind of botanical experiments she'd ever heard of called for laboratory mice.

Most sinister of all was his condemnation of Bunny. It sounded like the accusation of a man who was personally affected by the woman's dirty tricks. Yet Louise had heard no such stories.

Giving Louise a penetrating look, as if he could read her thoughts, Newcross suddenly stopped talking. He bent his head and peered at her over the top of his glasses, like an indulgent professor with a foundering student. "I see your mind is busy. You've not paid a bit of attention to my plan for your shoot. Maybe I should tell you everything you want to know—though you will be able to prove nothing."

A cold chill swept through her body, and for a moment she thought she'd faint. She closed her eyes. It had been insane to trust this man, for he was one of the dozen people that she herself had so painstakingly placed near Bunny's wineglass the night of the Christmas ball. In her naïveté, she'd accepted important figures like Nathaniel Poe and Shelby Newcross on face value, failing to apply good sense. Now her hero suddenly materialized as a dangerous old man. She needed to get out of here—but she was trapped, psychologically and physically.

Her eyes opened a slit and surveyed Newcross. If it weren't for that little gun tucked in his sweater pocket, she was sure she would prevail against him if it came to a physical fight. She'd simply grapple with him for his door keys and run out that front door to safety. But in her trusting way she hadn't even thought to carry Bill's gun in her jacket pocket; it was in her purse, far down on the floor beside her.

And if she did escape from this locked house, she would leave the truth behind, and the deaths of Bunny Bainfield and Joanna Heath might never be resolved.

She opened her eyes. "Tell me everything."

"Indeed I will," said Shelby Newcross. He nodded at her wineglass. "But you must drink your sherry, Louise."

She looked at the half-empty glass of amber liquid, and a thrill of fear went through her. *This is the man who has killed two women already. Am I going to be the next?*

34

If Shelby Newcross were to live up to his bargain to tell her everything, Louise would have to finish her wine—or at least to appear to. The glass was half-empty, so what was done was done: if he'd put a slow-acting poison in her drink, she was already as good as dead. She brought the wineglass to her lips as if drinking, let it linger there, and then set it down again.

"Now, your story," she urged, keeping her eyes away from the tape recorder for fear he'd have her turn it off. Newcross seemed to have forgotten it was running. She was going to need more than her word to prove this prestigious scientist was a murderer.

She sat back and listened to the tale of a man who had lived and breathed gardening since it became his obsession when he was in his mid-thirties.

"I started out in the service of the British government, as certain of us who came down from Oxford and narrowly missed service in the Second World War chose to do for reasons of patriotism. Because of a set of circumstances that I will tell you about later, I changed careers. It was a shocking change at first, but soon I realized it was my soul's salvation, to turn from the dark side of man's affairs to the fair side of nature's wonders.

"I began the study of botany, and became totally enamored of plants and their origins, of gardens and all their dignified and exciting tradition and history. I went on plant exploration trips"—he lowered his eyes modestly at this point—"and had a good eye for finding new species, including a wonderful field orchid about which you may have heard, and those other plants that have now become part of every plantsman's catalog."

He looked dreamily into the distance. "What a happy and felicitous find that orchid was."

But then he gave a short, cynical laugh. "It is sad that even in gardening, there is much competition, some of it vicious, and much attention paid to those who *discover* new things. My trips to find plants, I must add, were totally benign and not fraught with competition or human travail of that sort, though they were arduous and sometimes hard on my health. But my point is this: because my new introductions were widely publicized, I prospered in my field. I began to have many offers to teach, both in Europe and in the United States, to head institutes and the like."

He smiled at the memory of it. "Research money was thrown at me, and it was truly a scientist's dream: so many choices and opportunities. But the years have gone by, and you, Louise, realize that we are now in the age of decline, the decline of good taste, of the small refinements in life, pleasing to the eye and the ear and all the senses, that make life worth living.

"Among the people who have aided this decline was Bunny Bainfield. Her influence in the world of gardening was truly amazing: to see horticulture perverted and cheapened by one enterprising woman with a loud mouth, world-class marketing skills, and brash manners, and just enough purported class to fool the public."

His eyes shone brightly, and he even sat up straighter, and Louise realized Newcross was invigorated by this confession, if it was a confession, and not just an enormous spoof on her.

He continued on, obviously not expecting her to comment. Nor did she wish to interrupt the flow of words. He said, "I have watched this woman mess about with my friends, one after the other, as she gained a stranglehold on certain markets and determined to dominate *all* of them. But worst of all, I've watched the insidious influence of her mediocre tastes affecting thousands of American gardens and homes. Take, as an example, her choices of what to raise in that tissue culture manufacturing plant nursery of hers: those outlandish, neon-colored impatiens the size of silver dollars, those coleus that look as if they've had a nervous *breakdown*—"

Louise's face broke into a reluctant smile at hearing his apt description.

"The fuchsia with its exaggerated and sexually explicit form that she and her experts selected out for production in the millions." He took a deep breath, as if realizing he was getting too excited for his own good, then continued.

"The companion loss of beauty and grace, elements that great gardeners have always cherished, is enormous," he said. "With Bunny, as with some of the worst elements in our society, the theme now is big, bold, brash, and bilious."

Louise had realized the man was eloquent, but on the topic of Bunny, he was more than eloquent; he apparently could talk for hours, and in the most colorful language she'd heard from him.

Newcross raised a spectral finger. "I go on too long, my dear. Let me get to the point. Now, in one of the most ignominious moments of this woman's life, Bunny phoned me a week before the First Lady's Christmas ball. She told me that she had the 'goods' on me. It was an old story about a fiasco that occurred when I worked for the British Secret Service. It was a muddled affair that took place in Eastern Germany, in which I was completely absolved of blame. This was during the fifties, when, as you know, a number of British agents became moles for the Russians. Though I was totally cleared by the Home Secretary, there still was the stain and the humiliation of being wrongly charged."

"You mean, Bunny intended to drag this affair up again?"

"Oh yes, and she knew the British press, at least the tabloids, would positively jump on it, as they jump on any morsel of scandal. She knew I was to be knighted, so this threat to 'expose' me came as I was about to receive the highest award of my career."

"I can see the tabloids loving it," said Louise. " 'OBE Candidate Once Accused of Treason,' or something like that."

"Exactly. A story that is half a century old, dragged up to blackmail a sick old man." He sat forward in his chair, his anger growing as he reviewed his grievances against Bunny. "But what was

so corrupt was her bargain: she said she'd keep
quiet with the British press if I agreed to come out
publicly and sponsor her garden products." His
pale eyes blazed, as if the woman had committed
the most heinous crime of which a human was ca-
pable.

"And of course you refused."

He gave Louise a sly look. "No, my dear, I didn't.
In fact, to delay her, I implied that I might con-
sider it. Then I went back to the laboratory, where
I found an answer."

Those beakers, Louise realized, were as lethal as
they looked, not the perfume experiments that
Newcross had implied they were.

"You did notice my beautiful beakers, Louise. I
saw your eyes attracted to them. In my experiments with plants, I *have* developed certain plant
perfumes. That was not a lie on my part. It is quite
an enchanting hobby. I've also developed certain
plant poisons, some lethal. Among the poisons is
one made from the essence of oleander. That's
what the mice are for: I've tested it and other poisons on the mice." He gave her a measured look,
as if to gauge whether or not she was ready to receive this information.

Louise felt tears pricking her eyes; she'd worked
in a biotech lab and seen beguiling little mice at
the mercy of detached scientists, but still, Newcross's
experimentation disturbed her.

"Finally, I used the poison to good purpose: to
murder Bunny Bainbridge." He let that statement
hang in the air for a while as Louise tried to control the tremble that ran through her body.

"You call murder a good purpose?" Her voice
came out louder than she expected.

"Yes, my dear, in this case."

The phone rang on Newcross's Chippendale

desk, and she started. Totally immersed in his story, the scientist took several moments to get up from his chair. He answered it on the fifth ring. She took advantage of the moment to pour the rest of her sherry into the orchid plant.

"Of course you may speak to her," Newcross was saying to the caller. He slowly took the pistol from his pocket and calmly pointed it at her. "It's for you."

She got up from her seat on the couch, feeling numb. "Thank you," she said, taking the phone from him. Newcross stood a few feet away from her, eyes glistening with attention.

It was Janie. "I'm home," her daughter said, "and I'm bummed. I read your note and saw that you're out gallivanting, so I got the phone book and tracked you down. What are you doing there?"

Janie had helped save her once before, and maybe she could again. "Dr. Newcross and I are tucked in here nicely," said Louise, in her most casual voice. How could she alert the girl to the danger she was in?

"We are having a nice talk, Janie, and I'll be home soon. Do me the favor of taking out the Julia Child cookbook; I'm going to try an experimental dinner out on you and Dad. I'll stop at the store for the loin of veal and mushrooms. You could harvest the tops of those chives from the pot on the kitchen window—that's part of the recipe. And one more thing: please walk the dog."

Newcross looked impatient now, but not suspicious: it sounded to him like a normal conversation between mother and daughter.

Louise had no pot of chives, of course, or window in her interior kitchen. Fella, the dog the Eldridges had been caring for, had been returned to its owners months ago.

"Ma!" cried Janie. "Are you crazy or something?"

"Yes, I am, my dear. I'll see you soon."

Louise hung up the phone and returned to her seat, trailed by the botanist. She'd sent enough signals. Janie should realize her mother was in terrible trouble.

35

Now Louise had the delicate job of bringing Shelby Newcross back to his story. The man sat quietly in his chair, the pistol restored to its place in his pocket.

For a moment she merely sat in silence. Then she said, "I wonder why a man like you would even *make* poisons. Was it your intention to use them on a human being someday?"

Newcross looked quite interested now, as if a student in a classroom were finally challenging him at his own high level. "Ah, interesting point, Louise. As a non-scientist, you probably don't think much about the concept of basic research." He laughed graciously. "It was as simple as this: the oleanders lining the back walk have been there for many decades. It was just a question of the challenge of seeing if I could do it. In truth, I think I'm normally *not* a killer. My experiences in the spy business left me wary and disenchanted with people and with human nature. Therefore I welcomed the more simple and rewarding pleasures of plant research and teaching the young. It was an extraordinary situation that pushed me into murder: a crass, blackmailing woman about to sully my reputation just as I reached the pinnacle of my career, and leaving me with no time to refute her lies."

"No time?"

He smiled again patiently. "Oh, I'll soon be dead, Louise, isn't that obvious? Bunny's falsehoods about me would still have been floating around me as I was in my death throes." He shrugged. "Then, perhaps within a year, the story would be straightened out, on page twenty-five."

"So you decided you'd solve your problem by killing Bunny. Was it that easy to do?"

"It was quite easy," he told her. "When the invitation came for the incoming First Lady's native plant party, I knew it was a good portent. With little effort, I found out the name of the musical group that would perform during the party. I simply phoned one of the musicians, Mr. Bryan Keller, carefully laying on an American accent, of course, and made a deal to pay him for an interruption to the musical program. Musicians are so terribly hard up that it took but a small sum to convince him to do it. The ensuing confusion allowed me to slip the lethal potion into the woman's glass."

He pointed a finger straight at Louise. "You, my dear, were essentially looking straight at me when I did it, and for a while I feared you had caught on to what I was up to."

She remembered that hubbub, a tangle of bodies, Gail falling, and men catching her—

She must have looked right through Shelby

Newcross, trusting, not being suspicious of the movements of a dignified old man.

"But the nerve it took to do this at a public event."

He sat imperiously, his head high. "Oh, I thought that the best part. Oleander has a massive effect on the heart, which thereafter creates the sweating, the vomiting, the diarrhea, the muscle spasms that we saw Bunny Bainfield undergo. To suffer and die in front of the many people she'd wronged was simply Old Testament justice."

Louise was so stunned by his cold logic that for a moment she couldn't speak. Finally, she said, "And Joanna—you killed her, too."

At these questions, Newcross's facade began to crumble. It was as if he were shrinking a little in the big chair. "Oh, poor Joanna," he said, and she thought she heard a tremble in his voice again. "It was equally easy to murder my old friend, though of course I deeply regretted having to do it. But Joanna *knew.*" Again, his eyes began to focus in the distance.

"She knew you poisoned Bunny?"

"Yes. She's been here, and she knows what I do in my laboratory. She also must have suspected that I was a person who would have both the courage to do it, and who would have nothing to lose." He smiled. "As you can see, I've already received my death sentence. Even as we speak, my cancer continues to eat into my organs."

This graphic description silenced her for a long moment. Then she asked, "Did Joanna say something to you? I noticed how upset she was all day yesterday."

"She was upset, but she didn't confront me, no." He shook his head. "In fact, had she done so, I might have refrained from killing her. I had to keep track of her for fear she'd go to the police. Fortunately, it was easy to follow her movements; she was monopolized by Fenimore Smith as he attempted to regain his nursery. Then, before checking out, I made a quick visit to Joanna's room. I had to persuade her that her suspicions were groundless, for I could see her determination to tell all to the authorities."

With a deep sigh, he said, "They would then arrest me for suspicion of a murder that I felt was fully justified. Joanna was drinking a highball when I arrived in her room. She drank quite a bit, you know."

He bent his head as if embarrassed by what he was to say next. "I fear I used my most genteel manner to lower her defenses, and successfully implanted in her mind the idea that it was Fenimore who had done the deed. But I couldn't be sure she wouldn't waver in her belief in me, so I decided it was safer to kill her. It was easy to slip poison into her drink. This time it was a slower-acting poison, one that takes about half an hour to act."

Louise felt her chest constrict as she looked into her empty wineglass. Her breath began to come in shorter bursts, and she felt suddenly as if she couldn't swallow. She sat back, trembling, and tried to control her breathing, forcing a swallow to move through her dry throat. How long had it been since she'd taken her first sip of the drink?

Then she looked at the magnificent orchid plant hanging nearby, and calmed down. Her breath slowed and became more even. Abruptly, she realized she hadn't been poisoned at all.

Newcross was too caught up in his story to notice her changing moods. "The poison would take effect after I left," explained the botanist. "Joanna was at least temporarily convinced of my argument that Smith committed the crime. She was happy to renew her trust in me, her old friend. So I also had the opportunity to place my extra poison vials in her purse. I fear I brought the extra supply for just such a purpose."

Louise looked in the man's face, which appeared so composed, so normal. "So both deaths were viciously premeditated," she said, in a cold voice.

"You could say that," said Newcross, and shrugged his thin shoulders, like a man dismissing a paltry insult. With growing horror, Louise saw that he enjoyed the gamesmanship involved in the killings.

"It was quite easy from there," he continued. "Upon leaving, I urged Joanna to throw the deadbolt on the door to safeguard herself against Fenimore Smith." He chuckled drily. "Poor Fenimore."

Louise leaned forward on the couch and burst out the words. "But how could a man like you murder a friend and cause another friend to be blamed for it?"

Newcross's wrinkled face suddenly collapsed, and for the first time she could see remorse in the man.

"You've cut to the quick, Louise. Joanna's was not an impersonal death, like the monstrous Bunny's, or a lab rat's, but the death of a friend and colleague I've admired for years, a woman who actually loved me for a while as a man, when we were twenty years younger . . ."

He slowly shook his head. "But Monday afternoon, she alarmed and *repelled* me. I needed a trigger to kill—I hope I made that clear to you. No problem with Bunny: Bunny was an insult to humanity. Joanna was a little different. After Bunny died, she began to act strangely, crassly, with wild boasts that shocked more people than just me. She said that she herself would take on Bunny's mantle, miming all of Bunny's more commercial stratagems. 'I can be as coarse as she was, given a little time,' she told me, and laughed like a harridan."

"In other words, she would sell out. . . ."

"Yes, to the tawdriness that was beginning to represent America in everything, including gardens."

Louise stared at him. "I think you killed her so that you wouldn't end up in prison for Bunny's murder."

He smiled benevolently at her. "You are partially correct, Louise. Her boasting was only an additional impetus to do the deed."

She sat for a moment, wondering where this conversation would go next. "It's a question of what you'll do now," she said. "Those beakers out there are evidence."

"Oh, no," he assured her, "they are perfumes, not poison. The lab is quite police-proof at this point; nothing incriminating will be found there, unless you can make the case that six white lab mice are evidence of something. My more lethal concoctions are now moved into a well-hidden colonial-era hiding place, which you, being interested in all manner of mysterious things, would probably be charmed to visit. Without my aid, these stores could remain hidden for generations."

He bent his head and stared at her over his spectacles. "And now you know why I did these things, and why I didn't fear the consequences."

She felt empty and as if the world were coming to an end. "So what now? Why haven't you tried to kill me, too?"

Wearily, Newcross sat back in the wing chair and said, "I wouldn't kill you, Louise, for several reasons. I admire you. And if I killed you, then I would have to kill the next person who came along and suspected me, and the next and the next. And as I tried to convince you, I'm really not the killer type."

During his narrative, Newcross had refrained from drinking his sherry, merely fingering the embossed crystal glass now and again. Now he put the cup to his lips.

"No!" she cried, and leaped over the side table bearing a priceless Chinese porcelain, knocking it to the floor with a crash, and shoved the glass from his lips. It sailed across the carpet and smashed into pieces against an antique brass wood holder next to the fireplace. The force of her landing managed to topple him sideways out of his chair, and he fell down and landed on the rug.

"Ooh," Newcross cried, and grasped his bony hip. She struggled to her feet and stood above him, panting, and saw that he was injured and in pain. Looking up at her with plaintive eyes, he said, "Why did you stop me? Now I'll have to end my life in prison."

She wanted to reach down and help him, but was afraid to do so. Instead, she went to the phone and started to punch in 911, but then heard a rubbing noise behind her, the sound of cloth on cloth.

It took a moment to perceive the danger. She turned to see the botanist using one arm to drag himself toward the table on which she had set her tape recorder. Her gaze went to the pistol in his other hand. It was pointed at her head.

She stood, frozen, regretting her naïveté about this clever old man. Her reactions were slowed, no doubt, by the several drinks she'd downed this afternoon. Perhaps she could talk him out of this, or wait until his hand became tired of holding the gun. She decided instead on a feint.

Turning toward the door as if she'd heard

something, she shouted, "Oh *no!*" Looking quickly
back, she saw Newcross's gaze had gone to the
door. Desperately, she dodged down and scurried
around the big sofa. Without hesitation, she approached him from the rear just as he turned to
see her. She batted the pistol out of his hand, then
rushed over and grabbed her tape recorder.

Newcross lay prostrate on the Oriental rug, a
look of reproach on his face. She saw the irony of
it all: this man's reputation as a horticulturalist
would be shattered when she called the police. He
would be hauled off to jail and, already near death,
would perish there in a matter of months. What
was the sense in disclosing that Shelby Newcross,
with his endless contributions to the science of
gardening, was a murderer? The man was helpless;
it would be easy to take those keys from his sweater
pocket. She could open the front door and depart
from the house, leaving him to poison himself, or
live out his remaining few months in solitude.

She went over and picked up his pistol where it
lay on the floor, shaking her head as if to rid herself of these empathetic thoughts about a murderer. Newcross had already killed two people to
keep them silent, and there was nothing to stop
him from tracking her down and murdering her as
well.

She turned to the telephone to call Mike
Geraghty. Even as she was pressing in the numbers, she heard the sound of police sirens and cars
screeching to a stop in the gravel driveway at the
front of the house. Car doors slammed, and then
someone beat on the old door and simultaneously
pushed the doorbell.

Above it all, Janie's voice demanded, "Open up,
or we'll break down the door!"

36

Louise was slouched in Mike Geraghty's inadequate visitor's chair in the Mount Vernon District Station, wishing she could go home and collapse with a good book and get her mind off murder. She'd just finished giving a lengthy statement to the detective, and he now sat back in his squeaky chair, looking inordinately pleased.

"According to what I hear is happenin' in the interrogation room, Newcross is ready to give it up." He leaned forward, his chair whining in protest, and tapped his finger on the tape player. "Even without his confession, this would have cinched it."

At that moment, Ron Goheen appeared in the doorway of Geraghty's office. Somber as ever, the Alexandria chief of detectives took one look at Louise and broke into a big smile. It was such a surprise that she could only stare at him.

"Case *closed,* folks, or as you people in television might say, Mrs. Eldridge, it's a wrap!" Then he came in and sat down in the chair next to Louise.

But the moment of friendliness was brief. Goheen took off his smile with his oval-shaped glasses, and by the time he'd cleaned the spectacles with a white lawn handkerchief, his somber expression had returned. Goheen tried to sit back and get comfortable in the pinchy plastic-covered armchair, but failed and sat up straight.

"Mrs. Eldridge, we solved this, partially thanks to you. But I can't say I approve of the way you operate. You're lucky to be alive, I hope you know that."

Geraghty intervened. "I told Louise she was perfectly safe to go to see Newcross since he was not a target of our investigation."

"You're right. We'd crossed him off our list. A worldwide reputation as a botanist. A man who was about to be *knighted,* for God's sake."

Goheen looked like a man who had been outfoxed.

"We might never have caught him if Louise hadn't wandered down there," said Geraghty.

"Wandered?" Louise gave a dry laugh. "I didn't exactly wander there. I had a great interview planned with the man—I was just scouting out the territory. What makes me so darned frustrated—" Inexplicably, she felt tears rushing to her eyes.

"I know, Louise, you admired the guy."

She unzipped her big handbag and groped for a tissue, and wiped her eyes. She looked over at Geraghty. "You don't know how hard it was to make that phone call."

"I don't know if Ron here agrees with me," said Geraghty, "but I'd guess that Shelby Newcross isn't going to do prison time. He'll probably end his days in a prison hospital."

Goheen put his glasses back on his face and nodded agreement. "He doesn't want to live. He decided that when Mrs. Eldridge was at the house and somehow discerned that he was the killer. Um, how you did that, I don't really know yet."

"It was just a few suspicious things: the path not taken, for instance."

"The path not taken?"

"He avoided going down the main path in back of the house. I caught a glimpse of it. It was lined with bushes with long, thin, pointed leaves. Oleander. And then there were those beakers with colored liquid, and the experimental mice that couldn't really be explained by a man who spent his time raising orchids."

"Once your suspicions were aroused, he decided he'd spill the beans to you, and then take poison himself."

"You mean he did poison his sherry?" asked Louise.

"Definitely," said Goheen. "Your antique-smashing vault over that eighteenth-century table saved his life, much to his regret."

Geraghty added, "And we've just found Newcross's poison cache on the property. He had to tell us where it was, in an abandoned root cellar down near the Potomac." Louise could just picture the botanist, operating in his usual organized, scientific manner, clearing his laboratory of any evidence that he made poisons, then packing up his stash of securely sealed bottles and carrying them down the stone steps to the secret place by the water.

Goheen consulted his notes. "That doesn't mean

he didn't still have a sample or two out for current use. He could hide it anywhere in that big house of his, just like he hid the poison vials from police in his room at The Federalist Hotel. He tucked them into the rim of one of those fancy light fixtures in his bedroom suite." He shrugged. "Of course, each potion was very small and exceedingly lethal."

Then the detective's swarthy face turned to her. "You're lucky you got out of there unharmed, Mrs. Eldridge. Lucky that your daughter Jane phoned and you were able to give her whatever secret message you conveyed to her."

"Janie realized I was in trouble when I began talking about making dinner from scratch out of a Julia Child cookbook."

"She did?" asked Goheen. "Why would that be?"

Louise waved a hand in a casual gesture. "Oh, just that I don't own a Julia Child cookbook."

"I see. Well, Shelby Newcross's dangerous. He's a killer. He killed twice, and he killed *deliberately*." He scratched his head in puzzlement. "There's one thing I can't understand: it's out of character with a person like that, but he made sure that we handed over to you some plant that he'd given you, that red orchid hanging from a lamp in his living room."

Her heart beat faster. The elderly botanist had forgiven her for turning him in.

"There's something you should understand. Shelby Newcross wasn't going to poison me." She said it with certainty, maybe a little more certainty than she'd felt when Newcross had begun to talk about slower-acting poisons.

"And just how would you know that?" asked Goheen. His tone was on the edge of rudeness.

With a sigh, she sat back and tried to get comfortable in the chair. This was going to take time. She explained it to him in detail.

When she was through, Captain Ron Goheen looked at Detective Mike Geraghty and they both solemnly nodded.

37

Louise carefully maneuvered her PT Cruiser out of its space at the police station parking lot, and let out a little yelp as she swerved to avoid an incoming heap of junk lurching into the space beside her. Inside the car were two long-haired young men. Probably involved in some murky criminal matter, she thought to herself, but then was overcome with a moment of shame.

Now that she no longer drove her dented Honda wagon, and instead a vehicle with lots of cachet, she realized she could become an elitist car snob. It was just what she'd always hated in drivers of other slicker cars when she herself was driving a junker. She would have to beware, for there was nothing she disliked more than a snob.

Just as she was approaching U.S. One and was about to pull into traffic, a red Porsche sped up and blocked her path. Leaving the motor running,

Charlie Hurd jumped out, leaving the driver-side door open.

Acting as if he'd found the mother lode, he whipped open Louise's door and leaned his thin form in on her. *"Louise!"* he cried, "I heard you cracked the case. Shelby Newcross, I heard. Son of a gun, I can't believe it! Have the Alexandria cops given you your reward yet? How about we go down the street and have a coffee and you spill all the details to me?"

His thin, pinch-nosed face was in her face, and it brought back all the pain and suffering: Charlie Hurd had recently endangered her life and limb just so that he could get a better story.

She would have grabbed the handle and closed the door, but his body was jamming it open. "Charlie," she said, "I'm not going anywhere with you. I'm giving you no interviews. I might give an interview to *another* paper, maybe to the TV stations, but not to you. And you know why."

She cocked her head in the direction of the Fairfax substation. "Go scrounge your story off Geraghty and Goheen. They're both there. They probably have a higher tolerance for you than I do."

He stood firmly in the door and said, "At least confirm this with me." His pale eyes shone with the excitement of a hunter who'd finally caught up with the fox. "Don't you think it's possible that if Shelby Newcross hadn't gotten to her first, that one of those other gardening characters might have killed our nasty friend Bunny?"

Louise shrugged. "Oh, I see. You're still clinging to that *Murder on the Orient Express* notion. Hmm. Maybe so, Charlie, but we'll just never know, will we?"

He stepped back from her car door, his face thoughtful. "On the matter of what happened on that island—I was a shit, wasn't I, Louise?"

☞"I'm glad you're finally admitting it."

"Look, it's Christmas. How 'bout sharing some Christmas spirit and forgiving me?" His pale eyes looked at her with a hangdog expression, as if he were on the list of the Christmas neediest.

Louise shook her head. "Charlie, you are a piece of work. Using a holy time for your own advantage. You're right—this is a time for healing. But if I forgive you, you'd better mind your p's and q's from now on."

"I will. Merry Christmas, Louise."

"Merry Christmas, Charlie." She closed the door and drove on, and crossed through a break in traffic to the median, then headed north toward the Dixie Pig.

It was a little after five o'clock. Geraghty and Goheen had both assured her there was no reason not to keep her rendezvous with Fenimore Smith at the restaurant. They themselves were too busy processing the case of the killer of Bunny Bainfield and Joanna Heath to accompany her. After all, the most they would do would be to chastise Smith and his wife for failing to check out of The Federalist Hotel as the police had requested.

She entered the restaurant, the sweet odor of grease assailing her nostrils. Immediately she was greeted by Dorothy, a dark-haired, lusty woman who'd been waitressing at the Pig for years.

"Louise! Como está?"

Louise grinned. *"Muy bueno,* Dorothy. And how are you?"

The Pig was a place of comfort for her, nothing

fancier than barbecue sandwiches, no bill larger than six dollars. No cover charges, no aloof Washington waiters, no highhat customers, just downhome types, many of them grossly overweight and willing to put on a few more pounds by tying into the Pig's renowned barbecue.

Dorothy swished her ample hips and eyed Louise curiously. "I'm great, actually." She lowered her voice. "But you've got some fancy folks expectin' you." And she pointed with a hand clutched full of menus toward the back booth.

The uptight couple sitting there eyed her without smiling. Louise noted that they both wore well-cut wool, while the rest of the clientele, as usual, sported Wal-Mart designs. She took a quick look at her watch; she was fifteen minutes late for this rendezvous.

"Well, Louise," said Fenimore, his hooded eyes on her, a semblance of a smile forming on his lips, "here you are, finally."

"Sorry I'm late," she said, and slid in next to Lily. "Hi, Lily, how are you?" Dorothy had set the tone of friendliness, and Louise was darned if she'd let the Smiths diminish it.

"Hungry?" she asked them.

Lily scanned the restaurant and with an air of dismissal said, "Yes, but I don't think we'll eat here."

"That's a mistake. They have great barbecue. And you two certainly look hungry. I'm starved." She lifted a finger, and Dorothy immediately approached. "I'll have the pork, Dorothy, plus a cup of coffee."

Lily's eyes widened. "Won't this just ruin your *dinner?*"

"Oh, no," said Louise breezily. "This is dinner. You can't let the chance go by to have the Pig's barbecue sandwich."

"Oh, well," drawled Fenimore, "when in Rome—" He looked at the waitress. "Bring us the same, please," and he handed the grease-specked menus back to her.

"Yessiree," said Dorothy, giving him a big grin, "and you won't regret it." Even Fenimore, she noticed, could not resist looking at her departing, swaggering rear, which was an echo, even though a very faint echo, of Marilyn Monroe's famous hip swing.

The Smiths were obviously under pressure. They sat stiffly, as if waiting for a reprieve of some kind. She should just tell them that the murderer had been caught, and they were off the hook. But something held her back.

"So you haven't gotten back to the police yet, have you?"

"How can you tell?" asked Fenimore, staring blandly at her.

Louise smiled. "You're far from relaxed. I'd say you are a couple of worried people, about something or other."

Fenimore leaned farther forward on the Formica booth, so that his eyes were no more than two feet away from hers. "Louise, I swear I didn't kill *anybody*. And *Lily* didn't kill anyone."

"I believe that."

He sat back. "You *do*? Well, then, help us. Tell the police to get off it. I know from the tone of the message we picked up that they're intent on pinning something on us."

"I wonder what that would be," she ruminated, "if not murder. Let me tell you what I think."

She described what she saw in The Federalist Monday afternoon, the bitter argument the Smiths were having with Joanna, the somber get-together in the bar. "I'm guessing you were trying all afternoon to get her to cancel that sales agreement."

Lily made a broad gesture with her hand. "Oh, just tell her, Fenimore. She'll get it anyway."

Smith leaned forward in the most dignified way possible and fixed Louise with his handsome gaze. "As soon as we signed the sales contract on Wild Flower Farm, we knew we'd made a terrible mistake. We came to Washington, knowing it was a good opportunity to talk to Joanna in person and get her to cancel it. We wanted our nursery back, despite its weakened financial condition. You saw us at the Christmas ball, talking about it before dinner, *arguing* about it, pressing the issue. Then, after Bunny died, we became more adamant, because we knew that with Bunny out of the picture, there was no doubt that Wild Flower could thrive and prosper again."

"You mean now that she's dead, Bunny's businesses will flounder?"

He sat forward, with an earnest expression she'd never seen before on his face. "You mustn't underestimate the *buzz* and the splash this woman's made in the garden industry. A great deal of her success was the sheer force of her personality, and her fantastic media exposure." He arched one elegant eyebrow upward. "Hadn't you felt the heat in the ratings of your show? If not, all it needed was time, and she would have encroached on you, too."

"She was formidable, I agree," said Louise.

He shrugged. "Look, it's not that I killed her to achieve such an end, believe me, but that will be the result. That's just how it is when a dynamic business leader leaves the helm of a going business."

With widened eyes, Lily reconfirmed this. "Of course we would never commit a horrible crime like that." Her perfectly made-up face and well-coiffed long chestnut hair convinced Louise that murder would be too messy for this woman to even think about. "But we knew if we could retrieve the business from Joanna, that we'd survive 'A.B.'"

"'A.B,'" repeated Louise. "Oh, I get it: 'After Bunny.'"

Fenimore Smith said, "Joanna, however, was very upset Monday, for some reason, and she didn't want to talk about tearing up our sales contract, even though we promised her a cash settlement for her trouble, that kind of thing. She even went off on some crazy ramble that made me think she now thought of herself as Bunny's successor." He shook his head. "That boggled the mind, since she disliked the woman so intensely."

Lily leaned over and touched Louise's hand with cool fingers. "I hate to say it, but we began to think Joanna had poisoned Bunny herself. And when we heard *Joanna* was dead, we realized she'd done it and then committed suicide."

"What I want to know is why you didn't go to the police," said Louise. "Instead, you made yourself into fugitives, more or less."

Fenimore stared down for a moment at the tan Formica. "That was disgraceful of me, Louise, and I hope I can rely on you to keep this among the three of us. But in the bar yesterday afternoon, Joanna was so distracted that it was easy for me to slip our sales agreement out of her big purse." He laughed bitterly. "She'd been waving the damned thing in our face all day—I told you she was acting funny. In fact—and Lily will tell you this was so— one minute, it was as if this good friend of ours *wanted* us to take back our sales contract. The next minute, she'd change her mind and play hardball, almost as if she'd taken on some of *Bunny's* persona. Believe me, it was scary."

Fenimore's glance encompassed the room, but Louise was sure he didn't see a thing: the overweight elderly customers, the men in jeans and work boots, work shirts, and billed caps, all happily eating. He was too caught up in his own story, and the personal shame it involved.

"When we heard Joanna was dead, we were trapped in this highly embarrassing dilemma." He opened his manicured hands in an expansive gesture. "It might have looked as if we'd killed her, stolen the sales contract, and sneaked out that back door of the hotel. And *that's* really why we phoned you—because it looks so hugely bad."

Louise stared over at the two of them. "I guess your family business must mean a lot to you. What you did is called theft. You'll have to go to the police with this and tell them the whole thing. Then maybe you can deal with Joanna's survivors and get your business back the legal way. As far as Joanna practically inviting you to steal the contract, that does sound a little odd."

Lily's hands made a graceful loop. "You would have to know her, Louise, to understand."

"Hmm. Well, I know the reason why Joanna couldn't keep her mind on business yesterday. It was on Bunny's murderer."

"Do you think she killed Bunny, and then committed suicide?" asked Lily.

"No," she said. "When the police told me that theory, I couldn't believe it. Joanna wasn't the sort to kill herself. And now, folks, let me tell you what really was bothering her."

Louise bent toward them and explained that

Shelby Newcross was Bunny's murderer, and that Joanna gradually came to suspect him. She described how Newcross went to her room and put a slow-acting poison in her drink, then urged her to double-lock her door against the prospective "murderer."

"Ah," cried Fenimore, "a locked room mystery: as a publisher, I can appreciate that. Who did Shelby lay Bunny's murder on?"

Louise gave him a long look.

"*Me?*"

"Yes, and when you and Lily disappeared, the police believed that, too. When you left anonymous calls for me, I thought you were chasing me."

"My God," said Fenimore, "Shelby killed them both!"

The looks of relief on their face were so guileless that Louise finally understood what a strain they had been under. Petty thievery of a sales contract was a source of great shame for Fenimore Smith, the powerful New York publisher. As someone had said, Fenimore Smith would do anything for Wild Flower Farm. Anything but murder.

Their food was brought to the table by Dorothy, who, being man-happy, lingered over Fenimore, seeking his attention. "How's that look to y'all?" she asked him.

He lifted one of the three barbecue sandwiches, took a modest bite, chewed it, and swallowed. Opening his hooded eyes all the way, he exclaimed, "Wonderful!"

Louise wondered if eating at the Dixie Pig could in any way be construed as a learning experience for Fenimore and Lily Smith. She hoped so. Maybe they'd talk about it sometime with their friends, or more likely, joke about it.

Whether it was the relaxed atmosphere or the

barbecue, Louise found herself having a fairly enjoyable time with the Smiths. Once past their haughty East Coast style, she found them an interesting pair.

When the meal was done, they parted with handshakes, and Louise started the two-mile journey home. She reflected on the past three days, still sad that she had to bring the great gardener Shelby Newcross into the arms of the police. Maybe the lesson was that great gardeners were no more immune from human malevolence than other people.

She was glad now that Christmas was almost here, for the challenge of handling young daughters in love, in-laws with differing political views, and another holiday dinner should take her mind off murder.

38

December 25

Louise looked into the faces of the twelve people around the dining room table and knew her Christmas dinner had been a success. They looked content, surfeited with three courses and dessert, and now happily drank coffee and nibbled chocolates. A certain tension was gone, since presents had been opened earlier in the day and now lay in pleasant clusters about the house.

It was a fleeting moment of family togetherness, but soon to be broken, for the young people, or at least Janie and Chris, were growing restless and would leave soon for more exciting pursuits. Martha and her boyfriend, Jim, older and calmer, were ready to hang out with parents and grandparents.

Bill's pride in Louise was obvious from the look in his eyes. He knew better than anyone else how anxious she had been to make this parental visit and dinner a success. Louise looked at her mother and felt like giving her a thumbs-up sign, for it was Elizabeth Sharpe who had inspired her and dredged up recipes for her, thus saving her from another lackluster culinary experience. At last, perhaps, she could call herself a good cook.

Her mother-in-law had been a great help, too. On Christmas Eve, when Louise's flan was removed from the oven looking as pockmarked as a moon rock, Jean Eldridge stepped in quietly and baked some of her renowned pecan pies. And even though she said she wasn't a cat person, Jean was kind to Hargrave. While everyone was absent from the living room, he leapt up the Christmas tree—far higher than Louise thought he could leap—and batted off a few ornaments that included Louise's favorite antique blue bauble with its unusual curves and knobs. Jean quietly cleaned up the pieces, and later tactfully told Louise of the loss, saving the cat from a sound scolding.

So far, the two sets of in-laws had gotten on well, with little discussion of politics because Bill and Louise kept them busy either sightseeing or visiting neighbors and friends. Martha's Chicago politician boyfriend had limited his political talk to one-on-ones with Bill.

There was plenty of discussion of the poisoning deaths, though Louise had taken little part in those discussions. In fact, since the murders, she'd not been her usual talkative self. Bill had explained that she was too distracted with the logistics of the holiday.

Actually, she was recovering from a period of mourning, though not able to explain to herself why she felt melancholy since the showdown with Shelby Newcross. Maybe it was the constant reminder, the orchid, that hung in her living room windows. Beams of sunlight passed through it, turning the red blossoms into patches that looked like deep-red blood. No wonder it was called *Dracula*.

Until the night of the Christmas ball, she hadn't known Newcross, only his reputation and his books. He'd been a remarkable scientist, one who'd fired her imagination, but one who'd now be remembered not for the precious plants he'd searched out and brought in from the wild but for the two hideous crimes he'd committed.

She welcomed the excuse not to talk about the matter. Instead, she hurried about, planning activities and fussing with food. Her mother stayed at her elbow in the kitchen, quietly giving guidance without making Louise feel she was in cooking school.

But she heard all the talk. Her husband, and sometimes Janie, filled in family members with bits and pieces of the story.

Bill: "Louise didn't believe the police theory that Joanna poisoned Bunny and then committed suicide. That was why she suspected there still was a murderer out there. . . ."

Janie: "Ma thought this guy was like God, so why would she suspect him of murder when the police didn't? So she innocently goes down there to interview him in his house. Good thing she told me where she was going. . . ."

Bill: "The First Lady's native plant program? Apparently, it's going on hold for a while. A committee is studying the need for it."

Their company had been there two days, so most of the questions had been asked. Louise's parents, as usual, were unruffled about their daughter's role in another detecting adventure. "This follows a pattern," explained her professor father. "Louise has always tended to operate outside the box. She was a very inquisitive child, always seeking out the truth. She hasn't changed much in that regard."

"You can say that again," said Bill.

Her father-in-law, Dick Eldridge, put it directly: "Well, I admire someone who can find a murderer when the police can't. That takes real smarts."

Louise glanced at her mother-in-law, sitting two places away from her. Since she'd arrived, Jean Eldridge had been her usual quiet self and had not entered the discussion about the murders. She was a comely woman, with lots of graying curls; she wore pearls with every dress. Now she fingered them almost nervously, and Louise could see she was working up to something.

"I hesitate to bring up this matter, Louise. But it's been bothering me ever since I heard the story of your encounter with this Dr. Newcross." Her round eyes blinked a couple of times, as if she were embarking on a very dangerous subject. "If *I* had been sitting there drinking that sherry, once I thought the man was a murderer, I would have bolted out the front door as quick as a rabbit and rushed to the nearest emergency room. I'd think that he'd poisoned me, just like he poisoned those other women."

This was the longest set of remarks her mother-in-law had made to Louise in years.

Dick Eldridge put up a cautionary hand. "Now *wait* a minute, Jean," he told his wife, "I don't know that you should ask Louise questions like that."

Jean blushed crimson, and her granddaughter Martha reached over and patted her consolingly on the arm. "It's all right, Grandma. We all want to know about that one."

Louise nodded. "I don't mind explaining it to

you." She looked at her mother-in-law with new interest. This upper-middle-class, bridge-playing matron might make a good detective herself: she got right to the point, as a good detective should. "Let's have a second round of coffee, um, Mom. Then I'll tell you all about it."

"Uhh," came from Bill, as if he had a bone caught in his throat. He coughed, trying to cover it up. "Sorry. I choked there for a minute."

Louise gave her husband a patient look. He'd been shocked when he heard the word "Mom" issue from her lips. He would just have to catch up to where things stood with these two women in his life. As for Louise, she felt a little movement in the universe, and she was glad.

Martha went to get the freshly made pot of coffee, then quickly returned to the table with it. Everyone sat looking at Louise expectantly. She had explained this matter only to the police and to Bill.

Jean accepted a refill of her cup, doctored it with cream and sugar, and then looked over at Louise as she took a sip.

"First of all," said Louise, "the man had a pistol in his sweater pocket, so dashing out the front door wasn't really an option. But maybe I should start at the beginning. After I arrived at his home, we toured his gardens and talked about plants. He was very solicitous, asking me all about my family. He has no family of his own."

"And you say he was quite ill."

"I discovered he had terminal cancer. After our garden walk, he took me into his laboratory. It was fascinating, a labyrinth of bottles and tubes and beakers. I began asking questions that he must have thought were suspicious. For all he knew, I could relay my suspicions to the police, and they'd come out to his house and find out that he was a murderer. He decided to tell me everything. He apparently decided I'd be the right person to carry his story to the world."

"He sounds like an arrogant man," said Jean Eldridge.

"He is. He was sure that he was ridding the world of evil by killing Bunny and Joanna. When he got to the part of his story where he described *how* he'd murdered Joanna, it terrified me. He'd used the poison at half strength, and it took half an hour to take effect."

Jean pulled in a breath. For the first time she was sensing the reality of her daughter-in-law's colorful life. "And *you*—"

"I'd just drunk half a glass of his sherry not fifteen minutes before."

"You must have been *terrified*."

"I was, for a minute. But then I looked at the orchid he'd given me, and I realized he wouldn't poison me. That plant was like a baby. He'd propagated it through tissue culture, you know, using a tiny piece of orchid corm implanted in a special medium—"

Jean shook her head in confusion. "I haven't the faintest idea about *that* sort of thing."

Louise sighed, happy to have the chance to explain it all. "His tiny orchids start their lives out in flasks—or test tubes—then graduate into pots. He had orchids at all levels of maturity, from baby ones, to ones in two-inch pots, to the large, mature ones in full bloom. The plant he gave me was in his greenhouse for years, and it's one of the hardest ones to grow. Believe it or not, you can get very attached to a plant that you live with for years." She smiled. "Now can you begin to see what I'm getting at?"

"Not really, Louise," said her mother-in-law, sitting forward earnestly. "Am I missing something?"

"He would hardly kill me after that, since he was trusting me to take care of it."

"Oh, *my,*" said Jean. "You mean on the basis of *that* you knew he hadn't poisoned your wine?"

"It's not a small thing, to give a person a plant. Maybe you have to be a serious gardener to know this, but such a gift is mystical, almost supernatural. After that, there's a special bond between you and the giver."

Jean Eldridge gave Louise a startled look, her lips parted slightly, and then a smile broke over her face. She was looking at something beyond Louise's right shoulder.

Louise turned and her heart beat faster. There in the corner was the graceful *Cyclad* plant she'd given Jean for Christmas.

GARDENING OUTSIDE THE LINES

A GARDEN ESSAY

When we were youngsters in school, many of us were handed coloring books with outlined pictures and told, "color inside the lines." This was the ultimate in respecting arbitrary boundaries just to please someone in authority. Breaking out, coloring "outside the lines," or in the business vernacular, "operating outside the box," is now much more acceptable, whether it's in our jobs, in our personal lives, or in the way we garden.

For many reasons, gardens these days are undergoing a revolution. Naturalistic landscaping, once a novelty in America, has now become the thing to do. Lawns have been revered for decades as something almost holy by Americans, and lawn *mowing* akin to going to church on Sunday. Today, lawns are not "out," but they've definitely lost cachet. Yards filled with native flowers, shrubs, trees, swaying long grasses, and groundcovers are definitely "in."

Plants in the neighborhood that people eyed suspiciously as possible weeds have turned out to be delightful, water-wise native specimens. We have scientists to thank for that—they've gone into the wilds of America and brought out native plants that now are available to us all in local nurseries. People in deserts are replacing bluegrass lawns with cacti and other native species. Folks building new homes are demanding that contractors save every tree and shrub on the property outside the immediate building "envelope" or site, so they can have a natural landscape from the day the house is finished.

It's remarkable that these treey, grassy, and shrubby landscapes are becoming the hot news stories in magazines and home sections of newspapers. They even make it to the front page of *The New York Times.*

This natural landscaping movement indicates that the country has awakened like Rip Van Winkle, and is surprised that God and nature had something really good going there on the land before the bulldozers swept it away. It is a far cry from the days, not so long ago, when nervous neighbors of homeowners who'd gone "native" or "natural" would call the police and complain about the wild state of things next door. A number of natural gardeners ended up in court, and the stories of how they eventually won their cases is a story of how America has gradually come to accept sensible gardening habits.

After all, these dauntless homeowners are only following the intelligent example set in the 1960s by Lady Bird Johnson, who pushed the cause of native plants in America. Because of her influence, the country's roadsides today are populated with native plants and trees.

When an individual yard goes native, many good things happen:

- The homeowner immediately has less maintenance work to do—including no more mowing, fertilizing, spraying weed killers, or raking leaves.
- Thousands of gallons of water are saved, for traditional lawns take more than half of all the water consumed by an average household. Natural landscapes take but a fraction of this amount.
- These almost magical gardens restore the earth to what it was in the beginning—a habitat for butterflies, small animals, and birds. Nothing is as moving, for a gardener, as to realize that the yard is no longer a chemically controlled rectangular patch of bluegrass, but part of a beautiful ecosystem. And the way the gardener tells this is by simply looking around, to see signs of avian friends, butterflies, and worms crawling in the soil.

When the idea of natural gardens and "back-to-the-prairie" landscapes first came up, lots of people shrugged their shoulders and suggested that this might be something for those living in drought areas but not for them. The years have demonstrated that drought can and will strike anywhere, even in the usually rain-filled northwestern states. National newspapers report more and more stories about the uncertain water situation in America. Even the mighty Lake Michigan, biggest freshwater source in the world, is dwindling, and drought conditions around its shores are predicted within two decades. That's a forewarning—join the prairie movement!

A companion issue is the pollution that results from using chemical pesticides and herbicides, with many ground wells and rivers in the United States affected by the runoff. The beauty of natural, native-oriented gardens is that they require few or no chemicals, including no chemical fertilizers.

To some, this landscaping reformation continues to be a far-fetched idea. There are those who are so tied to tradition, or so orderly in their perception of nature, that they cannot think of relinquishing their bluegrass lawn. But as cities face drought and impose sprinkling restrictions, homes with big, water-guzzling lawns eventually will look like horticultural dinosaurs.

Good news for the traditionalist, however: native/natural gardens can be designed in any style, from the wildest and most informal, to the most formal and conventional— Versailles-style gardens, if someone likes them, but filled with xeriscape plants and trees. Homeowners with children also might want to maintain a patch of turf for play, but they needn't use demanding Kentucky bluegrass. There are numerous turfs that require less water, each of them geared to a different region of the country.

Even if homeowners agree with the arguments for making these radical changes in the landscape, they may have no idea about how to start. It is best to have a careful plan, made with or without the help of a professional landscape designer. Many people do an excellent job simply by imitating what they have seen in xeriscape or native gardens in their own hometown.

A few guidelines on natural landscaping:

• Soil comes first, and should be enriched, whether it's for a field of grasses and flowers or for specific garden areas. These latter garden beds should be specially prepared with good subsoil and rich topsoil. This motto, "Soil First," will give gardeners years of trouble-free success with regional plants and trees.*

• What to plant: native or locally adapted plants, grasses, flowers, and trees, varieties that are now called, and sometimes even labeled, "water-wise" plants.

• How to fertilize: leaves from your trees, plus applications of manure-fortified compost once or twice a year are all a natural garden needs in the way of nutrients.

• How to control weeds: weeds must be controlled in this natural horticultural setting though thick planting of native species, either grasses or plants, and good mulching will minimize the problem. Organic control of weeds and even burning of fields may also be needed once in awhile.

• How to water: a xeriscape rule for growing plants sensibly advises gardeners to group plants according to water needs, high, medium, or low, remembering that even the most drought-resistant plant needs water in the dog days of summer.

It is better to be the tortoise than the hare when planning a big change to natural landscaping. Andy and Sally Wasowski, garden writers and authors of *The Landscape Revolution,* are avid believers in natural gardens. Yet it took six years for them to transform their property from grassy lawns to native gardens.

Doing a little at a time also eases the discomfort of neighbors, for in spite of natural gardening's new popularity, there still are many people operating inside the landscaping box who may be

---

*An excellent guide to the details of planting natural, organic gardens is contained in Ann Lovejoy's *Organic Garden Design School.*

threatened by change. Start with the strip between the sidewalk and the street. Replace the turf with interesting native plants, grasses, trees, or a combination of all three. This requires putting in that base of good soil, and finishing the planting by applying several inches of mulch to protect the individual plantings from extreme temperatures and loss of moisture.* Even native plants take regular and frequent watering until they become established, probably for an entire year. Many a gardener has made a misstep by believing that native plants as a group have no water requirements at all.

Definitions can be stumbling blocks when talking of "native," "indigenous," or "regional" plants. Clearly, "native," synonymous with "indigenous," does not mean the same thing for all regions of the country. Thus, go for "regional" plants—ones that suit your area.

Yet what to do when a plant only bears the description "native?" One scientist thinks the range of a native plant is no more than 1,000 feet, and the wise gardener knows this is true, in a sense, for every yard has microclimates within it. Another botanist sets this rule: if your "native" plant was grown within 100 miles of your home, it's native, all right, and is going to do well in your wild garden.

By reading, and keeping their eyes open, gardeners can find out what will grow best for them. Botanical gardens, county extension services, and garden books are filled with ideas about native plants and how to use them. And don't think only

---

*An excellent guide to the details of planting natural, organic gardens is contained in Ann Lovejoy's *Organic Garden Design School.*

natives are useful: responsibly "introduced" plants also can be part of your landscape. Be sure to avoid plants that can become pests—and remember, a well-behaved plant in the arid West, for instance, can become a real thug in a region with more rainfall. These pestiferous varieties get loose in the wild and crowd out native plants.

There are endless choices of plants for the naturalistic garden. As any experienced gardener knows, we should "layer" plants, so to speak, so that when one diminishes, another comes forth and fills the space. No need for this, though, if a western gardener chooses to plant native grasses studded with wildflowers such as gaillardia, coneflower, and larkspur, for the grass hides the dying flowers. An eastern gardener might carpet the landscape with native ferns, hellebore, ginger, and pulmonaria, with native dogwood trees and azalea bushes rising out of this handsome groundcover. The Sonoran desert gardener will rely on the many beautiful cactus plants, palo verde trees, and a patch or two of penstemon and other desert-ready perennials.

Since newly installed natural landscapes replace a good deal of space previously occupied by lawn, gardeners have all sorts of freedom to "color outside the lines." They can let plants flourish as they will, adding new varieties to the gardener's taste—or, better still, to the taste of the hummingbirds and butterflies.

It is amazing how, in a natural garden filled with the sound and movement of bees, birds, moths, and butterflies flitting above, and the tiny mouse and garden snake silently moving below, we find ourselves at one with these small living beings. We even go out of our way to grow the special nature treats they like best, such as clusters of dill plants, butterfly bushes, or bright red–flowered plants. Suddenly, the garden becomes an earthly paradise, and we're right there to enjoy it.

<u>BOOK YOUR PLACE ON OUR WEBSITE</u> <u>AND MAKE THE</u> <u>READING CONNECTION!</u>

We've created a customized website just for our very special readers, where you can get the inside scoop on everything that's going on with Zebra, Pinnacle and Kensington books.

When you come online, you'll have the exciting opportunity to:

- View covers of upcoming books
- Read sample chapters
- Learn about our future publishing schedule (listed by publication month *and author*)
- Find out when your favorite authors will be visiting a city near you
- Search for and order backlist books from our online catalog
- Check out author bios and background information
- Send e-mail to your favorite authors
- Meet the Kensington staff online
- Join us in weekly chats with authors, readers and other guests
- Get writing guidelines
- AND MUCH MORE!

Visit our website at
http://www.kensingtonbooks.com

Mischief, Murder &
Mayhem – Grab These
Kensington Mysteries

__Endangered Species   1-57566-671-5   **$5.99US/$7.99CAN**
by Barbara Block

__Dying to See You   1-57566-669-3   **$5.99US/$7.99CAN**
by Margaret Chittenden

__High Seas Murder   1-57566-676-6   **$5.99US/$7.99CAN**
by Shelley Freydont

__Going Out in Style   1-57566-668-5   **$5.99US/$7.99CAN**
by Chloe Green

__Sour Grapes   1-57566-726-6   **$6.50US/$8.50CAN**
by G. A. McKevett

__A Light in the Window   1-57566-689-8   **$5.99US/$7.99CAN**
by Mary R. Rinehart

Available Wherever Books Are Sold!

Visit our website at **www.kensingtonbooks.com**